WOLF & PARCHMENT

VOL. 2

NEW THEORY SPICE & WOLF

BY ISUNA HASEKURA

ILLUSTRATED BY JYUU AYAKURA

THE YOUNG MAN
ASPIRING TO BE A PRIEST
COL

THE DAUGHTER OF A
WOLF AND A MERCHANT
MYURI

"WHAT A SURPRISE,
HEIR HYLAND."

HE CALLED HER NAME,
AND HYLAND, WHO
WAS A TRUE NOBLE,
THE BLOOD OF THE
KING OF WINFIEL IN
HER VEINS, DISPLAYED
A HINT OF FATIGUE
BEHIND HER SMILE.

MONK OF THE
BLACK-MOTHER
AUTUMN

"DO YOU NEED
SOMETHING?"

COL JUMPED
AT THE SUDDEN
VOICE.

"I AM TRULY
THANKFUL
THAT YOU
WORRY ABOUT
ME FROM THE
BOTTOM OF
YOUR HEART."

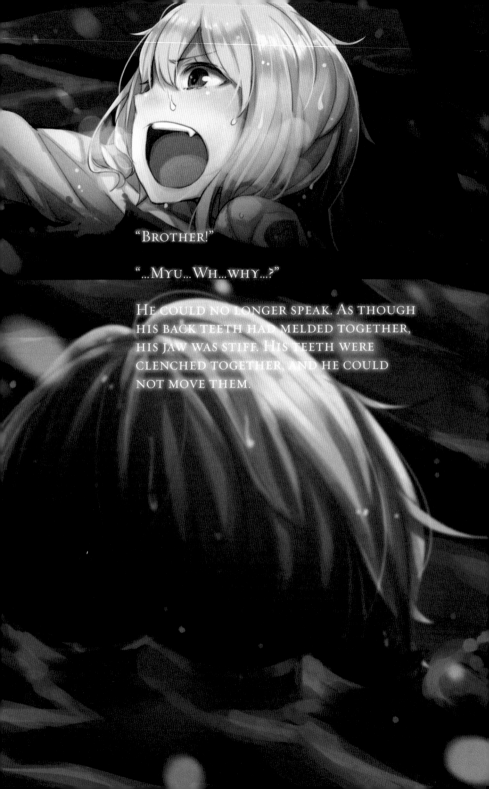

"BROTHER!"

"...MYU...WH...WHY...?"

HE COULD NO LONGER SPEAK. AS THOUGH
HIS BACK TEETH HAD MELDED TOGETHER,
HIS JAW WAS STIFF. HIS TEETH WERE
CLENCHED TOGETHER, AND HE COULD
NOT MOVE THEM.

MYURI WAS SWIMMING IN SUCH THIN CLOTHES THAT HE ALMOST SIGHED; PERHAPS SHE HAD REMOVED HER BULKY OUTER GARMENTS BEFORE JUMPING IN.

HE WANTED TO SAY, *YOU'LL GET SICK.*

Contents

WOLF & PARCHMENT

❖ NEW THEORY SPICE & WOLF ❖

VOL. 2

ISUNA HASEKURA
JYUU AYAKURA

YEN ON

NEW YORK

WOLF & PARCHMENT, Volume 2
ISUNA HASEKURA

Translation by Jasmine Bernhardt
Cover art by Jyuu Ayakura

WOLF & PARCHMENT
© ISUNA HASEKURA 2017
Edited by ASCII MEDIA WORKS
First published in Japan in 2017 by KADOKAWA CORPORATION, Tokyo.
English translation rights arranged with KADOKAWA CORPORATION, Tokyo,
through TUTTLE-MORI AGENCY, INC., Tokyo.

English translation © 2018 by Yen Press, LLC

Yen On
1290 Avenue of the Americas
New York, NY 10104

Visit us at yenpress.com
facebook.com/yenpress
twitter.com/yenpress
yenpress.tumblr.com
instagram.com/yenpress

First Yen On Edition: April 2018

Yen On is an imprint of Yen Press, LLC.
The Yen On name and logo are trademarks of Yen Press, LLC.

Library of Congress Cataloging-in-Publication Data
Names: Hasekura, Isuna, 1982– author. | Bernhardt, Jasmine, translator. | Ayakura, Jyuu, 1981– artist.
Title: Wolf & Parchment : new theory Spice & Wolf / Isuna Hasekura ;
translation by Jasmine Bernhardt ; cover art by Jyuu Ayakura.
Other titles: Shinsetsu ookami to koshinryo: ookami to youhishi. English
Description: First Yen On edition. | New York, NY : Yen On, 2017–
Identifiers: LCCN 2017035577 | ISBN 9780316473453 (v. 1 : paperback) |
ISBN 9781975326203 (v. 2 : paperback)
Subjects: CYAC: Adventure and adventurers—Fiction. | Fantasy. | BISAC: FICTION / Fantasy / Historical.
Classification: LCC PZ7.H2687 Wo 2017 | DDC [Fic]—dc23
LC record available at https://lccn.loc.gov/2017035577

ISBNs: 978-1-9753-2620-3 (paperback)
978-1-9753-2709-5 (ebook)

1 3 5 7 9 10 8 6 4 2

LSC-C

Printed in the United States of America

WOLF & PARCHMENT

WORLD MAP

CAESON

DOLAN PLAINS

ATIPH

ROEF MOUNTAINS

YOITSU

NYOHHIRA

JIIK

TAUSSIG

ROEF RIVER

SVERNEL

KERUBE

LESKO

TOLKIEN

KINGDOM OF WINFIEL

LENOS

ROAM RIVER

TEREO

ENBERCH

PLOANIA

N

W   E

S

KUMERSUN

LAMTRA

TRENNI

POROSON

RUVINHEIGEN

PAZZIO

YORENZ

SLAUDE RIVER

PASLOE

Map Illustration: Hidetada Idemitsu

PROLOGUE

Dawn had yet to break as he felt his way through the darkness to the well in the courtyard. He had been bedridden the past few days, so quite a while had passed since he last woke up this early. Even in the trading house he was staying at, now filled with rich merchants, he was still the first one here.

Using the pole that rested against the side of the well, he broke the thick ice that had formed. The water that bubbled up was painfully icy, and washing his face felt like a knife chiseling away his drowsiness. Wiping his face, he breathed in a lungful of cool air, then gazed up toward the starry sky, feeling so refreshed that he smiled.

Then he kneeled onto the frozen ground. There was no need for a woolen mat or anything of the sort. Enduring pain and the cold meant his prayers to God would be filled with passion.

The tranquil atmosphere always gave him the urge to pray, but as the sky grew brighter, early risers among the merchants began to appear. If he took his time here, there would no doubt be a line of people asking him to pray for the prosperity of their business. It would have all been for naught if he fell ill again from that.

After reaching an appropriate stopping point, he returned to his room, then prepared paper and ink on the desk. He had to write a letter, though it was rather late for that.

He was writing to the couple who had taken care of him since he was a child. Including various details of his travels, he wrote about the trouble he and his companion had gotten caught up in during their stay at a port town. The couple was sharp eared, and news of such a large commotion would reach them before long. He considered that writing in detail would be more calming than not.

Still, he carefully chose the words in his letter, cautiously laying out the truth. The reason was simple: He was currently caring for the only daughter of his benefactors, and he could easily imagine the look on her father's face, filled with worry for her safety.

He wrote that their daughter, practically of marrying age, was unharmed. There was emphasis on how she had shown a girlie side for once when he collapsed from overwork, leading her to take care of him. He added that though she was still a big eater, selfish, and a prankster to boot, she had been a great help with her courage as well as her intellect. *Then…*He began to write, but his hand suddenly stopped.

During the commotion several days before, he discovered the secret that their daughter had been hiding for several years. Her mother also knew already; the oblivious ones were the men. Her father should probably hear this, but there was a serious reason why the pen did not move. That was because there was a young man his daughter fancied, and he was that very boy, the one on a journey with her now.

From her father's perspective, it was as though she was traveling with a wolf. The young man in question had no undue intentions, of course, but confident as he was that a misunderstanding was unlikely, he still thought that writing about the matter would perhaps cause unnecessary anxiety. He hesitated for a moment, and in the end, he chose to not include it.

It seems we will be safely able to continue our travels. May God watch over you.

After writing that, he signed his name: *Tote Col.*

He really should have their daughter, Myuri, sign as well, but there was no doubt she would attempt to change the contents if she saw the letter. Simply thinking about it seemed like quite the hassle, which he wanted to avoid.

When he sealed the letter, he could not help but feel a twinge of guilt, as though he was sealing away a secret.

CHAPTER ONE

As the sun rose, the church bell rang loudly.

It was the sound that signaled the opening of the market and an announcement that another day had begun.

Of course, working artisans and merchants had been going about their business long beforehand, but they seemed a bit hesitant prior to the bell chime. Afterward, there was no need to keep voices low or mind footsteps. Though it was the middle of winter, all the windows in every house were open, and even the children of noble families who drank too much the night before would be chased from their beds.

Once the echoing of the bell faded away, Col closed the scripture and inhaled deeply.

"Myuri!"

He called her name, and for just a brief moment, the mound of blanket atop the bed wavered in protest. He thought for a second that she would awaken, but she immediately fell silent again.

He sighed and stood up from the chair, then pulled back the blanket that covered the sleepyhead staying with him.

"Ugh..."

With the bright morning light pouring over her, the silver ball of fur curled up even tighter. It was a young girl, her hair a curious hue, like flecks of silver mixed with ash, and she hugged a warm-looking ball of fur that ran with the same color.

Myuri had stowed away in Col's luggage when he left the bathhouse that had cared for him for ten years in the hot spring village of Nyohhira. Now she was shivering while covering her head with her arms to block out the bright morning sun. It was a sight he often saw back at the bathhouse.

"...It's cold..."

He could hear a reproachful voice from the face pressed against the bed. He could also see animal ears poking out from between her arm and her head, which someone else could have easily mistaken for a sort of fur hat.

"You will quickly warm up once you get up and eat breakfast."

"..."

Myuri fell silent in protest, but he suddenly heard a quiet rumble. It seemed her body reacted on its own upon hearing the word "breakfast." Col had known Myuri since she was a baby, and he knew how to handle her. He cleared his throat once and spoke as he folded the blanket.

"I'll start by putting some rye bread on the stove."

"..."

The animal ears poking out from behind Myuri's arm twitched.

"At the same time, I'll sprinkle rock salt onto some fatty bacon and fry it with onions. Perhaps I should add a clove or two of the leftover garlic from last night?"

Her tail shivered in her own grip, and she squirmed in her curled position.

"Once the smell of garlic fills the air and enough fat drips from the bacon, I'll add a fresh egg. *Fshhh...*"

He could hear her gulp.

"After scrambling the egg a bit, once it sticks to the juicy bacon,

I'll remove it from the heat and place it on the warm bread before the yolk hardens completely. And once the soft-scrambled egg and the salty fat from the bacon soak into the bitter yet slightly sour rye bread...*Yum.*"

"Aaaghh!"

Myuri gave up and released herself from her ball, sitting up.

"Brother, you bully! You don't even have any food like that!"

"Breakfast itself is a luxury. We still have pork sausage from last night."

He placed the folded blanket onto the bed, and he could tell that she was tempted to fall back asleep, but she was now completely focused on breakfast. She glumly slipped off the bed and sneezed loudly.

"Here, fix your hair and your clothes."

"...*Hachoo!* ...*Sniffle.* It's too much work. I want to eat breakfast here..."

"This is not the bathhouse, and we are not patrons. Go to the kitchen yourself."

He spoke calmly, and Myuri pouted, reluctantly changing out of her clothes. Though Col treated her like his actual sister, having cared for her since she was a baby, Myuri was getting to be that age. He turned his back to her as she changed.

"Okay, Brother, I'm ready!" she called out to him grumpily, and he looked back over his shoulder.

She had a rabbit fur cape wrapped around her shoulders, bear fur wrapped around the waist where her trousers cut off at the hips, and linens on her legs that emphasized the lines of her body.

It was a look that stood out even in a busy port town.

Col could still see something in particular that would draw the gazes of others, so he quietly pointed it out.

"Your ears and tail."

Then Myuri patted the animal ears and tails before they

disappeared. They were not fake, but actually a part of her. It was a characteristic of what would be called demonic possession in human society, and it was because her mother was the embodiment of a wolf who resided within wheat.

Though Myuri was an incorrigible tomboyish prankster that he could do nothing about, he could say with conviction that God had not cursed her. Moreover, since she could voluntarily hide her ears and tail, it wasn't too much trouble for her to live alongside humans. However, if she became angry, surprised, or experienced other large swings in emotion, it wasn't uncommon for her ears and tail to pop out on their own.

"Is this okay?"

He shrugged, and Myuri copied him.

"Aw, I'm hungry. I'll do my hair later…"

She placed her small hands onto her stomach, and the ends of her eyebrows drooped. If her tail was out, it would have definitely been sagging lifelessly. She passed in front of him, and just as he considered seeing her off, she suddenly grabbed his sleeve and pulled him forward.

"What? Wh-what are you doing?"

Just as he was about to fall over, Myuri turned back to him in exasperation.

"What do you mean, what? It's my turn."

"…Your 'turn'?"

Col was perplexed as Myuri gracefully hugged his arm. She beamed a cloudless smile at him from below his shoulders.

"This is a contest, and it has to be fair. No hogging allowed."

Myuri smiled at him innocently, but he did not know what she was talking about.

Contest? Hogging?

His efforts to try and piece those words together went unnoticed as she intertwined her fingers with his.

The reddish-amber eyes she inherited from her mother glinted, ready.

"Did you forget? The contest between me and God. *Who are you going to fall in love with first—me or God?*"

"…"

Myuri was around twelve years old, and her smile was still filled with innocence.

Just like a real sister, he had cared for her since she was a baby, but he had just learned a few days ago that she had, at some point, begun to see him as a member of the opposite sex.

For ages, she professed her love for him, and he knew that she admired him, of course. He never doubted his relationship with Myuri. However, it was a different story when it came to her liking him in *that* way.

Above all, he was someone who aspired to be a priest, and he had sworn vows of abstinence. Therefore, it was not possible to answer Myuri's feelings. He had explained this to her clearly.

She was smart, understanding the logic completely. It was pointless to indulge her feelings and throw temper tantrums. The problem was that Myuri was also too clever, and she would continue on the path of what she considered right without any hesitation.

"It's not like we're related by blood. There's no problem if we like each other, so I just have to get you to like me more than God, right?"

She explained her rationale calmly. When he voiced his rejection, Myuri had not been sad or upset, nor did she begin to doubt their relationship and act awkwardly. As always, she would slip into his covers during the night, cling to him at every opportunity, and her ears and tail, wagging happily, would be out whenever she could manage. Rather, it was as though she stopped holding back once she made her feelings known. Her displays of affection were even more intense than they had been back in Nyohhira as she practically threw herself at him.

In the face of this, a priest's vows of abstinence seemed like nothing more than sheltering in the shade of a tree to escape the intense midsummer sun bearing down on him. To top it all off, Myuri was even planning to cut down that tree. With the intelligence she inherited from her parents, she had come to one conclusion after reading the scripture from top to bottom.

Though priests were not supposed to give in to bodily desires, laypersons were not forbidden from loving priests. In short, as long as the priest himself did not try anything, there was no problem. What's more, Col had indeed sworn vows of abstinence, but he was still not a full-fledged priest!

Col did not have anything in his arsenal to fight back against such an argument.

The logic was sound after all.

"Come on, let's go have breakfast! It'll be *way* more fun than talking to a God who won't ever listen to a single prayer of yours!"

Though she spoke confidently in such a faithless manner, she was generally correct, and it made his head hurt. He looked down at her smiling face out of the corner of his eye and spoke wearily.

"If we want to discuss who listens to me less, then you may be winning in that regard."

"But as long as you can touch me, I haven't lost."

Her tail, which should have been put away, was swishing happily, and her head was pressed against his chest, not minding if her animal ears bent.

There was not a single hint of sexual attraction in her actions; a child's crush was exactly what it was.

However, he remembered how hard she worked to take care of him after he collapsed from exhaustion these past few days. In his hazy bouts of consciousness, he occasionally saw her praying expression, and he could not imagine that was insincere. He could also take her onslaught of affection as an indicator of how much she had worried about him. When he thought about that, it was even more difficult to act indifferent.

"Right, Brother?"

"...Very well."

She pressured him, and he responded with a sigh.

"However..."

He changed the tone of his voice, and Myuri quickly loosened her grip on his arm. She knew that he would get angry with her, and she did not want to do anything that upset him.

There was no doubt that she was a good girl.

"Your ears and tail are still out."

"Oh."

She hurriedly patted her head while retracting her ears, then tapped her tail, making it disappear.

As she did so, Col walked to the door, reaching for the knob.

"And one more thing," he said as he opened the door, Myuri jogging up to him. "Don't eat too much."

She widened her eyes blankly at him, then grinned, baring her fangs.

"Okay."

That was most certainly a hollow promise.

He did not feel like being cross with her; she really did have him in the palm of her hand.

They exited into the hallway, and as the door closed behind them, Myuri's small hand naturally slipped into his.

He sighed, and she beamed a cheerful smile.

It was another lively day for the Debau Company trading house they were staying at.

15

There were many jobs that had to be done in such a large company, and it was rather flexible when it came to taking breaks. Anyone who sat at one of the tall, worn-out tables by the wall in the kitchen could watch the errand boys and experienced merchants stream in when they managed to find a free moment and eat while standing before heading to their next job.

Among all the hustle and bustle, whenever the errand boys came in, their eyes would widen as they saw Myuri leisurely dipping bread into her soup.

Rather than being captivated by her elegance or extravagance, they were surprised because Myuri had worked as an errand boy for the trading house for a short while. It seemed they were surprised that one of the friends they worked together with was actually a girl.

"I did the best work, and I was the bravest."

Myuri puffed out her chest in pride, but when Col thought about how she would soon be of marriageable age, he wished she would be a bit more ladylike.

"Hurry and finish eating."

"What? But you always get mad when I eat fast."

She pouted.

"…That is because you would always have meat in one hand and bread in the other like a bandit, stuffing it into your face all at once, then going to play in the mountains."

It was written all over her face how much of a pain she thought his remarks were as she scraped the bottom of the bowl with her bread and tossed it in her mouth.

"But you have nothing better to do, right? All the commotion in town's died down."

That commotion was exactly what had caused him to collapse from exhaustion and the reason why they had come to the port town of Atiph in the first place. The issue was the standoff between the Church that headed the world's grandest religion and the Kingdom of Winfiel that stood against it.

The Church, holding the same seat of authority for a thousand years, had forgotten the meaning of faith and instead wielded its power to satisfy personal desires. Needless to say, the clergy indulged in debauchery and other transgressions. They extracted taxes at every opportunity and exploited their privileges. Lately, they had been drawing the ire of the entire world due to their tithes, originally levied to pay for a holy war against the pagans, which were still being pried out of the people's hands even though that war ended.

Thus, the Kingdom of Winfiel finally stood up to the Church's tyranny, spurring Col to leave the rural mountain hot spring village of Nyohhira to become a collaborator in the kingdom's efforts.

Then he and Myuri got caught up in a big incident right as they were attempting to persuade the church of the port town Atiph, but somehow, it all managed to end up being okay.

"I do have better things to do. After this, I must go to the church and help Heir Hyland."

Hyland, an illegitimate child of the king of Winfiel, was a respectable noble of royal blood who had directly asked Col for help. She had a virtuous will and, despite the overwhelming odds in the aforementioned incident, had calmly put her own life at risk for the sake of her faith.

If everything Col had learned deep in the mountains could be of some help, he wished to use it in service of a person like her—someone who embodied his ideals.

"Aw, what?"

However, when Myuri heard Hyland's name, she made a clear frown.

"You don't have to go…That blondie said so herself. You should concentrate on getting better. So after this, we should take a walk in town or even rest in the room."

She called Hyland "that blondie."

He wondered why she disliked her so much. Perhaps it was because Hyland was a beautiful woman who dressed as a man.

It vexed him, but it seemed that his respect and vassal-like attitude toward Hyland looked quite similar to love for Myuri.

"I have spent an entire week in bed. And there is a mountain of things that need to be done in order to correct the wrongdoings of the Church."

"Hmph." Myuri snorted, uninterested, as she splayed her upper body on the table.

"Of course, if you decide to quit this troublesome journey and return to Nyohhira, I will allow you to do so."

Still bent over, she lifted her head and glared at Col for his comment.

During the whole commotion, Myuri had supported him both physically and mentally. It was clear that without all her help, things would have gone very differently for him, so it was necessary to recognize her outstanding strength and wit. That was why, if he sent her home without hearing what she had to say, he felt as though he would be the one at a disadvantage.

Even though it was typically unthinkable that such a young girl would go on a journey, she made her way in the world much better than he did, so he could do nothing to convince her.

Myuri, currently staring at him, was more than clever enough to grasp all this.

"Fine, fine." She said as though she had given up, and she looked up at him from the corner of her eye, anticipating what he would say next.

"Then go and put your dishes away. Or would you rather stay behind in the room by yourself?"

"No."

"Then please clean up."

"Fine."

As though with great effort, Myuri did as she was told and went to the kitchen to return her tableware.

Before long, she returned with a piece of dried meat in her mouth.

Col could not summon the will to remind her that girls should not stand and eat.

"The church, then?"

"Yes. Oh, before that, we should go say hello to Mr. Stefan. I haven't been able to see him since becoming bedridden."

Stefan was a part of the Debau Company, which had branches all over the northlands. He was responsible for business conducted at the Debau Company's trading house in the port town of Atiph, where Col and Myuri were borrowing a room.

But when he said that, Myuri was astonished, and it was not as a joke.

"You probably shouldn't, Brother."

"What?"

"Did you forget you mercilessly threatened him during all the uproar? Beardy was really afraid of us…of you, really."

"…"

It was true that during the crisis, Col had needed to persuade Stefan to cooperate with them in order to save Hyland. Their plan involved convincing him of a massive misunderstanding. To put it simply, they made it appear as though they were truly instruments of God.

Though they had been captured, the fact they escaped so easily must have seemed like the work of God anyway. On top of that, when Stefan saw Col free from his prison, a silver wolf stood at his side, potentially a proxy for carrying out God's punishments

19

on earth. From an outsider's perspective, it should have been easy to see there was something supernatural at play.

Of course, if anyone were likely to anger God, it would actually be that wolf herself—Myuri.

"You probably shouldn't deal too much with him, so he can relax a bit." She smiled dryly before adding, "I feel kind of bad for him." There was a particular look on her face that she only showed when she knew one of her pranks had gone too far.

"W-was it that terrible?"

In response, she shrugged like a little girl who couldn't help but want to seem like an adult.

"…Very well, then."

"It's fine, I think."

Col had no wish to hurt others.

"Then, let's head to the church for now."

Myuri nodded, munching on her dried meat.

In larger towns, it was a typical sight to see the retired elderly remain in the church once morning prayer ended. With this in mind, Col was bewildered when he found an entire crowd after opening the door.

"Line up, line up please! We ask that you take any requests not related to the church to the council!"

A young man, perhaps a deacon, literally stood out from the rest of the crowd, perhaps because he had climbed atop a crate or something, and was yelling as loudly as he could in the hallway. Much like the hallway, beyond the crowd Col could also see that the nave was overflowing with people. From the clothes of the people packed inside, he discerned a diverse group of merchants, artisans, farmers, shepherds, and even some who, for whatever reason, held up flagstaffs bearing association crests.

"Haven't we seen a scene just like this one, Brother?" Myuri asked as she tilted her head a bit, but he did not know.

As he was in complete shock at the sight of what seemed like the church holding a festival, someone bumped into him from behind.

He turned around, and there was a stout man who looked like a merchant.

"Oh, pardon me! ...Mm? Oh, a man of the Church! Perfect. I wanted to ask where we might be able to discuss the wine tax."

"Huh?"

"I've heard there've been reforms enacted by the archbishop, so we from the Brotherhood of Taverns and Inns from Schulaze Parish Alley wish to request he reconsider the contributions for ceremonial wine, you see."

The man seemed sad, and he lowered his head, placing a hand on his large stomach.

"Ah..."

"As you know, on top of the tax we already have to pay when we import wine, oftentimes we can't get any because the ships don't come in. So to bring a contribution of wine whenever we come to pray is too much...Oh, here are pastries baked by the girls from our parish and candles. Please accept these."

As though the man thought he had spoken too one-sidedly, he joyfully produced a package and pushed it onto Col.

Because Col was dressed like a priest, it seemed this petitioner had completely mistaken him for a member of the Church.

It seemed that the entire building was overflowing with people like this.

"O-oh, I'm sorry, I am not a member of the Church. I'm a traveler..."

"Oh? Ah, is that right? Then how about it? Why don't you come stay at an inn in the Schulaze Parish Alley while you're in town? We have great food and comfortable beds ready for you. And of course, if you happen to see the archbishop, please tell him of our integrity and piety and to reconsider the tax on wine—Wh-what? Hey!"

At this rate, they would be talked into staying at some inn by this pushy merchant. Col took Myuri's hand, who had stood beside him grinning for some reason, then apologized while pushing his way through the crowd to head farther into the church. It seemed that the aftermath of the recent tumult that consumed the town just a few days before had morphed into something bigger, throwing the people into even more disarray.

To put it simply, though the townspeople had stood up and denounced the evil practices of the Church, it seemed too rash to assume that everything would be all squared away once they won over the archbishop. Along with the city council, which managed the government of the town, the church was a place with a large influence on the town's administration. All the inhabitants followed the Church's decisions, which meant collecting taxes on a great many things. Any time the archbishop changed his mind and wished to enact a new policy, he could not avoid dealing with many people. And if the townspeople thought a change could be for their benefit, they would rush over to his side, asking to be included.

As one of the people partly responsible for this trouble, Col cringed in regret and horror.

However, what he was working toward was not a small adjustment in a northern port town.

It was to right all the wrongs that the Church had accumulated over a thousand years. If that came to pass, it would surely cause chaos ten or a thousand times bigger.

This was no time to be horror-struck by such trivial matters.

"…Oh God, please give me strength." Col murmured under his breath, encouraging himself.

Hyland was likely at the center of the commotion, and he

concluded that she was probably in the meeting room. The flow of people seemed to be vaguely heading in that direction. He and Myuri shuffled through the crowd until they could finally see the entrance of the meeting room.

The large doors to the room had been left open. A maidservant emerged from the crowd inside, carrying an armful of parchment. Though her head and face were wrapped in cloth, perhaps out of respect for the Church, the long hair that spilled out from beneath the veil gave her an image of exhaustion. Her eyes were cast downward as she made her way meekly through the frenzied throng.

She was a sight to behold; her height pairing well with her brilliant, albeit frazzled, blonde hair.

But Col could not stare for too long lest he be rude, so he immediately looked away. Then, he suddenly remembered that Myuri was beside him, which made him grow nervous for some reason.

"What is it, Brother?"

Myuri posed the question while trying her best to avoid being crushed by the crowd. There was a puzzled expression on her face, denoting that the short Myuri had yet to catch a glimpse of the maidservant.

"Oh…It's nothing."

A few moments after he responded, he looked back to the maidservant, like being drawn in by a fishhook.

He opened his mouth but unwittingly closed it, because the maidservant had noticed him as well, and she softly placed a finger to her lips. Then, with a surprisingly clean-looking finger for a working girl, she pointed farther inside the church before walking off briskly without waiting for his response.

Dumbstruck, he had no other choice but to follow her. He grabbed Myuri's hand, and they pried their way through the press of people.

They followed the woman for some time before finally arriving at the stairway that led up to the bell tower, where there was no sign of any others.

"Well."

The woman threw the parchment she was holding onto some crates that were stacked in the hallway, removed the wrapping on her head, then ran her fingers through her hair to fix it. It was strange, since as she did so, she looked like upstanding nobility from the shoulders up.

And for some reason, she also looked like a beautiful widow.

"What a surprise, Heir Hyland."

He called her name, and Hyland, who was a true noble, the blood of the king of Winfiel in her veins, displayed a hint of fatigue behind her smile.

"I wouldn't have been able to leave that room if I didn't do this. The townspeople swarm me when I try to get back to the trading house, even late at night, so I'm staying here. That being said, I'm glad I can't be recognized in this disguise, but it also feels a bit strange."

At the end of the day, people often judged others simply by their appearance. Col recalled how he had mistakenly assumed Hyland, who had dressed as man for her travels, was male, even though they had quizzed each other on the scripture in the hot springs, so he could not exactly bring himself to laugh.

"Hello there, little miss. How are you doing?"

It seemed Myuri had immediately recognized who it was when she saw her dressed as a maidservant, and her mood instantly grew sour. On the other hand, Hyland was rather happy to elicit that response from her.

"Myuri."

Of course, Col had to rein in her rude behavior. When he admonished her, she looked away in a huff.

Hyland's shoulders shook with laughter.

"I guess it's because I don't have any candies today. Oh well."

"I am so sorry..."

"I'm just having fun; it's like I've made a sister much younger than me. Well then, how are you doing?"

"I am much better, thank you."

He thanked her like a vassal would his lord, and from his side, Myuri shot him a dispassionate glare.

"You should be thanking the little miss here. I'm not the one who took care of you."

Myuri slapped Col's back in agreement with Hyland.

"And I should be the one showing you gratitude. You saved my life, as well as the flame of righteous faith."

He looked up and Hyland was smiling.

Nobility did not easily bow their heads, but her feelings reached him well enough through her smile.

"I didn't..."

"You'd act like that even if you saved the world." She chuckled. "Well, no matter. As your superior, I shall simply show my thanks through action. It's not quite a celebration for your recovery, but why don't we eat together? I've been working since before the sun rose, you know."

Like Myuri, she pressed a hand on her stomach.

"Can we have meat?" Myuri butted in.

Col wanted to scold her for the audacity of such constantly rude behavior, but Hyland seemed to be truly enjoying it. Besides, he did not have the heart for it. Of course, Myuri was doing it precisely because she knew that Hyland would not get angry with her.

"I don't mind. I'd like some meat with plenty of salt, too."

"Yay!"

It would have been pointless to remind her that she had just eaten breakfast.

"Then let's leave through the back door. Bear with me—I don't have a covered carriage to take us. And while we're on the way, I want to tell you about what's coming next. A lot happened while you were asleep."

They did not come to this town to enjoy a relaxing vacation.

Col straightened up and nodded, while Hyland dipped her head slightly in turn.

They exited through the back of the church into the street, which was as quiet as the front was loud. Though people seldom passed through here, it did not feel empty or desolate. It would be more appropriate to call it tranquil.

Perhaps the sky was so clear because the air in seaside towns was known for being remarkably dry. And maybe it was because the sounds of housework and a crying baby could be heard from a small window of one of the buildings that lined the street.

The town was undoubtedly filled with the energy of people going about their daily lives.

"For now, everything's going perfectly." Hyland spoke as she gracefully lifted the hem of her skirt and stepped across an old, thin dog that lay on the ground, blocking the street.

Col carefully moved to the side of the street and went over its tail instead. When Myuri followed, the old dog respectfully curled its tail out of her way. To the dog, it was not nobility nor a lamb of God who stood at the pinnacle, but a girl with the blood of wolves.

"The town's archbishop has promised to rethink the rights he had taken for granted as well as the indulgences, opting to live a simple life from now on. Of course, when he says that he means a lifestyle that is not too meager for an archbishop, but it is still an enormous step. Tithes are nothing compared to using the offerings he gains every week, every month, every season from prayer and festivals for his own private use."

"The moment I entered the church, a person from the brotherhood of one of the town's parishes came to talk to me about contributions of wine."

The priests in town had a great deal of perks.

"Yes. Those crowding into the church are people of that sort. There are fourteen parishes that call themselves alleys in this town. The artisans and merchants of each parish have their own associations, and there are even several brotherhoods for their peace of mind. You could easily find fifty of them in this town alone. There are also individuals who come with their own interests in mind, so it's been quite the handful dealing with them."

Even in a place like Nyohhira, where everyone knew one another, community management was still challenging.

Col could not imagine how much trouble it was for Atiph, a large town that needed a greater amount of resources to operate properly.

"On top of that, the churches of the surrounding independent cities and monasteries have learned about the terrible degree of the people's anger toward the Church, and there have been throngs of their emissaries. They're asking, 'Should we change our policies as well?' and 'How much of a shift is necessary?'"

Though there must have been criticisms of the Church in the past, rarely has it led to open defiance.

No matter how questionable its actions, no one could challenge the Church. The people had given up, grown accustomed to the idea that no matter how rotten the institution became, it was still better than any alternative.

"In addition, there are many questions about the common-language translation of the scripture that you worked on. There were many people who were upset that priests held a monopoly on reading the holy works. Acts meant to discourage the Church from more audacious behavior are spreading like wildfire. It's all thanks to you two."

Col could think of a hundred reasons why that was untrue, but he considered it polite to accept Hyland's compliment without fuss, so he smiled shyly and filed her words away in his mind.

Still, their job was not yet over.

"But fire must always be kept under control."

Leaving the embers of reform to spread and burn—that line of thinking would only bring about civil strife. And they were up against the Church, which had more bastions across the world than even the biggest trading companies. They could not haphazardly throw themselves into fights with them.

"Exactly. We need to add the right amount of fuel to the fire, then watch the way the wind blows."

"So what can we do next?"

After continuing along the back street, they eventually entered an area referred to as the Old Town, from when Atiph was still small. Col knew this because the stones on the ground were worn down, having clearly been around for some time. There was also a bronze plaque on a building that actually read OLD TOWN. He could feel the pride of the longtime residents in how brightly the plaque shone.

Though it was a bit small to be called a proper square, food stalls had been set up around a small well, while cobblers repaired shoes and the neighborhood elderly played cards in the gaps between. What grabbed Col's attention most of all was the number of large nets that covered the entire walls of buildings. They surrounded the entire square and even hung from the roof of a five-story building.

It looked as though the whole square was caught in it.

"Brother, what's that? Is it for a festival?"

Myuri tugged Col's sleeve as she spoke.

"It would seem so...There's something on it. Is that dried grass cut to resemble fish?"

"This is apparently a festival hoping for a good catch in anticipation for spring. This neighborhood is where Atiph's fishermen live."

As she spoke, Hyland bought four skewers of fried herring from a stall.

She gave one to Col and two to Myuri.

"Fish fills the belly more than wheat does in this land. And no one can fight on an empty stomach. By the way..."

Hyland paused briefly before continuing.

"How well can you two swim?"

She smiled meaningfully, flashing her sharp teeth, then took a bite out of the back of the fried fish.

Violent winds roared like a war cry. Mountainous waves reached high into the sky. Water pouring in from the deck; food already chewed through by rats. Unable to sleep as the ship rocked so intensely that there was no discernible difference between floor and ceiling, he found himself exhaling water more than drinking it. With no place to run, there is nothing to do but pray. Even if he could continue to bear such fear and pain, it would all be over once the ship capsized with the next gust of wind. On the seas, unbeknownst to anyone, he would simply disappear.

On the other side of that, the names of ships and their value were posted on large sheets of paper in the port town taverns, the crests of various vessels on display. Rather well-dressed merchants would stand all day in front of these papers, hands folded, praying. At the very top of the sheets, written with rough strokes, were the words:

By the will of God.

In that tavern, a bet was being wagered as to whether or not the ship would sink. This test of chance was sometimes called by its other name: insurance. The owner would give 15 to 20 percent of the worth of the ship's load to his betting partner, and if it sank, then he would take the money back. If it did not sink, then the betting partner would be able to keep the money. In essence, it was estimated that there was a sinking in one out of every five sea journeys. This included pirate attacks.

Anyone who looked out beyond the town on a gray and windy day would find villagers who lived along the coastline standing on rooftops, staring at the sea. They would be on the lookout for foolish merchant ships greedily trying to make their way on the white waves. They could make a profit on the cargo that drifted ashore if those boats were wrecked by the winds, thrown onto the rocks, or simply sank. However, through arrangements between large mercantile entities and landlords, any freight that drifted ashore lawfully belonged to the landowners. That was why it was unthinkable for the villagers to provide assistance to the ship-wrecked vessels. It would mean trouble with the higher-ups. If they wanted to be saved, the castaways should have wrapped themselves in gold—but then again, it would be worse to sink under the weight of the coins.

This world was hell. Truly, the epitome of an adventure.

God bless those who navigate the seas.

"Well, that's the gist of it."

The noble of the Kingdom of Winfiel, a country surrounded on all sides by water, mischievously licked the chicken fat that coated her fingers. Before Col lay a massive feast. They were in a tavern where local fishermen gathered, whose work began on the sea before dawn and ended before noon.

He had not touched his food, though—not because he was

shying away from meat as a person who aspired to join the priest-hood but because of Hyland's story.

On the large model ship hanging from the ceiling, there were wings made of chicken feathers—perhaps someone's idea of a prank. After hearing her story, it almost seemed as though there was a deeper meaning to those wings.

"...Are you requesting us to go on such a sea voyage?"

Col raised the question in a thin voice, prompting Hyland to look up at him as she bit into her chicken thigh. Her refinement shined through even more as she ate, oddly emphasizing her femininity.

"Oh, my apologies. I didn't mean to threaten you."

It was like she had seen right through to the heart of his troubles. After she placed the chicken onto a bed of oats—a replacement for a plate—she wiped her mouth.

"My country is surrounded by water, you know. We talk about ships and the ocean more than any other place. We love tales of adventures on the seas. When I was little, the old sailors would often scare me with their stories."

When Col imagined a young Hyland, wrapped in a blanket in front of the fire, enthralled by grand stories, he could not help but smile.

There was no mistake, however, that the sea was a terrifying place, even more so in the dead of winter.

"Of course, what I just told you was an exaggeration, but there are times when such things can...Hmm?"

Col followed Hyland's gaze, and beside him, Myuri had gripped her bread and it crumbled out from between her fingers.

She was leaning forward, her mouth slack-jawed and her eyes wide open.

When Myuri spoke, her voice was practically a groan.

"Ad...ven...ture...!"

Had he poked her cheek, which was nearly bursting with excitement, her ears and tail might have popped out.

"Don't expect too much. I might end up disappointing you this time."

Hyland smiled wryly, and Myuri quickly collected the scattered crumbs and sprinkled them over her soup as a topping so as to not waste it. A part of Myuri still seemed like a seven-year-old boy on the inside.

"But—but a ship? On the sea? Brother?"

"Calm down. Come on, let go of the bread."

Myuri had thrown a fit of excitement over hearing about pirates when they came to the town of Atiph. To a girl who was born and raised in Nyohhira, a hot spring village surrounded by mountain views, exciting stories about the sea were much too thrilling.

It also took quite some work to loosen her fingers from the bread she gripped.

"We'll be taking a ship, but it won't be a long journey. It's short enough that you'll always be within eyesight of land, and no ship will risk the trip if the weather is even slightly agitated. You'll be at sea for half a day at the longest. It's just a bit of a trip from port to port. And it won't be a problem if you get seasick, since you'll be at the port by the time you wake up."

Hyland laid out her explanation, which helped ease Col's nerves but left Myuri visibly dissatisfied.

"But it doesn't mean there won't be any problems. The seas are difficult around the islands even farther north of here, beyond the diocese of Atiph. No authority of any country reaches that far. They have their own rules and are harsh with outsiders. The weather often changes suddenly, and the shadow of the island can disappear when it needs to—it's a perfect trap. We call those who control those islands…"

She paused and looked straight into Myuri's eyes.

"…pirates."

"Pirates! …*Guh—!*" Myuri yelled, standing from her chair, and Col, flustered, pushed his hand over her mouth and sat her down.

Luckily, the tavern was filled with leathery-skinned, red-faced sailors, who were unfazed by such terrifying words.

Hyland smiled, delighted, and it seemed she was intentionally egging Myuri on.

Though perhaps it was the kind of joke a noble would tell, but there was likely truth in what she said.

"And are you saying…to convert those pirates?"

Though he had knowledge of the scripture, he could not stop violence with aphorisms. He was grounded in reality enough to realize at least that much. Anecdotes of missions where ruffians instantly transformed into obedient puppies after a round of preaching were obviously fantasies.

"If you have a holiness that puts saints to shame, perhaps, or…"

Hyland narrowed her eyes in mischief and smiled. In her hand, she held the low-quality ale that the sailors drank.

But she was clearly not drunk. Even when she stayed in Nyohhira, he did not once see her drunk, and high alcohol tolerance was a sign of nobility.

"Of course, I won't ask you to do something so reckless. I'd like you to make the most of your scholarship."

"…And that means?"

"Mhmm."

Hyland nodded, gazed into space, and the innkeeper, who had been standing in front of the counter, hurried over to attend to her. It seemed as though it was not a coincidence they came here.

Then, after she said a few words to him, he disappeared into the back and then returned carrying a small wooden box. It was bound with an odd cord, and upon closer inspection, Col could tell it was fish leather twisted together like yarn.

She released the string and opened the lid, and laying on a blanket of straw was a black figure.

"Ooh, a doll?"

Myuri's voice was surprisingly girlie and pleasant.

That being said, when she happily stood from her chair to get a peek inside the box, the color suddenly drained from her face.

"...Whoa, that's...weird..."

He could not bring himself to laugh at how straightforward she was, since it mirrored how he felt.

"Isn't this...the Holy Mother? But why is it this color?"

He thought it was a wooden figure that had been seared. There was, however, a beautiful glint to it, and the craftsmanship in the details was superb. He could tell it was a completed piece and that it was meant to look like this.

"It's made of jet," Hyland said and picked up the black figure of the Holy Mother. "You can sometimes find it in regions where peat and amber are gathered. It's an odd stone."

Hyland handed it to Col, and for a moment, he thought he had dropped it.

It was that light—completely different from what he imagined by looking at it.

"They say that it is amber that has turned into coal. Like amber, polishing it attracts sand and wool; but unlike amber, it burns without melting once placed in a fire. It smells like something between peat and coal. That smell reminds me of home."

Peat and coal were abundant in the Kingdom of Winfiel. Nyohhira was rich in timber while peat was impossible to find there, so it was never used. During his travels, he had used it occasionally as fuel during his travels.

He handed the jet to Myuri, and she was also shocked by how light it was, admiring the fantastic decorations.

"They sometimes whittle it down into small balls and call them black pearls as a scam. It's merely rare, not precious. It doesn't have much value."

A figure of the Holy Mother made of jet.

Hyland took it from Myuri and gently returned it to its box.

"And there is a land that makes these jet figures of the Holy Mother and fervently worships them."

"You mean the islands in the north, correct?"

A region of harsh environment controlled by pirates.

"As you can see, it's a very well-wrought figure of the Holy Mother. However, since they have traditionally regarded the mainland as enemies, they've kept their distance from the power of the Church that is the foundation of the mainland. In the past, the Church once made various attempts to bring this region into their sphere of influence, but in the end, it was too costly to force them into submission, so they gave up."

No matter how he looked at it, the black figure of the Holy Mother, sealed with a string of fish skin, seemed heretical.

It would not be strange to consider this religious witchcraft.

"And so...," Hyland said, "I want you to go see if we should bring the believers of this land into our fold."

He returned her gaze. What he saw were not the kind eyes of a distant friend but the sharp glint of his superior.

"The Church sometimes suspects them of heresy, but their faith may be the real thing. Or perhaps, though they are creating such wonderful figures of the Holy Mother, it might also be a cover against actual subjugation if they were to be called pagans. I know you can connect with them and determine if their faith is true or not."

"That's—"

"Let me rephrase that. Whatever your judgment is, it will play a large part in my considerations."

What she showed him after was a smile for fooling people.

36

In their present situation, the number of allies they gathered was not a problem. On the other hand, if one of their allies was a strange religious group, it would create an opportunity that the Church could take advantage of, potentially leading to doubt in the righteousness of the Kingdom of Winfiel. That being said, he could tell that lip service would not be enough. That was because she had qualified her statement with "play a large part in my considerations."

Of course, it was the way of the world for people to bow down and follow the orders of a noble. He and Hyland were never equals to begin with; their relationship would typically not allow them to share the same table.

However, jesters aside, the only ones allowed to butt heads with rulers were priests.

Hyland continued to smile, and temptation spurred Col on.

"Very well. By the light of my scholarship and faith, I shall see if their conviction is true."

Still smiling, she stared at him and nodded, satisfied.

Her gaze suddenly turned to Myuri, who sat beside him.

"And is there anything you'd like to say, little miss?"

When she said that, her smile was clearly personable and gentle.

"My brother's a coward." Myuri chewed on the cartilage of some chicken thigh as she continued. "I don't want to watch him be used like a tool."

He looked to her only to see her staring back at him.

She was carefree, mischievous, always seemed like she thought of nothing but food, and her intelligence was beyond expectation. Her mother was known as the wisewolf who was worshipped as a god once upon a time, and her father was a sharp merchant, highly regarded by a select few in the northlands.

With such a pedigree, one could not disregard Myuri's keen

insight simply because she was a child. She clearly noticed that he had swallowed every doubt that occurred to him about this job.

But though he admired her quick-wittedness, she was still a child.

"It is not because I am afraid of her authority that I do not ask Heir Hyland questions."

"Then what is it?"

"Because I trust her."

Myuri widened her eyes in surprise, then frowned.

"Little miss, your brother isn't the obedient lamb you think he is."

"...What?"

Really? Myuri looked at Hyland doubtfully.

"He trusts that with the requisite information, I will pass a proper judgment. Those expectations need to be met. Your brother understands that I am serious about my obligations."

Hyland added that therefore, there was no need to put everything into words. For some reason, she seemed to be having fun.

Myuri often put adults to shame, but she made a face as though Hyland was speaking to her in a foreign language.

That being said, she had stayed quiet for so long because that was not what she was thinking about.

"When I think about that, I believe that one day he'll get into a lot of trouble because he really didn't know anything."

"Myuri."

He admonished her, and she glared back at him.

She pointed at him and said, "You can only see half of half of the world!"

Her logic was that the world was filled with men and women, so his lack of understanding of women was half of the world. Then, because people had both good and bad sides, when he did not notice the bad, he lost another half there. Myuri sincerely believed that without her, Col would immediately stray from the path and fall head over heels into the pits of oblivion.

"You two make a great pair."

Hyland smiled with her eyes and spoke with a slightly envious expression on her face.

"That's why I feel comfortable leaving it to you."

Then she took the cheap ale in her hands. Maybe it was because from the perspective of others, she would be worried unless she drank.

What she said next made that seem about right.

"When the Church deemed the Kingdom of Winfiel enemies that should be subdued, the strait between Winfiel and the mainland became a militarily critical area."

The talk suddenly shifted from faith toward bloodier talk.

That was what she had not spelled out when she said she would take his judgment into consideration.

"We do have a substantial force. The pope lacks a true fleet of ships to call his own. He would likely go to war using ships commandeered from coastal towns. That is why I came to the port town of Atiph, to create as many allies on the mainland side of the strait."

She sipped her ale and gently placed it onto the table.

"And if war did break out, it would interfere with imports into our island nation. Our wheat would never arrive, requesting wine would never amount to anything more than wishes. So what would be left?"

What sort of people gathered in this tavern?

Col's gaze drifted down to the soup on the table, chunks of fish floating in it.

"Fish?"

"Right. The pirates in the northern islands have a firm grip on the areas with good sources of northern fish, including herring.

If they become our ally, it would a secure a food source for us, and if they become our enemy, the opposite would happen."

The world was made of a complicated map of power.

It could not be freed so easily, like untying a knot.

"On top of that, they are incredibly skilled with all sorts of seafaring vessels. They will be the deciding factor in whether we gain mastery of the open water. However…"

Hyland pressed on.

"Our just cause is based on righteous faith. No matter how important they are strategically, we will not accept those with twisted beliefs as our companions. A rotten fish will spoil the other fish in the same barrel."

He trusted Hyland—had anyone else said the same thing, he would not have believed them.

However, her expression suddenly relaxed, and her smile dripped self-mockery.

"That being said, I sincerely hope they aren't rotten…But you can still eat rotten fish after cooking it through thoroughly, if you're even a bit worried. All of my companions, though, are starving."

No matter how careful Hyland was, she did not command this fight alone. The other nobles under the king of Winfiel might elect to take an easier route.

While that was happening, what Hyland could achieve in her position depended on how much correct information she could obtain. For that purpose, Col was to be her eyes and ears.

Before him was a great responsibility, but it was worth the effort.

Above all, he was simply interested in seeing what an unfamiliar faith looked like.

And so, there was only one thing left to ask.

"When shall we go?"

Hyland drained her ale, then spoke.

"How about tomorrow?"

Hyland had placed her trust in Col and assigned him a mission. Now he had to live up to those expectations.

And his judgment of the Black-Mother faith would have an effect on the greater flow of things. If they were too hasty to make the pirates their allies, it could become the source of trouble later, even if things seemed fine at first. It was also possible that these people were exactly what their cause needed, even if they seemed heretical at a glance.

At any rate, he was both scared and happy that she was relying on his insight.

It seemed that Hyland had not been kidding when she talked about setting out the next day, so they immediately began preparations to secure a ship. Though it was urgent, he could tell that if he stayed behind, there would be nothing for him but paperwork. The draft of his common-language translation of the scripture, which he had undertaken here in this town, had been sent off to the scholars in Winfiel, and Hyland said all there was to do was wait for their thoughts. It would take some time for a reply to come.

And so, if there was someplace else he could demonstrate his knowledge, he wanted to head there as soon as possible. The northern seas were, quite honestly, an unknown, frightening place to him, but it would be the perfect opportunity to broaden his worldview. It was a chance to push himself to do everything he could.

"Hey, Brother?"

Myuri's carefree voice cut through his ruminations as she pulled on the hem of his clothes.

"Which is cuter, this fur wrap or this leather one?"

After finishing their food and parting with Hyland, the two headed out to Atiph's marketplace. They most certainly did not have enough warm outfits for a journey to the northern seas. Luckily, though, the town offered many clothes, since the frequency of long sea journeys meant a large volume of people coming and going.

The abundance of options was a good thing, but since there were so many shops, Myuri spent the past while taking him from one storefront to the next. Then, when they arrived at a new spot, she would gather clothes from every corner and ask him what he thought about this or that.

But he simply was not interested and only answered mutedly.

"Choose something cheap and warm."

Every time, Myuri would consistently wear a flat expression, but she suddenly asked, "Fine, then let me ask you a different question. Which one do you like better?"

Instead of a cute smile, she directed a glare at him.

It seemed so innocent and cute that she hoped to draw the attention of her crush with clothes that he liked, but her mimicry always fell flat. She was overflowing with youth and energy but also a short temper.

"…Cheap and warm…Fine. Fine, then."

To appease Myuri, who had bared her fangs at him, he compared the two wraps and pointed to the fur one.

It seemed to have been made of deer fur, and he felt that a rough lay of fur suited her much better than something soft and fluffy.

Myuri looked hard at the one he pointed to and sighed.

"You have no eye for clothes."

He held back from scolding her that she should not say that after making him choose.

"But you chose it, so I'll take it!"

She suddenly smiled and happily hugged the fur.

For a moment, there was a pang in his chest as he thought about how he would have chosen more carefully if he had known she would be so happy. Ultimately, it did not matter since he could not reciprocate her feelings, so this was all right.

"*Sigh*...Well next, we need gloves, hats, and sachets for pocket warmers..."

There were many things they had to buy. It was at least a relief to know that Hyland would be footing the bill, but whenever he paid with the silver coin of the sun that was in circulation in this region, he felt something akin to guilt.

He had grown rather distant from moderation and frugality recently.

As he thought about how he needed to concentrate, Myuri suddenly spoke with a serious expression.

"We're going to need a sword and a shield, too, right?"

It seemed that the image in her head had completely turned into an adventure story once she caught word of pirates.

"No."

"Aww..."

Her disappointment was obvious. She took the fur coat they had just finished paying for and quickly rolled it up to carry on her back. Even though she proved that she could successfully work as an errand boy for a company with such skill, all that came out of her mouth was fantasies and daydreams. After thinking about how far her good name would echo throughout the world if she pulled herself together, he sighed.

"What we'll do is crash into our bounty from the side, then, with our swords in our mouths, we'll raise a battle cry and leap onto the other boat, right?"

She placed her hand by her mouth and gnashed her teeth, as though she really was gripping a sword with her mouth. Col was exasperated, and not just because her gnashing made it look like she was biting into skewered meat.

"How would you be able to raise a war cry with a sword in your mouth?"

"…Uh. Wait, what?"

Her expression was blank.

"See, you cannot simply accept stories about pirates when you don't know if they are true or not. Think more seriously about the cold that you need to face soon."

Myuri wore thin clothes for the sake of fashion and her body was slim without much in the way of fat. Though she did have her tail, that was not something she took out in front of regular people.

There was no such thing as too many pieces of thick, warm clothing in a place where freezing rain and the frozen sea were constant companions.

"I'm fine. Nyohhira's full of snow, too."

"There's no wind in Nyohhira. The wind on the sea will chill you to your bones."

On top of that, if the cold of Nyohhira's nights ever became too much, people simply jumped into the hot springs.

When he said that, Myuri suddenly fell silent and stared at him.

"What is it?"

"Have you ever been to the cold sea, Brother?"

Though she sounded a bit skeptical, she also sounded surprised. Or perhaps, she meant to express how unfair he was being.

"I have. I went to the Kingdom of Winfiel by ship in the dead of winter. It was bitterly cold."

"Really? When?!"

"It was when I had just met your mother and father, so…quite a long time ago."

In the face of the cold, Myuri's mother, Holo, had gone onto the deck to enjoy the scenery, but Col was still a child and afraid of ships at the time, so he clung to her father, Lawrence—that part he kept to himself.

"I have much more experience than you when it comes to traveling. So you need to listen to me."

Experience, rather than logic, resonated most with someone of Myuri's personality.

She still seemed dissatisfied, but she nodded half-heartedly.

After buying plenty of gear for their trip, they returned to the trading house to begin packing all the warm clothes and preserved foods they bought. Since they could be leaving the very next day, it would be bad form to dillydally if the order to depart suddenly came.

The sun was already setting when they finished up.

"I'm…tired…"

Once she finally wrapped the luggage in a blanket, Myuri collapsed onto the bed.

"This is a lot."

If Myuri carried the set of luggage sitting in the corner on her back, it would probably be bigger than her.

When Col imagined that, he smiled slightly.

"It's almost like—"

"A big adventure!"

Myuri leaped up, sitting cross-legged on the bed and smiling happily. He found himself troubled, because it suited her so well it almost felt tactless to scold her for being unladylike.

"A big adventure…Well, you're not wrong."

Though the tomboy was tired from travel preparations, it seemed she grinned in anticipation whenever the luggage caught her eye. Col, on the other hand, could only sigh.

"Brother, what's wrong? Are you hungry?"

"…"

He couldn't tell if she was joking, but it seemed to be a serious question.

"*Sigh…* No. It's not that." He answered and placed his hand on the leather cover of the scripture that sat on the desk in the room. "I don't know what will happen in the northern seas during this season. When I think about what could happen…"

He would likely not be able to help her. Though dangers were part and parcel of traveling, the place they were headed for was particularly unforgiving. Warmth wafted up into his palm that touched the cover of the scripture, where he believed a power rested. He had poured his whole body and soul into translating the inaccessible script of the Church into the vernacular, and he felt that in doing so, his faith had deepened.

His faith was true. God was lighting his way.

But despite that, his worries were not easily lifted.

"Brother." A voice came from behind him. "It's going to be all right."

He turned around, and there was Myuri, smiling triumphantly as always.

"You are always so optimistic."

"And you're so pessimistic. You'll age faster that way, you know."

It was nothing good for men who looked so young at his age. If anything, he wished what Myuri said would happen.

His expression asked, "Who on earth do you think I'm worried about?" and she grinned, baring her teeth.

"It'll be fine."

She spun around him and jumped to sit on the desk behind him.

"If you fall into the sea, I'll definitely go save you."

She only said that because she knew what he was worried about. Even if he continued to warn her, she would plug her ears and pretend not to hear.

He really was worried. If something happened to Myuri, he would never be able to explain it to Lawrence and Holo waiting for them back in Nyohhira.

He thought it might be best to leave her behind, even considering how furious Myuri would be, but she suddenly smiled calmly. That expression looked exactly like her mother's, the wisewolf, Holo.

"Well, you probably wouldn't be able to save me, but I can say one thing."

She then reached out to gently touch his chest and continued.

"If you fell into the cold, dark sea, I would absolutely jump in after you. I won't leave you alone, and as long as I'm with you, I wouldn't mind the depths of the sea."

Myuri adored tales of heroes and love stories. Her distinction between fiction and reality was hazy. She always believed that she would be the main character.

That she seemed slightly embarrassed after saying such things was proof she had grown up a little.

Then, as though hiding her embarrassment, she began to twist her finger on the leather cover of the scripture.

"M-Myuri, stop it, you'll mark the leather."

He voiced his protest, flustered, but she had already turned back to her normal, cheeky self.

"Hmph. What's so great about this book? I bet the God they talk about in it would just keep on sleeping if you fell into the sea, Brother. But I'm different."

She smacked the cover of the book, and she drew her face closer to him, a satisfied smile on it.

"So, you'll pick me, right?"

Her logic was like a hatchet that chopped through everything.

Myuri always kept her eyes on her goal, chasing it at top speed and biting into it with all her strength. Though she was a bit shy, she did not hesitate. She was straightforward, like a ray of light piercing the thick cover and lighting the ground on a cloudy day. That was her charm, and it often brought about good endings.

However, she was becoming old enough. She needed to know that not properly considering the consequences was not courage, but immaturity. She liked him as someone of the opposite sex because she had felt safe around him since she was a baby. This feeling was likely born as an extension of how lenient he was with her in one thing or another.

"I can say one thing."

He reached out to touch her cheek as she sat on the desk, and she closed one eye and tilted her head.

"I have an obligation to get you home safely to Nyohhira. You must prioritize your own safety. If something happened to you, I would never be able to face Lawrence and Holo again."

With his hand on her soft cheek, Myuri closed both eyes and tapped her feet.

But she did not answer.

"And what do you say?"

She opened her eyes and looked at him. He was perplexed because in her eyes, he could see a bit of maturity. She must have felt this was the place to say something serious, but as she began to speak, she stopped.

The tomboy closed her eyes again and said, "Okay."

He was disappointed in her half-hearted response.

Or perhaps he was just imagining it. As he looked at her, he could hear her stomach growl.

"I'm hungry."

When she declared that with a smile, every trace of the atmosphere from moments earlier had already vanished.

"Hey, Brother, we won't be able to eat meat at all when we go to the islands, right? So I want meat today."

She hopped down from the desk and returned to her usual self. She was like a puppy, begging for food.

"...You had meat with Heir Hyland during lunch, and this morning you had dried meat, and you had some sort of grilled meat yesterday, didn't you?"

"You're so nitpicky...," Myuri complained.

She grabbed her coat, wrapped it around her shoulders, then ran toward the door.

"Come on!"

She opened the door with one hand while offering her left to him. Her smile showed no doubt that he would reach out and take her hand, and he could not help but smile in return. He accepted her hand, and she gripped his firmly.

At the end of the day, their relationship was steady and would not change so easily.

There was no need to force it into something different.

As he watched her run innocently around the stalls, he prayed that they could continue to live in peace like this for a long time.

CHAPTER TWO

The ship they were to sail on was much nicer than Col had imagined, large enough to squeeze a hundred people if they were herded on board like sheep.

However, it was not a vessel meant only for them, nor did it belong to the Debau Company. One of their trade ships was apparently just now on its way back from the northern islands, and it would have been a waste of time to wait the several days it would take to unload then reload cargo. Instead, they decided to contract the ship of another company.

They did not tell the captain of the ship their true intentions, since if the pirates who controlled the area found out they were working on behalf of the Kingdom of Winfiel's political motives, then they might be watched or cause unnecessary misunderstandings. So they were acting under the premise that they were traveling priests, journeying all over to find a place to build a monastery on the orders of a certain noble.

It seemed Hyland was aware that Col was rather conscious of how lying went against God's teachings because she told him that one of her aristocratic relatives was truly thinking about searching for a spot to build a monastery. There were several deserted islands in the north, and as they were all desolate, their story would not attract doubt. What's more, under the pretense of a monastery, it would be easy to ask about the Black-Mother, so it was the perfect plan.

Their destination was a port town on the biggest island among the northern islands, Caeson. The journey was roughly two, three days long, and they went from island to island as if they were stepping-stones.

They were instructed to ask the large number of merchants more about the northern islands while at the Debau Company trading house where they would be rooming on the first island.

For the time being, they had to make sure they did not attract undue attention from the pirates who controlled the northern seas while investigating their true beliefs. The decision of whether or not to court them as allies was also a political decision, and of course, even if their faith was heretical, they would certainly make no attempts to convert them.

"I'm grateful to hear that"—or so Hyland had said to them through the mouth of a messenger as they were about to depart.

Considering how busy she was and how many subordinates reported to her, there was no way she could hold their hands for every step of their journey.

Her consideration for them was clear enough in that she had sent them a messenger and put them on the biggest of commercial ships. Col had renewed his determination to work his hardest.

"Well then, we will be your eyes and ears in their land."

He relayed that to the messenger, exchanged a firm handshake, and crossed the ramp onto the ship. The port town of Atiph was lively as always. Overhead was a beautiful blue sky, and there was no harsh wind. Col considered that it could be an easy journey.

"I saved us a spot, Brother."

As he stepped onto the deck, Myuri's face popped out from among the cargo. She was already wearing the practical deer leather wrap he had picked for her in the market around her waist and a woolen scarf from the Kingdom of Winfiel around her neck. On top of that, a hooded linen cloak rested on her shoulders. She was more than ready to face the coming cold. She had complained that it was not very cute, but that meant it had the advantage of making it difficult to discern her gender. A wandering priest searching for a site to build a monastery who traveled with a young girl would only create bad rumors.

"You didn't need to get any sort of...What, you mean here?"

She was waiting at the back of the ship, beside a mountain of leather.

"Why not the hold below deck? Isn't it too cold to be out here?"

The spot may have felt open underneath the sky, and perhaps the cargo was packed in a way that offered some protection from the wind, but he at least wanted walls. It was decidedly cold on deck.

Then Myuri put her hands on her hips and tilted her head in astonishment, sighing.

"Sheesh. This is why you are a novice when it comes to ships."

"What?"

"The hold is dark and damp and a hotbed for rats, mites, lice, and flies!"

The ship Col boarded on a long time ago had not been so bad, but Myuri had recently done a bit of menial work for the companies here in Atiph. Her experience from unloading cargo at the port could not be disregarded.

"Erm...Fine. However, if it gets too cold, we'll go downstairs."

Myuri shrugged.

The work crews finished loading all the cargo before long. The ramp and the rope mooring the ship to the pier were removed, and then the anchor was lifted. There were about five people who were running the ship. There were about three or four others traveling as passengers besides Col and Myuri; they were all merchants.

"Brother, look down."

Myuri, clinging to the ship railing, pointed to the surface of the water. He peeked over and watched just as long oars that reminded him of the bones in a bird's wings slithered out. There were two on this side, so he surmised the ship was steered by four in total.

"It's because they can't really use the sail in a port without wind. The plan is that once they get offshore and set course on the current, all that's left for them to do is sleep until they reach the north."

He was shocked by Myuri, who delivered a confident explanation about something she likely overheard while working as an errand boy. Col smiled as he leaned against the railing and looked up at the sky. He could see a fine sail, waiting for its turn, as well as two masts for it—one in the front and one in the back.

The ship was half as wide as it was long, seemingly stocky. It was typical of commercial ships to be filled with cargo instead of people. Coming from the northern seas, it would be laden with fish, amber, and ores such as iron; on the way there, it would carry wheat, wine, and dried meats, as well as finished metallic or wooden goods, or even leather goods like what surrounded them today.

There were other larger ships moored at the port, but this was more than enough to store the entire market of a small town on board. Though he had traveled with a merchant when he was a child, Col keenly felt that trade conducted on the seas was on an entirely different scale.

The ship drifted from the port toward the river by going under the giant chain that prevented naval attacks from the sea. He was finally starting to feel like they were truly departing on a sailing journey.

"By the way, Myuri, do you get seasick?"

From what he had heard from a merchant earlier, the best way to prevent seasickness was to avoid standing on deck as much as possible, focus on something far away, or simply sleep. He also warned him that no matter what, he should not look down and stare at his feet.

"No, not at all. Look, Brother, look at all those fish! I want to jump in with a harpoon!"

If her tail had been out, it would have been wagging excitedly. He looked up into the sky in exasperation at her typical attitude only to spot singing seabirds above them, perhaps suspecting there was fish in the cargo.

Before he knew it, the ship had exited the port at the mouth of the river as the oars steered toward the coast. When he finally began to feel the wind on his cheek, he noticed he no longer heard the oars on the water, and then sweaty men emerged from below deck. They manipulated the rope that connected the yard and the sail, slowly turning the ship's course northward.

"Brother, Brother, we're on top of the ocean! It's so cool!"

Myuri's eyes sparkled beneath her hood. She had been born and raised deep in the mountains, so everything about the sea was new to her. Even if that was not the case, she was still much more excitable than others, and she would be adorably satisfied with her trip even with the wind gusting in her face.

As Col watched her, he thought that allowing her to come along with him was really not that terrible a thing. At the end of the day, there was nothing better than Myuri being happy.

The sky was clear, the wind was not too strong, and between the cries of the seabirds and the lazy rocking of the ship, it felt like a drunken weekend day. In reality, he wanted to think about conveying the scripture into the common language and translations of abstract words that he would be satisfied with, but he suddenly felt drowsy. He suddenly found himself soaking in the baths back in Nyohhira during the daytime. Even though he knew it was a dream, he could not fight how relaxing it felt.

While that was happening, the sound of rustling cloth jolted him awake.

"Mm…Myuri?"

He looked beside him, and there sat Myuri, hugging her knees. Her eyes were closed, but she did not seem sleepy, and her throat occasionally moved as though she was swallowing something.

The ship was rolling back and forth, back and forth.

She noticed him, and she looked as though she had heard a suspicious noise in the middle of the night.

"Myuri, you're pale…"

That was all he managed to say before she suddenly stood and stuck her head out over the side of the ship. Before he could say anything, her back shivered and he could hear her retching. It seemed she could not stay the energetic and invincible girl she was.

But for some reason he was glad, and though he felt sorry for her as he stood, he could not help but smile when he rubbed her back.

"This is because you do not listen to me."

He took the opportunity to scold her and she glared at him, her face pale, but that energy was once again overwhelmed by nausea.

She groaned for a while, but sicking up seemed to relieve her discomfort for the time being. She rinsed out her mouth with a drink from the waterskin, then spread her wrap out on the floor and loosened anything that was snug on her body, like her scarf.

From what he had heard from the merchants at the Debau Company beforehand, the last step was to lie with one's back on the floor and sleep; she would feel much better afterward.

Laying her on her back, her complexion was terrible, and her breathing was quick and shallow. And yet, when he placed her head on his lap, she felt around for his hand and gripped it tightly. She was always throwing barbs at him for being an idiot or this and that, but there was still this sweet side to her, too.

He felt safe in knowing that people could not die from seasickness as he felt the need to get some payback.

"How would you be able to save me when the time comes like this?"

Her eyes that were scrunched up in pain opened slightly as she pursed her lips, annoyed. To top it off, she sunk her fingernails into the palm of the hand she was gripping.

"Brother, you…bully…"

"I know, I know."

He patted her head. She immediately closed her eyes, perhaps thinking that she could not win no matter how hard she tried. He looked down at her, smiling, wishing she would behave at least half as well as this normally.

"…Brother?"

"Yes?"

"I'm gonna barf."

"What?! Just—just hold on a second!"

Disregarding how flustered he was, Myuri rolled over onto her side, then glanced back at him. Her curled back shook violently several times as though she would vomit, and even Col's face lost its color.

He did not know whether to keep holding her thin shoulders or let go, but he needed to get her to the edge of the ship…And then, he finally realized it.

"Eh-heh-heh…"

Her expression still strained, Myuri smiled, having somehow gotten back at him.

He would never be able to beat her in teasing and trickery.

"Honestly…"

He sighed in relief and irritation as Myuri rolled onto her back again. Of course, her head lay on his lap once more, and he had not let go of her hand. She was as white as a candle, but her stiffened lips had relaxed a bit.

He was more impressed than angry with her spirit.

"You've beat me."

He admitted defeat, eliciting a slight smile from Myuri, who then exhaled deeply. It seemed the tension in her body had eased; her breathing slowed.

The best way to overcome seasickness was to sleep, he had heard.

As he stroked his tomboyish little sister's head, he bade, "Sleep well."

They passed several small islands and skerries, but there were no places that looked like they could serve as a stopping point for the ship. Journeys where he could not grasp the direction and distance were rough for Col, which was only exacerbated by traveling on unfamiliar seas.

While he occasionally adjusted Myuri's covers as she turned in her sleep, the sun finally started setting. The wind stung him while the sound of the waves grew steadily more unbearable, when a rather massive silhouette of an island came into view. Realizing the ship was headed straight in that direction, he felt relieved. It was likely where the Debau Company had a trading house that Hyland had described.

"Myuri."

He shook her small shoulders and she opened her eyes, seeming quite groggy.

"We're almost to the port. It's almost time to get off."

Though she was most certainly looking at him, he was not sure if she was completely conscious yet.

"Do you still feel sick?"

There was no response besides an unsteady stare. Then, she closed her eyes and nodded once.

She seemed like a weak, young child.

"So you're all right."

He patted her on the head, and she groaned deep in her throat.

"We have lots of luggage, so I won't be able to carry all that plus you. You'll have to get ready on your own."

She was sulking deliberately, which meant she had recovered considerably. After finally conceding, she sat up either because she knew he saw right through her or because she remembered that she was in the middle of an adventure. That being said, she was still not in the best condition, so he wrapped the blankets and other bulk items onto his luggage.

"When we get off the ship, make sure you don't fall into the water." He spoke seriously, but she just lightly slapped his back with a frown.

The ship steadily drew closer to the port. By the time Col could see the faces of the workers on the ships moored there, the sailors had already begun to efficiently fold the sail. Then, the pilot stood at the bow and shouted orders to the helmsman at the stern of the ship. The vessel glided across the water and safely came to rest in port.

A ramp was set into place, and soon men who looked like dockworkers rushed onto the ship at the same time. The sailors and merchants began their exchange with them.

Col was unsure if it was all right for them to simply disembark, but it occurred to him that he and Myuri would only be in the way if they stayed on deck, so he pulled Myuri's hand and they quickly got off. The ramp was not as solid as the one in Atiph, which made him nervous, but they crossed safely in the end. Feeling solid ground after half a day at sea gave him a great feeling of relief.

"All right, next, we'll be staying with the Debau Company trading house..."

In the middle of readjusting the luggage on his back, he noticed Myuri had stopped, staring blankly. He approached her, thinking it could have been vertigo or anemia, but as she gazed at the island, she murmured, "...It looks so sad."

The chaotic sight consisted of seabirds circling annoyingly above people jostling or hustling against one another, while stray dogs and cats skulked around, hoping to pilfer fish from fishermen who were nowhere to be seen. There were several docked ships, including many large ones, but besides the sailors actively working on them, there was no one around. He could count the number of big buildings on one hand, and most were fenced in.

On top of it all, behind those buildings were bare hills without a single tree in sight. Had they been blanketed in snow, it would have been a different story, but the remaining patches of snow that dotted the landscape only made it seem even colder. White, bone-like driftwood was scattered along the beach that extended from the port, emphasizing the loneliness.

Even the sailors who had arrived on the same ship as them had not let slip a peep of chatter as they walked hunched over toward the building that would be their inn for the night. This was not the sort of place that impressed the need for friendly banter.

To a girl born and raised in Nyohhira, a village filled with song, dance, and the sounds of laughter nestled deep in the mountains, such a bleak atmosphere was unimaginable.

"I'm here."

He gripped Myuri's hand through his deerskin gloves, and she stared up with beautiful eyes between her hood and scarf.

"You remind me of yourself sometimes, Brother."

After she said that, she bumped him with her shoulder.

"And? Where are we staying tonight?"

"We're about to search for someplace to stay, but I do not think we'll get lost."

"I want to be by a fire as soon as possible!"

The coastal sunset was certainly terrifying and cold. Together, they walked along the empty, lonely port.

There were few buildings along the beach, so it was not difficult to immediately pick out the Debau Company trading house. It looked like the stately house from Atiph was trying to pass the winter here as the wind blew against it. The raised flags also blew lifelessly in the cold wind, almost as though they had long given up resisting.

He knocked on the heavy door, perhaps meant as a measure against storms. Before long a hairy, round-bellied merchant appeared.

"Oh? This is unusual. A traveling father?"

"We are on a journey to the northern islands for certain reasons. Here is a letter of introduction from Sir Stefan from the trading house in Atiph."

Of course, it was something that Hyland had written on his behalf.

"Oh?"

The merchant narrowed his eyes, and when he took the letter, he moved his large body to the side.

"Well, it's cold out there. Why don't you come in?"

"Thank you."

They stepped over the threshold into a needlessly large atrium where the floor was exposed, packed earth, exactly the same as it was outside. Obligatorily placed there were small tables and chairs, ill matched for the size of the space. Far on the opposite wall hung a map of the region and a flag displaying the company's emblem. The room's leisurely atmosphere slightly softened the bleak air that permeated from outside.

"Please take a seat by the furnace. I'll bring you some drinks."

The merchant motioned toward something resting squarely in the atrium's center that could only be termed a furnace. It was metallic and stout, with a chimney extending up and out of the ceiling. From its wooden mouth, Col caught a glimpse of what seemed like an unreliable flame.

"They get their firewood from the sea..."

Sitting by the hearth was the kind of driftwood they saw on the beach. Myuri had perhaps imagined someone hunched over and shivering, gathering firewood under leaden skies on a beach beaten by icy waves. Collecting such firewood seemed like hard labor, almost like it was some sort of punishment.

"We finally have fire. Let's go ahead and place our things by it."

It was completely silent in the trading house, as though not a soul was present. Though they placed their things by the fire, they kept their coats on. Even with a roof and walls surrounding them to shelter them from the wind, it felt just as cold as it did outside.

Col went to grab chairs from a nearby table, but when he touched them, they were oddly soft from the salt and humidity. He was not sure whether the room was finished or not, but because of how wide it was, the shadows in the room grew darker even before the sun had set—it was depressing, perhaps even more so for a girl who had come from a lively hot spring village.

He considered this and turned to Myuri, who was holding driftwood that she never saw in Nyohhira and was studying it.

"Myuri?" he called to her, and when she looked at him, her eyes were shining.

"It's like an inn at the edge of the world. It's so exciting!"

"..."

Though she had been throwing up and her face was a bit pale, her spirit was recovering quickly.

Myuri's youth and the ability to find enjoyment from anything she found in front of her warmed Col more than the furnace did.

"I didn't think we'd be getting guests today, so I apologize for the appearance."

As they were doing all that, the merchant who came out to greet them brought over steaming tin cups. They took them, and inside was a mixture of goat's milk and honey. Perhaps the drink was a staple in these parts. He imagined that goat's milk after throwing up would not be very good for Myuri and looked at her, but she sniffled from the steam and eagerly drank it.

"It's quite a large building, but is it typically livelier than this?"

"Yes. The winter fishing season is over for now. This hall was filled with barrels of herring for sale to merchants and couriers who were sleeping in every cranny, leaving no room for anything else. Every day, commercial ships were arriving at all hours. What a riot it was."

Despite what the merchant described, the atrium did not particularly smell of fish. His story sounded almost like he was reminiscing about a castle that was lively once upon a time but long since destroyed by war.

"And it will be filled again with migrant workers in the coming seasons; only this time, it'll be those eyeing the spring storms."

Col sipped his helping of goat's milk. It was sweet enough to melt his teeth away, but perhaps it was just what he needed in such a cold and dark place.

"For the storms?"

"We say storms, but we really mean the things that get washed up by them. We sometimes get sea creatures with horns or even giant sturgeons washing ashore. All sorts of things."

Myuri's eyes went blank when she heard "sea creatures with horns." It sounded mythical, and it seemed she had thought it was made up.

But Col had seen them before in real life. The animal's horns were sometimes said to hold the power of granting immortality and traded as snake oil. The sea was truly full of more mysteries than land could ever be.

"Also amber. A mess of it washes ashore after the storms."

When the conversation turned to easily understandable gems, Myuri's eyes sparkled.

"You can gather even the smallest bits on the beach, but the largest pieces are deep in the sea. That's why they make large sieves in town, then pack them on boats to ship here. Greedy folks bring ones so big they can't carry it alone. Then they head out to all these different islands and wait for the big storms to come. When the time is right, they go out in the raging wind and waves, wade out waist-deep into stinging water, then search along the floor underwater. To make sure they don't faint from the cold and drift away in the water, they tie ropes to one another. Even then, it's never-ending, dangerous work."

It was terrifying just imagining it, the very thought giving Col a chill.

But Myuri was so enraptured by the story to the point she barely noticed snot creeping down from her nose.

"That goes on until the flowers on the bare hills behind us begin to bloom. All these folks hoping to get rich quick come flooding in. It's amazing how lively it gets. Sometimes there are amazing individuals who have earned their entire fortune with a single pull. And in the summer, this island becomes a base for people gathering peat and coal or mining iron ore. Well, that business has been in a slump recently...But still, what I mean to say is, you two arrived at a very rare moment of quiet."

The merchant smiled merrily.

"So, the cargo on the ship we traveled on is meant to prepare for what's coming?"

"Yes, I think so. Or it could be for islands even farther north of here. The Debau ship isn't due for a few days still, so my buddy and I have just been relaxing."

The merchant smiled and pointed with this thumb to a room connected to the atrium, where a dog sat, peering over at them with an air of intelligence.

"He's usually friendlier, but maybe he's being a little nervous around God."

Col of course did not mention that he guessed it was due to the blood of wolves in Myuri's veins.

"But still, I guess there's a reason you've gone as far as hitching a ride on another company's ship?"

The merchant spoke calmly as he added a piece of driftwood, white and smooth as a deer's antlers, to the furnace.

As Myuri drank the goat's milk, her eyes were trained on Col.

Her cheeky gaze seemed to say, "Are you going to do it?"

"And both of you are quite young."

As he tended the fire, he glanced back at them over his shoulder with a very merchantlike, openly scrutinizing look.

That being said, both of them were already quite aware that together they drew unnecessary attention. Col straightened his posture, placed his hand on his breast, and dropped into a bow.

"My name is Tote Col. This is Myuri. I have been studying theology since a young age as a wandering student. Now, I am in the care of a certain noble."

"Huh."

The merchant left the wood he had been fiddling with as is inside the furnace and lifted his face.

"Well, well. I am the master of this trading house, Yosef Remenev."

He extended his hand, and when Col took it, he noticed it was as hard as a mountain animal.

"But a wandering student. It's like I'm seeing a miracle."

Yosef flashed a carefree smile. It seemed he knew all about wandering students.

"A wandering student is just another name for evil debauchery and thievery. I was no different from any beggar. I was so desperate to obtain more of what little money I had that I was tricked by a swindler. I was at my wit's end."

"Well, that's..."

"In my hardship, through the guidance of God, I found a traveling merchant who took me in, narrowly rescuing me from death. He taught my ignorant self many things, was accommodating enough to give me time to study every day, and here I am now."

"I see."

Hearing the heartwarming tale of a fellow merchant, the likes of whom were often censured by representatives of God, Yosef seemed rather proud.

"And your companion here?"

He gestured with his hand, and Myuri, who only ever behaved at times like this, straightened her back and smiled.

"When I was chosen by a certain noble and departed from the village, she was hiding in my luggage. I should return her, but...I, too, was once a wandering student."

"Ha-ha-ha! I see, I see."

By the teachings of God, Col could not lie. However, even the scripture was filled with ambiguities. Smart conversationalists would fill in the blanks on their own, while the intelligent, confident ones especially would not ask for more details.

Yosef nodded deeply, slowly, and knowingly.

Myuri did not refer to him as "Brother" because anyone familiar with the wandering students knew these children called the elders in their group "bro."

"And so, you are traveling today for this noble?"

"Yes. It is an urgent request. We've heard this area hosts a harsh environment and is a place that people cannot easily get to. It would be perfect as a place to practice profound worship."

These were also words that were not a lie but still misleading.

"I see. I've heard that there was a big commotion about faith in Atiph. If someone who knows of irreverence is building a monastery, then that means they want to tighten the leash on faith, huh?"

Yosef's round, drumlike belly shook as he spoke merrily. It seemed news of what happened in Atiph was spreading far.

"There are a number of small, remote islands in this area perfect for a monastery. We sometimes deliver the materials, but…at the most, they last about three years. Ah, my apologies."

Searching for salvation, monks often built monasteries in remote places, but due to the severity of the environments, many wound up leaving. Or when the rich who originally funded the endeavor passed away, there was no one to deliver materials.

Monasteries could not remain standing on their own, and even monks could only endure so much. A house of prayer and asceticism had to be supported by worldly gold and a certain level of comfort.

"There are many forms of faith, and passionate prayer will reach God, whether it be from the top of a mountain or the bottom of the sea."

Col responded with a smile while Yosef, who had let his true opinions slip free, rubbed his belly, perhaps out of relief. Then he spoke with an uncomfortable smile as a pretense.

"Well, I don't want you to misunderstand, but there are many around these parts who hold fast to true faith. It may come across somehow as an incredibly touchy time, but I will stake this on the honor of this region."

"Of course."

Col had no intention of questioning faith here, and though he took it as small talk, Yosef said something he could not ignore.

"Sure, belief in the Black-Mother is often met with doubtful eyes, but the crewmen are more passionate than anyone else, and they are all of the purest faith. God's teachings are firmly rooted in this land."

From the way he was speaking, perhaps Yosef was also a native of an island in the area.

Then, this was the point that determined if Myuri would be calling him an idiot or not.

Col spoke, making sure his voice did not raise out of excitement, in the most natural manner he could muster.

"The Black-Mother? Are there black-and-white versions of the Holy Mother?"

Yosef seemed to be one who was exceptionally passionate about his work and the land he lived in.

So when Col feigned ignorance, sure enough, Yosef's eyes widened.

"Oh, you don't know. That's no good. You can't get around the islands without a boat, and any journey by sea is uncertain without the protection of the Black-Mother. Please wait a moment. Living by human power alone is almost impossible in this land, so this benevolent Holy Mother is our constant friend and companion."

Yosef shot up and went into the adjacent room, almost toppling his chair over in his haste.

The driftwood crackled in the furnace.

Myuri sipped the last of the goat's milk in her tin cup and burped.

"That was all right, I guess."

She shrugged as she sassed him, chuckling.

Yosef brought over a figure identical to the one that Hyland had showed them in Atiph. The only differences were that his was a bit smaller and all the details had been worn away.

"Everyone born and raised in this region will wear this on them when they go out to sea."

He spoke as his rough hands gripped the figure of the Holy Mother. A small bag with a string attached sat beside him. It appeared he wore that around his neck with the figure inside whenever he traveled over water. As she listened, Myuri rustled around near her chest because she, too, had a small pouch hanging from her neck, though containing wheat.

"Is it different from the Holy Mothers and saints on the front of the ships that regularly embark on long journeys?"

Yosef shook his head woefully in response.

He was about to speak forcefully, but his eyes suddenly turned to the skewered fish standing before the furnace.

"Oh, it's almost time to eat. These fins around the body here are crunchy and very delicious."

It was flounder—flat, skewered, and then seared over the heat. Myuri knew of them in a fashion, but her eyes widened when she saw their strange shape for the first time.

"The kind we catch in our nets are usually the size of a plate, but when the big storms come, huge ones wash up from the depths of the sea, and they're like this! This big!"

Yosef demonstrated, drawing his arms in an arc that made it seem like they would come out of their sockets. Myuri was honestly surprised and her eyes glinted, but Col only pretended to be polite. The stories of merchants entertaining guests always had to be taken with a grain of salt.

"The sea is full of such giant creatures just roaming around that are unimaginable on land. Many legends still remain. But if we leave it just to fish, then the smaller ones taste the best. Please help yourselves before it goes cold."

The flounder, typically found clinging to the bottom of the sea, had been grilled and skewered. Its meat was soft and flaky, making for a tasty meal. The fins, which had become crunchy and charred from the fire, were salty and delicious. Myuri ate two, perhaps because she wanted to fill her stomach after throwing up so much on the trip.

Col nearly scolded her for being unladylike, but Yosef seemed quite happy that a guest was enjoying the local fish, so he stayed quiet. Myuri's puppy-like appreciation for the meal may have made Yosef feel like he was giving her a treat.

"Well, about the Black-Mother, it's not like an *amulet* for a boat. The Black-Mother truly does protect us."

On this wide, empty, cold earth, there were only three people and one dog in the darkness around the furnace. It was already pitch-black out and the cold wind was unceasing. There, the more Yosef passionately spoke, one word came to the forefront of Col's mind.

Heresy.

The devil always showed people miracles before snatching them all away.

"No, I understand. Both mainlanders and merchants who

72

come all the way from the southlands to buy herring all wear a skeptical look on their face."

Col, flustered, brushed his cheeks. Yosef laughed while Myuri glared at him.

"But those who won't be swayed when it comes to doubt all believe it. Monasteries built here do not last long because the people of this land will not go near them. That is also a factor."

He could not help but imagine that something devilish was at work here, if this statue of the Holy Mother attracted faith so desperately.

Yosef continued to talk.

"There are many stories about ships that have been saved by the statue of the Black-Mother, and there are many that start with, *Long ago, my gramps heard a story when he was a kid...*I, too, have seen it with my own eyes."

As though he was not trying to convince him, Yosef closed his eyes and pressed the figure to his chest, recalling his story.

Perhaps the details on the figure had worn out so much because he did that every day.

"It was a sea voyage in the fall."

The wind howled outside.

"The earth was barren, damaged by seawater, so we were transporting the sheep and goats. They were thin from malnutrition, unable to give milk to the young—the meat and milk that is our livelihood. There were also humans with them trying to stave off the cold with what little wool they could get. We didn't know if we should save this one poor island village."

It was a bleak sight that greeted them when they got off the ship, to the point that Myuri was left speechless. The farther north people traveled, the more inhospitable the environment became and the more difficult it was to live there. Perhaps before

73

becoming a member of the Debau Company, Yosef was born in these seas and labored as a villager on one of these islands.

"For every day we delayed our departure, one animal died. And with every death, we could no longer support another member of our families. One morning, with a tepid breeze and thin clouds that dampened the walls, the elder fisherman opposed us, claiming we should not go out to sea. We knew the dangers, but we had no choice but to go. It was days like these that it was said the white devil would come swallow us up, but we were so concerned with the troubles before us."

The wood in the furnace crackled and popped.

Yosef did not fidget.

"But the nearest island with grass was just a few hours away by boat. On sunny days, it looked close enough to swim to. And the surface of the water was quiet and calm. We were sure this was our chance. The next day, humidity would become rain, the winds would descend, and the waters would become agitated. Once that happened, we would lose all our livestock."

Col imagined them, about to go out to sea, betting on their will to live.

"Then, in the haze, we set off. Every time the oars hit the water, the ripples spread into the distance until they disappeared into the mist. We headed for the island in what was supposed to be a straight line. But no matter how far we went, the island's shadow never appeared, and our view grew whiter and whiter. It was like the devil had placed his hand over our eyes."

"...The mist?"

Myuri, born and raised deep in the mountains, said the word with dread.

Sometimes mist grew so thick in the mountains, it became impossible to see your own outstretched fingers. Myuri understood that fear well. Even Myuri's mother—a large wolf that towered over people and could only be described as a god—could lose her way and quail in such a phantasmal world.

What would happen if someone tried to curl up and cower in the mist, only to have their feet swallowed by the sea?

Yosef's despair showed in the depth of the wrinkles on his face.

"We often say that this kind of mist is something you can grab, break, and eat. But it was nothing like that. It would have been better if we could grab it. The mist covered everything and everyone. We couldn't see one another's faces even though we all stood on the same deck. We stayed strangely quiet, like when goats or sheep sense something off. I've been caught in storms that whip up waves as big as hills and always stood steady. But in that mist, my legs were a shaky mess, and I reeled so many times."

"When that happened to me on the mountain, I just kept screaming."

Myuri sounded as though she was trying to comfort Yosef, who may as well have been still lost in the mist.

Yosef looked surprised before he smiled.

"Me, too. I didn't know where I was, and I yelled with everything I had. My buddies later told me they did the same thing. But that thick, white mist swallows everything up. My voice barely reached my own ears."

He gazed off into the distance before adding a little wood to the furnace.

"The rowers believed their heading was true, so they continued to row. No turns left or right, only straight ahead. Usually, you can tell where you are in the water by the current and resistance of the waves, even when your eyes are closed. But because it was so calm, we couldn't tell anything. In the end, some of them started to randomly hit the water with their oars. By then, I was gripping this figure of the Black-Mother so hard I thought it might break. That's a story we believe—that by this point, the Black-Mother will come to save us."

Whenever matters were beyond the power of humans, they turned to the gods.

Yosef gripped the figure of the Holy Mother at his chest and continued.

"Creeping along the side of the ship, I made my way to the front, where I discovered all my buds had thought of the same thing. We didn't have to say anything. Our lips drawn, we all nodded, and everyone held a figure of the Holy Mother in their hand."

As though he would do just that, he held the figure of the Black-Mother up high.

"O, Our Mother, guide these pitiful lambs...We literally had lambs on board, too, but we chanted this and tossed our figures of the Black-Mother along with our prayers into the sea. Then..."

Myuri gulped and leaned forward, and Col found himself enraptured as well.

"The ship shook with a loud *thunk*. Someone yelled that we'd hit a reef. The seas around here are difficult, and accidents happen if the pilot doubts himself. I had been trembling in despair, but in the next moment, the ship began to move on its own."

Col looked at Yosef as he spoke, and an odd state of mind overcame him.

It sounded too much like a made-up story, and he doubted that such a miracle could really happen so conveniently. But rather than obvious apprehension as the listener, it was the speaker himself who wore a complicated smile on his face. His expression suggested that it was they themselves who doubted if it was reality or fantasy.

"As though guided by a powerful force, the ship moved slowly across the water. Honestly, I thought I'd already died in a shipwreck and was being led to the underworld. But after a while, a large shadow suddenly appeared from the mist, and it was the island we always saw. The ship glided smoothly across the calm water before finally grounding on the shore. We stood on the tilted deck for a while, only looking at one another. We couldn't believe that we were alive."

Yosef shook his head and sighed.

"We just thought the gods had protected us, then let the sheep and goats onto the island, and then something happened when all our work was finished. Once the mist cleared, the wind came back, and the sea started to make waves again; the figures of the Black-Mother that we threw into the water washed up onto shore by the ship. It was like we'd ridden on her back, and she was the one who brought us there."

He claimed the story was not mere hearsay, and it did not seem like he was lying.

Whether it was because she had been so excited or relieved that Yosef and his friends had made it out safely, Myuri's eyes were watery and her nose was runny.

As though he was calming his own grandchild, Yosef smiled and wiped Myuri's nose.

But Col was someone who wished to be a good priest, and he could not let his eyes be clouded.

"Has the Holy See requested to see the miracle?"

Col mentioned that any good believers would have done so. The Holy See was at the very center of the corrupt Church that needed to be reformed, but if they officially recognized a miracle here, it would raise the authority of the churches in the region whether anyone wanted that or not. It would also be an honor for the faith as a whole. In more ordinary terms, more pilgrims would visit and the land would profit financially as well.

On the other hand, the Holy See would certainly send inspectors to inquire about the veracity of the event.

As though Yosef had already anticipated Col's thoughts quite a while ago, he slowly shrugged his massive shoulders.

"We argued about that. Even I think it was half miracle, half coincidence."

"...Coincidence?"

"The sea is a complicated thing—no matter how calm the surface looks, it's hard to tell what's going on underneath. Boundaries between currents are clearer than mainlanders think, too. Once you pass a boundary, it sometimes feels like you've run into something."

He meant it was quite possible they collided with a current when their senses were heightened after their vision had been taken away by the thick mist.

"And that beach has always been a common place to find things washed ashore by the current. Had we drawn close enough, we would have arrived there eventually, even without touching the oars. If we make all this fuss about what happened and then it comes out that moment wasn't a miracle, we would accomplish nothing but draw even more suspicion to this region, which people already suspect is a place for heathens."

Like yourself—Yosef's eyes glinted with a hint of mischief and he smiled.

"That is why we decided that it was half miracle, half coincidence. Personally, I've been taking greater care of the Black-Mother ever since."

Col could see the determination that, even if he was declared a heretic, he had no intentions of changing his mind.

And Col had not come here to convert these people.

He had come to determine if those who believed in the Black-Mother would be strong allies in their fight against the corrupt pope.

"And there are other stories that could be either coincidences or

78

miracles, like a fire on a boat put out by a big wave after the men on board threw their figures of the Black-Mother into the sea or those saved by the Black-Mother after falling into the water."

When he mentioned falling into the water, Myuri glanced at Col with a bit of a meaningful gaze, but he pretended not to notice.

"Of course, the biggest one..."

Yosef, who had spoken fluently thus far, cut off his words and smiled shyly, having strained himself, then continued softly.

"No, you should see the traces of it for yourself. Would you be heading to the main island by any chance?"

The island called Caeson was the pirates' stronghold. Col heard from the Debau Company that it was the center of the northern islands.

"I was told that I must go there if I hope to venture into the waters beyond."

"That's because there are many poachers and outsiders who plunder defenseless villages, you know. If you make yourself known on the main island, then you'll avoid larger problems. Especially if you want to build a base on an island somewhere. It doesn't matter which noble's patronage you have; we are all powerless at sea."

The authorities of the Kingdom of Winfiel and Ploania, the northernmost country on the mainland, did not reach this far.

"The only thing that can protect us is the Black-Mother, then."

Yosef showed his polite merchant's smile in response to Col's sentiment and nodded.

"The main island also houses this region's only monastery. You may find it useful to visit the monk there. He is the one who crafts all the figures of the Holy Mother. Though rather old, he is a pious and outstanding man."

It seemed that his figure and the one Hyland showed him looked similar because they were made by the same person.

And since the Church's jurisdiction did not reach this far, it wasn't impossible that this man simply called himself a monk and his house a monastery. Monasteries did not have the privilege of collecting money each time one presided over baptisms, marriages, or funerals, so the Church was generally not too strict with their organization. Problems only arose if they got in the way with the pope's business.

Nobles wanted to build monasteries instead of churches because they were less likely to cause trouble.

"But recently, all the big coal mines on every island have been cleaned out. Production of jet has drastically decreased. The less we find, the more our trade will naturally thin out, but so will the protection for the people of the sea—in other words, us. What a dilemma."

Yosef likely did not mean to grumble so. After finishing his reflection, he suddenly came to himself and seemed uncomfortable, as though he had just heard his own complaining.

"How boring all this talk must be for travelers."

In a merchantlike manner, Yosef suddenly smiled and directed his gaze to the furnace.

"Have you had enough yet? There's plenty of fish, so feel free to have as much as you like."

Six skewers were lined up at Myuri's feet, the ends all burned. They all seemed to be of the same length and thickness in the trick of the long, dark night.

"No, thank you. We are grateful for your hospitality."

"By God's will."

Yosef proceeded to show them to their room. The reason the two were given a whole room to themselves was due to the lack of sufficient fuel, which meant the furnace could not be left on all night. It would be much too cold to sleep in the empty, vast atrium. Instead, their host gave them each a stone that had been heated by the furnace. Once placed inside a sack, the stone would warm them until morning if kept under the covers.

Then he brought them to a room that seemed to be typically offered to honorable captains of large commercial ships, and Myuri's eyes widened at the sight of the woolen bed.

"I might get hungry sleeping in a bed like this."

Myuri sounded like the daughter of wolves, but Col knew her being hungry was simply a matter of course.

As Myuri bounced around excitedly, Col found a worn metal washbowl, so he took out a handkerchief from his luggage, sprinkled the contents of a waterskin over it, and wrung it tightly.

"Look, Myuri."

"Huh?"

Myuri had been sitting on the bed, staring blankly. He sighed because he noticed bits of charcoal from the fish still around her mouth.

"Honestly."

Exasperated, he did not have the energy to point it out to her, so he walked over and wiped her face with the wet handkerchief.

"You are a girl. Are you not bothered by how salty your body feels after a day at sea?"

At first, it seemed as though she would resist, but then she started to point out places she wanted him to wipe. He wiped her cheeks, her temples, her forehead, and both sides of her nose. When he refolded the handkerchief to switch to the clean side, her wolf ears and tail popped out. She showed her neck to him as a sign for him to wipe that, too, and her tail began to wag out of impatience.

"This really goes to show how thankful we are for the baths at Nyohhira."

Myuri's ears and tail twitched in comfort as he wiped her neck, and then she sneezed, perhaps from the water.

"*Sniff*…Brother!"

Her nose began to run and she looked at him.

"After I wipe your face."

When he quickly began to wipe her face with the few remaining clean parts he hadn't used yet left on the handkerchief, Myuri immediately began to rub her nose with her sleeve.

"But still…"

As Myuri began to speak, she insisted he continue wiping, so he had no choice but to look after her thin ankles and small feet as well.

"…that was an amazing story."

It was truly amazing that she was making him, the closest thing she had to a brother, towel off her feet as though he was her servant, but he knew it was partly because he couldn't help but meddle whenever it came to Myuri.

"If it is true, that is."

In the scripture, saints always washed the feet of the poor starting with the left foot for some reason, and it was done this way in ceremonies as well. Col had never thought about it, but he understood when he did it himself. It was simply because it was natural to start on the left for people who were right-handed.

"You don't believe the story about the black Holy Mother?"

When he finished wiping her left foot, it felt rather cool. They had the heated stone, but Col was still worried that Myuri might get frostbite, so out from his luggage came a shell packed with bear oil for warding off the chill. With a knife, he chiseled a bit that had frozen from the cold, then warmed it with the fire of a fish-oil candle.

"Or maybe…there really is a witch."

Myuri mused on her theory as he scooped the softened oil onto his finger and rubbed it along her foot. He looked up, and her expression was rather serious.

"Because the boat moved on its own and the water poured on them, too!"

She sounded slightly angry, perhaps because the expression on his face was irritated.

As he rubbed the oil into Myuri's delicate skin, he spoke.

"Mr. Yosef said it himself—it was a coincidence."

"...A coincidence?"

"It could even be called a misunderstanding or bias. In any case, nothing good will come of assuming these things are a blessing from God. It will most likely only lead to bad things."

When he finished with her left foot, he started on her right, swabbing his finger into the oil.

"There are so many examples of this happening if you learn theological history. A mistaken faith is more wicked than no faith at all. It is not that difficult to teach people new things, but it is not easy to change a person's way of thinking."

Like making someone give up her crush on her older brother. The words came to mind, but he swallowed them.

Perhaps the story of the Black-Mother fell into a similar vein.

"So you must be cautious. There, all finished."

Once he had finished coating both her feet in rubbing oil, he tapped them lightly and urged her to stuff them under the blanket. He used his hardworking handkerchief to plug the gaps in the window as its final job.

"But isn't it the same as a person helping them? Is that still wrong?"

As he stuffed the cloth into the gap of the window, he turned back to Myuri because he thought she seemed rather stubborn on this topic.

Under the blanket, she was thinking hard.

"Someone who is oddly nice to you in town might want to kidnap you. It is the same thing."

It was not something that could be easily believed. The scripture expounded the importance of not taking God's name in vain.

He finished stuffing the cloth in the gap, and as he checked to see if the cold wind was no longer coming through, Myuri had pulled the blanket up to her nose.

"You're always so mean whenever you talk about God."

And for some reason, she was pouting.

"I am not being mean, just calm."

Myuri did not respond. Only her ears twitched.

"Besides, our host told us we can see what remains of the miracle. It won't be too late to pass judgment after actually seeing it for yourself."

There were several similar sightseeing spots throughout the world. Col had heard many behind-the-scenes stories from guests who came to stay at the bathhouse he worked in for over ten years. He had the confidence that he would immediately be able to see through any false faith.

"Come now, move in a bit more."

He blew out the light, and the room suddenly fell into darkness. Groping around, he tried to slide under the blanket when Myuri, who could see well in the dark, reached out to him. As he had just wiped her hands with a wet handkerchief, they were rather cold.

And yet, under four blankets, it was already much warmer thanks to her body heat. On top of that, the bed was woolen instead of straw, and there also was her fluffy tail. There was little chance they would get sick.

"Aren't you cold?" he asked only tentatively.

Without any hesitation or consideration for him, Myuri buried her face in his chest, yawned, and shook her head. Maybe she was not answering his question but actually wiping away tears in her eyes. Either way, she did not seem discontent.

84

Once the light went out and they both stopped stirring, suddenly a number of sounds became clear. There was the sea wind knocking on the window, a clattering on the roof of the trading house, the bending of wood. Oddly louder than the rest were the waves.

This was not the bathhouse in Nyohhira that Col had grown so used to living in but a practically empty building on an island even closer to the edge of the world.

"Hey, Brother?"

Myuri whispered so quietly into his chest it was almost as though she had not spoken at all.

"It almost doesn't feel real."

Her whisper was almost drowned out by the crash of the waves outside.

"It doesn't?"

When he responded with a question, her pointed animal ears twitched, brushing lightly over the tip of his nose.

She commented on the driftwood that looked like a deer's antlers and the inn at the edge of the world.

They truly were near the world's boundary in the middle of an adventure. This was not a place that could be reached with only the commitment for a leisurely stroll.

Myuri inhaled deeply in his arms until her body puffed out a little.

"I'm happy."

Perhaps the adventure she had always dreamed of felt just like this.

She exhaled, and her body shrunk and grew softer. A helpless, fragile girl who seemed like she might break if he squeezed hard enough.

He could tell that she fell asleep right away.

He usually found himself frustrated with how easily she fell asleep, but earlier that day she had thrown up everything, then filled her stomach with a strange-looking yet delicious fish.

She was so very much a child still. He patted her head, smiled slightly, then relaxed, too.

Sleep came for him quickly and wrapped his consciousness in bolts of silk.

He had a tough time accepting the story of the Black-Mother at face value. Though it was a problem that would require much investigating and thinking, he was only supposed to fulfill his given role.

His role as a servant to Hyland and a good guardian to Myuri as her elder brother.

The waves tirelessly lapped up against the shore. And the inside of the blanket was very warm.

The next day before they departed, Yosef gave them a fragment of flat wood with a letter inscribed on it.

"You are honored guests from Sir Stefan in Atiph, after all; there are lots of rowdy folks out there. When your ship is inspected, please show them this piece of wood."

An insignia was burned onto it, likely written in the local language. It must have been some sort of passport.

"Show that letter to the people of the church in the port town of Caeson on the main island. They should welcome you with hospitality."

"There is a church there?"

Col had heard that the northern islands were rather far from the Church's sphere of influence, so that was unexpected. He thought that only monasteries for worshipping the Black-Mother had been independently established.

"We might call it a church, but it's more of a place to stay, paid for and managed by the big companies that want to do trade in the northlands. Because we have to work together in foreign countries, of course."

It was very mercantile logic to work together where there was profit to be gained even between otherwise fierce competitors. In this harbor, where each company split off into their own trading houses, Col and Myuri were still in familiar territory. From here on out, they would be stepping foot into an unexplored world.

"They may tell you more about the Black-Mother."

"Thank you."

"Then, you must go to the monastery on the main island. If the brother there accepts you, there will be nothing you won't be able to do."

The building of the monastery may have also originally been meant to influence the people to stand up to the pope's army that could try to cross the sea.

And its monk, who sat at the center of the Black-Mother faith, would be the key to determining whether this faith was genuine. Col had to meet him.

"Safe travels."

Yosef smiled while bidding them farewell, standing in the doorway of the trading house. His canine companion sat obediently at his feet. Perhaps it was because Myuri was not nearby, but the dog seemed a bit friendlier.

Col bowed and headed to the port, and the morning sun stung his eyes.

The moment they had gotten off the ship yesterday, they were greeted with a fierce feeling of desolation, but seeing the small island under a clear, pale-blue sky made it seem less oppressive.

There was greenery visible against the snow on the rocky, bare hills, and goats dotted the scenery, wandering about grazing on grass. Even on the beach, which looked like the end of the world yesterday, there were seabirds resting on driftwood, along with islanders busily gathering seaweed that would be used for fertilizer—it was a lively place.

Among the islanders was one nosy traveler child, trying her best to peek at the seaweed. It was none other than Myuri.

"Myuri, we're going!" he called out to her.

She immediately looked at him but reluctantly gazed down at her feet again before giving up, hauling her luggage on her back. He had noticed that she had gotten up surprisingly early, but he now knew that after wolfing down her breakfast, she had come to the beach to search for amber.

"Did you find any?" he asked with a dry smile, but she glumly shook her head. "It will not be easy."

Though it was cheaper in value compared to other precious stones such as gold or silver, amber was more popular as jewelry.

If it were that easy to find some on a beach, they would have no problems.

Myuri sighed and exhaled breathily from her nose like a cow, blowing out white vapor, and then opened her gloved hand. There were small brown bits that looked like earwax.

"When I went to go look, they found some right away for me! Even though I couldn't find any after looking so hard!"

There were children about the same age as Myuri among those gathering seaweed. They were probably showing off their kindness as locals to the outsider who had come from the distant south. Of course, the kind of amber that she had in her hands was much too small to have any value.

"Of course. There have been many times when others easily found truths in the scripture that I could not, even though I read it so much."

Then Myuri, who was wearing so many layers that the outline of her body had grown square, shrugged her shoulders.

"That's especially true because you only see half of half of the world."

He sighed, thinking about how he had spoken out of consideration for her only to be met with such a response, but then he noticed Myuri looking up at him happily.

"But don't worry! Instead, I've found a lot of good things about you that no one else has noticed yet!"

He truly felt exasperation when she said that.

He could not bring himself to let that stand, so he replied, though it made him a bit embarrassed.

"Let me just say this now, but when I worked in the bathhouse, I had to turn down invitations from many women, you know."

There were a great many beautiful dancers and musicians at the bathhouses in the hot spring village of Nyohhira. Of course, they were not children like Myuri but wonderful women who could navigate the world by their own wit.

But instead of becoming angry with him, Myuri grinned, unaffected.

"You didn't turn them down, you just ran away."

"Urgh—"

Much like how Col had watched over Myuri ever since she was born, Myuri had also been watching him ever since she came into this world. He did not hide how he acted before women that decorated themselves like birds, with chiseled chests and necks.

He was silent as Myuri had nailed him where it hurt. She grinned again.

"Well, Mother says a good woman can love everything, including the pitiful parts. So no need to worry, okay?"

"…"

There were no words. Then, he looked down at her and smiled back.

He did not know if he should point out the insolence of calling a man who was practically her older brother and twice her age "pitiful" with a smile, or if he should describe the arrogance of believing that she was a good woman even though she could not tell if he was a grown man or not.

But he shook his head, changing his mind. Myuri was a smart girl. She would naturally learn her place in the world as she got older. His job as her brother was to trust that she would manage that. Though some of her bites stung quite a bit for a pup, he decided to be the adult and weather through them.

"Of course. I look forward to the day you won't give me any worry."

He smiled, while Myuri looked as though the prey she held firmly in her teeth had just slipped away.

"Sheesh, Brother, I'm being serious!"

"I am, too. Besides, my head is filled with worry about our journey to the next island. You had three servings of fish soup for breakfast this morning. Will you really be okay? You were gobbling up all those fine-looking sardines, head to tail."

"Urgh..."

This time, it was Myuri's turn to be speechless. As though she was vividly recalling her terrible seasickness yesterday after seeing the ship, her face stiffened.

"I-I'll be fine!"

Of course, there was no proof of that. But positivity was one of her good points. At the very least, Col would trust in that.

"Be sure to lie on your back and look at the sky."

"...If I do that, then I won't be sick?"

Her cheekiness had completely disappeared. She was staring at him, uncertain.

"Of course. God is up there, you know."

Then she suddenly frowned and spoke with a pout.

"But the one I believe in is you, Brother."

She was pressuring him with her stare, but it made him smile instead.

"Then, I would appreciate it if you listened to me a little bit more."

Then he patted the hood that covered her head.

"No, that's not it!"

She started to protest, but he smiled and dismissed it.

The sky was blue, and the breeze was calm.

Even if a witch really was waiting for them beyond the sea, he had a feeling that it would all somehow work out.

Good weather meant good visibility.

Yosef saw them off as the ship circled the island and began heading north. They were finally entering the northern islands proper. They were continually surprised as little islets appeared one after another.

"It's just full of islands. I would never be able to tell them apart."

Myuri, unable to stay lying down the entire time, would sometimes suddenly get up after tossing and turning. At the moment, she rested her face on the ship's railing and gazed out across the water.

"I can't find trees anywhere. It looks so cold. They should just bring some from Nyohhira."

Every island was rocky, with only a bit of grass growing on each. There, they saw the daily lives of wandering goats and their attendant shepherds, craftsmen repairing rope on the beach, or people drying fish in front of their houses.

Serene was a nice word for it, but Col easily imagined how every day must have been a struggle.

If they could not go fishing for several days after a storm, then their food supply would suddenly dwindle. If their house was damaged, no trees grew around these parts, so supplies would have to be ordered for any repairs to be done. Even the boats, which supported their entire livelihood, were fashioned out of wood; the foundations of their lives were terribly fragile.

The ship they were riding on had unloaded most of its cargo at the previous port, but the villagers along the shore would stop moving once the commercial vessel came into view, their eyes blank with desire. An image appeared in Col's mind of a ragged little girl gazing up at a noble on horseback, wearing jewels that she would never touch. If the villagers had just one crate of cargo that was packed onto the ship, then their lives would improve greatly.

"I'm sure the faith here is real."

"...?"

He murmured absently, and Myuri looked at him with a questioning expression on her face.

At the end of the day, people had no choice but to pray if, after gathering everything they could, it was still not enough.

It was a real crutch in order to persevere against the blustering wind.

"I pray that those gaps are filled with the right thing, however."

The people born in this region kept the figure of the Black-Mother on them every time they got on a ship not simply as a precaution. It was because they desperately wished for something to support them.

And it was a single monk who created the figures of the Black-Mother that formed the bedrock of this region's faith. If that monk was spreading the figures in accordance with the true faith, then Col could expect that the followers were genuine as well. That was his hope now.

The ship pressed forward. On the way, the weather occasionally worsened—it even snowed once—but the wind was never terrible, and nothing hindered their trip.

On one island, they stayed the night at the only man-made structure, which seemed as though it crouched beneath a sheer cliff above. Before the sun rose the next day, they were already departing. It was terribly cold but there was no wind, and as he huddled together with Myuri, whose eyes suggested she was still half-asleep, he watched over her while they meandered along the forest on the small island. But things changed just as the sun rose.

They suddenly exited into an open area.

Col thought the sudden change in scenery had given him a dizzy spell, but the truth was that the ship suddenly began to rock. Unlike the narrow passages between islands they had traversed up until that point, the waves were taller now since there was room for the wind to blow freely. The sail billowed painfully in the wind, and the mast creaked with the sound of gnashing teeth. Their sea journey had quickly become an adventure.

"Are you all right?"

A wave crashed against the ship, and the wind fanned the water across the deck.

Col hurriedly tried to fetch his oiled, leather cloak, but Myuri had awoken and was gripping the side of the ship with both hands, staring out at the sea, enraptured.

"Wow…There's a lake…in the sea…"

When she said that, he thought he saw a clear line drawn in the sea. There the color grew darker. It was likely because the seafloor suddenly dropped off at the bottom, but at a second glance, he could see that the boundary was strung out along the islands, circling them. There was most definitely a lake in the middle of the sea.

Another gust of wind came. It blew back Myuri's hood,

whipping her long hair about. However, the silver-haired girl paid no mind to it, enthralled by the severity of the north.

The wind started to feel like ice at some point, leaving no difference between the cold and pain. In just a few moments, they became aware that the season they had felt before was more like spring. Then, when he considered that this was how it usually was only after the most difficult part of winter, he was hit by something similar to fear.

But disregarding that, it seemed that the lake in the sea was a kind of crossing for aquatic journeys because they soon began to see other ships. Ice clung to Col's eyelashes, and no matter how many times he rubbed his eyes before looking out across the water, he could always see the imposing figures of massive ships built for long ocean journeys with three or even four decks, as well as commercial ships for transport operated by only one or two crew similar to the one they were riding on.

Everywhere people were carrying out their lives as normal.

Myuri, who was typically noisy, quietly watched the other vessels crossing the sea. As she breathed puffs of white, her hands grew red, gripping the railing against the buffeting wind, ice, and waves. It seemed she had even forgotten about her ears and tail, which usually popped out whenever she got excited.

"...Is that...a ship?"

It seemed she did not even have the time to be seasick, murmuring like she was finally coming back to reality.

"But...it's pitch-black...and so...huge!"

He stood next to her as she doubted the way ahead of them. Widening his stance, he planted his feet in anticipation of the rocking and rolling of the ship as he looked forward.

"That...doesn't seem like a ship. More like a mountain. The black parts are a forest."

"Mountain?"

It sounded like she was asking why there would be mountains in the sea, but on closer examination, anyone could tell almost instantly that it was their destination. Once they could clearly see the ridgeline of the mountains beyond their hazy vision, the number of ships around them grew. This must have been the main island, the center of the northern islands.

Col brushed off from his clothes icy drops, which no longer melted when he touched them. He covered Myuri's head with her hood again, then stuck the woolen scarf around her neck.

She seemed rather bothered by it, but she did not make the greatest effort to resist as she watched the route ahead of them.

Fair winds allowed the ship to head straight for the island at a great speed.

What finally came into view was the first decent, stylish-looking port town they'd seen since leaving Atiph, along with a mountain that sat like a king in his throne, lording over the lake behind it.

There was no other mountain that could be called so majestic.

As Col stood, awestruck, Myuri suddenly giggled.

"Heh-heh, look, Brother. That mountain looks like a king pulling up his pants."

"What?"

When she mentioned it, he saw that the foliage was different around the center of the mountain and the foothills were darker than the rest. It certainly looked like someone pulling up their pants to their stomach. Then, he noticed the snow on the treeless peak resembled a crown, and everything suddenly looked silly. At the same time, his eyes were filled with mirth as he admiringly glanced out of the corner of his eye at Myuri, who was staring innocently at the scenery.

The world she saw was always colored with a fun and exciting light.

"Hmm? What's wrong, Brother?"

95

She noticed his gaze, her eyes wide.

"It's nothing. You are always just like yourself."

"Huh?"

She looked up at him blankly, like a cat that had been tricked. He merely patted her on the head through her hood, dodging the question.

"Oh God, please watch over us on our journey."

The ship rocked, and water from the waves sprayed them as they made their way to the mountain king.

The roofs on the buildings were large and steeply slanted, perhaps to keep the snow from building up. They were built closely together, resembling a group of people huddling low after being blown together by the wind.

Caeson, the port on the main island, was certainly quite large and packed with both people and ships, but perhaps it seemed that way because Col and Myuri had grown so used to the lonely sights since leaving Atiph. If they bothered to stop and spend the time, they would have easily been able to count the buildings and people they saw up until then.

And yet, Col was relieved to see people chatting and laughing by the snowy roadside. The bustle and warmth of many people was present. On the corner, there was a large snow sculpture, its hands and face made out of sticks.

"Is that the church? Thank you."

He asked directions from a passerby, who pointed upstream of the river that flowed through the port. It was rather wide and deep. As no bridge had been built, the townspeople used ferries to get from one bank to another.

Perhaps that was why there were not many people on the streets along the river, and even snow that had been marked with footprints was still piled rather high. He looked at the river that flowed from its mouth up on the mountain, thinking it looked like a rip, as though someone had tried to tear the island itself in half.

"Come, Myuri, let's go."

He pulled his scarf up to his mouth and held Myuri's hand as they made their way toward the church in town.

"Is that where the guy making the dolls is?"

"They are not dolls. They're figures of the Holy Mother."

"And that's different?"

It would be difficult to explain the significance to someone without faith, so he could only groan.

"And we're not going to the monastery?"

"We'll be staying at the church. The monastery is different. By the way, as we were nearing the port, the monastery was visible from the ship. Did you see it? There should have been a smaller island a short distance away, and I believe it is located there."

"What? Oh, uh, I think I saw something like a small shrine, but...Wait, someone lives there?"

Sharp-sighted Myuri had indeed found it. They probably passed it when he was putting warmer clothes on her while she stared out at the passing scenery.

Then her eyes suddenly began to sparkle.

"No way, someone actually lives in a place like that? Seriously?"

Her nose, bright red from the cold, was twitching, as though she had caught the whiff of adventure.

"Is it really that exciting?"

"Definitely. The waves were crashing up against it, and there were huge rocks all over the place. It was really cool! I was sure it was an altar for sacrificing goats, but...Mhmm. It definitely looks like a house for a sorcerer who controls lightning and walks on the sea."

In the decades of war between the Church and the pagans, the Church tried to eradicate the kind of faith where people worshipped those very sorcerers. After the war, there were few who still held on to such beliefs, but those legendary figures still remained alive in people's minds as the subject of adventure tales and in writing.

Though they were often depicted as evil people who needed to be subdued, anything was fine for Myuri as long as it excited her.

"Oh man, I can't wait. I bet there are stairs leading down to underground mazes and doors we should never, ever open!"

There was certainly a big misunderstanding occurring somewhere, but Col did not know where to start.

"Oh, Brother, what should we do if there's a dragon down in the labyrinth? Should we get Mother?"

To Myuri, the line between dreams and reality was fuzzy. She really looked like she was enjoying herself. The problem was that her mother was indeed a kind of spirit, one that normally lived deep in the shadows of the woods.

But still, in order to make sure that such a young, easily influenced girl would not grow up oddly, he had to draw the proper lines and teach her the proper ways of the world.

Though he was cowardly and weak in many things, Col could still teach certainty in a world full of uncertainties. He had, at the very least, studied hard every day to know what was right.

The two of them continued on and eventually came to a large portcullis. He could tell it was a church because he could see, on the other side of the stone wall, the crest of the Church fluttering in the wind. But if he had to describe what he saw, he would have called it a fortress.

"Wow..."

The portcullis was currently raised and was fashioned from thick wood—a sword or ax in the hands of a human would not make so much as a mark on it. It appeared to have been designed with war in mind, an impression that was only reinforced by the length of the path extending from the portcullis and how thick the stone walls were. On top of that, there were unique-looking holes looking down through the ceiling above the path, and Col could see that they were charred. They were holes meant for pouring boiling oil onto attackers to force a retreat.

"The...church?" Myuri asked.

Even she was dumbfounded by how imposing it seemed.

"Even Mr. Yosef said so—it is likely a sanctuary."

"Huh...You mean, like there's important treasure inside?"

The optimistic Myuri's eyes were sparkling, but that was not it.

"No. I am talking about rules of the adult world."

While she stared up at him blankly, Col pulled on the cord that was dangling by the gate, which rang a little bell. Before long, a door on one side of the path opened, and a soldier holding a spear appeared. He wore hard leather rather than metal armor because the latter would have stuck to his skin.

"Oh, a traveler boy, 'ey?"

He had the same reaction as Yosef, but he did not seem surprised because traveling clergymen often came to borderlands.

"An introduction from Sir Yosef of the Debau Company."

Col presented the letter and the piece of wood, just in case.

"I don't need that."

The soldier did not take the piece of wood, which meant this really was a unique place.

"Under the orders of a noble, you have traveled through Atiph to the distant northern seas to survey...I see. You've come far."

The soldier shrugged his shoulders, neatly folded the letter, and returned it to Col.

"If at all possible, we would like to stay here while we are in the area."

"Of course, I don't mind. That's what it's here for. A guest of the Debau Company is a guest of ours."

The soldier walked off, his body language inviting them to follow.

"Let me just say this now, but missionary work is forbidden in town. The folks here follow God's teachings, but it's a bit different from how southerners see it. Are you aware of that?"

"The Black-Mother, you mean?"

The soldier nodded, relieved.

"Also, I've heard there's been religious riots down in Atiph. The people here are sensitive about tension with the Church. Don't let anything funny happen."

It appeared that the effects had already rippled this far.

They soon passed through the walls, exiting into a rather spacious courtyard. With one glance, Col could tell why straightaway. Crates and trunks wrapped in straw were stacked here and there, all of them under the banners of large, familiar commercial firms. There was of course the Debau Company, as well as that of the Ruvik Alliance, which once owned more ships than any king, lauded as the strongest at sea the world over. This was a place without any greater authority to rely on, a shared base maintained by the merchants from large companies engaging in long-distance trade and a sanctuary to which they could escape to if something happened.

Though the Church would have typically taken similar measures in pagan land where its authority did not extend to, this place also fell under that umbrella.

At that very moment, there were a multitude of merchants all around, accounting for cargo and maintaining their draft horses. Myuri was looking around, entranced by everything, but the soldier pointed at her and looked at Col with inquiring eyes.

"And one important thing. This is a church, after all, and a small one. Women are seeds of trouble. Wives that come with their husbands and maidservants all sleep in special accommodations. The same goes for slaves."

It was not odd for the slave trade to be present in economically depressed areas. From the disgusted look directed his way, Col could tell that soldier may have thought he was a softhearted priest who had come to take home a slave girl who he had found in the south.

But whatever the truth may be, what he needed to think about first was that he could not leave Myuri alone in this place where they had no one else to rely on. One of the few rules he gleaned from traveling in the past was to always keep valuables within reach.

However, there was no doubt that Myuri was a girl, and no matter how convenient it was, this was still a place of rest for the lambs of God who wore the crest of the Church around their necks. Col, who was striving to become one of those servants himself, could not bring himself to lie.

As he stood speechless, Myuri removed her hood and scarf and revealed her long silver hair in the snow.

"There are lots of perks to dressing like a girl," she said and grinned.

The soldier studied her as she did so, and he suddenly bared his left canine.

"Clever kid. You're gonna make something of yourself one day."

"Heh-heh, thanks."

She smiled freely, her expression calm.

"There should be someone in the biggest building there. You can ask them your other questions."

Long ago, Col had once stayed on the grounds of a grand monastery. What they saw now had a very similar feel to it.

A big church building stood in the center, and starting from the south there was the courtyard, vegetable garden, stables, then dining hall and such all surrounding it, as well as residence halls for guests.

Since it was a base for merchants, the courtyard was bigger than that of the monastery, as were the places to eat and sleep. The stables were not as spacious, however, since this area relied mostly on ships for transport.

"I see. Thank you very much."

"Not at all."

Before the soldier returned to his post, he showed how he had grown to like Myuri by bumping fists with her.

"How was that, Brother?"

He had just witnessed a moment of the tomboyish Myuri gaining a strange sense of confidence again.

"Honestly, you spout lies so easily."

"What? But I didn't lie."

It was certainly true that she had not told a lie. Her words were simply the truth. It was the soldier who had misunderstood, and Col himself had used that technique several times before.

But there was a clear difference between the two of them. Myuri was using it to enter a place she was not allowed. He could not come to terms with his conscience as to whether or not he should overlook it.

His reproach and confusion must have been visible on his face because his companion wore an offended expression.

"But, Brother, if you really thought it was that bad, then you would have confessed the truth then and there."

"..."

"You didn't because it was convenient for you, right?"

It was true, so he could not utter a sound.

"Then, it's fine. It wasn't my pure and righteous brother that lied anyhow," Myuri said, her words sounding like satire, and she hugged his arm.

103

Nothing frightened a girl who did not believe in God at all.

"My faith feels like it's about to waver."

"You can give up whenever you like, you know. Then we can get married."

"…"

It seemed this was her trap. She had just chased him and he fell for it. His only response was to stare at her with tired eyes. It was like she was grinning down at him from the lip of the hole.

He sighed; then knowing he could not continue like this, he spoke.

"Act properly next time."

Myuri shrugged as though placating him.

Then, as the soldier had suggested, he opened the door to the big building, white smoke puffing from its chimney.

The hallway extended straight ahead of them and seemed even colder, made of stone, but there appeared to be an open hall just to their left. He could hear merry voices coming from beyond the door standing ajar.

"It seems like a good, lively place…What's wrong?"

Myuri had her nose shoved into the open part of the doorway.

"It smells…weird…," she said, and he sniffed the air.

"Ah, that's the smell of peat."

"Peet?"

"Do you remember the story about what jet is? It's like muddy coal. They gather it in fields and grasslands. It's cheap, but it's flawed in that it does not burn well and has a peculiar smell. You may be able to find it on this island as well."

Myuri had a good sense of smell due to the blood of wolves flowing through her. Perhaps that was the reason.

"If it's too much, we can arrange other accommodations for you."

Even in Nyohhira, there were quite a number of people who left the mountain because they could not stand the smell of sulfur. While some residents were used to it and it did not bother them at all, there were others who could not stand it.

That was what he had in mind when he made his offer, but Myuri, pinching her nose closed, glared at him for some reason.

"Wh-what's wrong?"

"That's how you're going to keep me from traveling with you, isn't it?"

It seemed she was now on guard, since he often scolded her, asking if she wanted to quit traveling whenever she overslept, overate, or said something selfish.

"I am just being considerate."

"...Hmph."

Though she did not say outright, *Brother, you idiot*, she did look away in a huff with a frown on her face.

"More importantly, let's quickly secure our room and go investigate."

He had not come this far to babysit or relax. The commotion in Atiph had created such big ripples that it could be felt this far out into the sea, and its effects would grow bigger yet with time. He needed to wrap up here in the northern islands as soon as possible, then head to the next job.

Myuri was still grimacing from the odor of the peat, but as they crept in through the door, a person approached from the hall.

"Oh!"

His voice was rather pleasant, perhaps because it reflected his personality, but it was more likely because they were wearing similar clothes.

"We don't get your sorts much this time of year—travelers?"

It was an elderly priest, the crest of the Church hanging from his neck. His cheeks were red not from the cold but probably from alcohol.

105

Setting that aside for now, Col gave him a visitor's bow.

"Pardon us. I am Tote Col. I have come to this land under the orders of a certain noble. Further details are in this introduction from Sir Yosef of the Debau Company."

"Oh-ho."

The priest blinked in surprise before walking over and taking the letter. His hands were soft and warm, though there was most certainly alcohol on his breath.

"I see, I see. I am the master of this church, Reicher Freedhoff. This means you must have come in search of land suitable for a monastery. Oh, no need to explain anything. Those sorts of people always come. For some reason, southerners have the misconception that this is heaven's front gate."

In addition to being drunk, it seemed he was typically like this. He plainly spoke of things that were not often said aloud, wearing the smile of a pleasant old man. Then he gave a troubled sigh that smelled heavily of liquor.

"Good or bad, this is just the edge of a cold sea. If you search too hard, you'll only find danger. Especially during this season, there'll be no help if you fall into the water, and there are the pre-spring storms. Occasionally, people like you obsessively investigate islands no one else goes near, and what a commotion it makes."

Reicher hiccupped and shrugged his shoulders.

"Do you mean a spiritual commotion?"

As Col probed, he noticed a strong light in the man's eyes, fitting for a priest who ran a place ringed by the stone walls of a fortress.

"Are you inquisitors?"

Had they both been knights or mercenaries, this would have been the moment they each put their hands on their swords.

However, after Reicher studied him, his gaze finally dropped to what was latched onto Col's back.

Col answered slowly as the priest looked at Myuri.

"If I were, then I think I would choose more carefully what I bring along."

Inquisitors, often called executioners or torturers for good reason, would not walk around with a young child in tow.

"So it would appear. Or if you two actually were, then it looks like the Church is managing to get away with keeping the people here and there in good faith."

Then the priest suddenly sneezed.

This man must have had some sort of reason why he occupied a place of worship in such a remote area, one where the Church had no official presence at that. It did not seem to be because he was a faithful servant to the Church.

"It's cold here. Why don't you come in...? Ah, we need to take care of your luggage first."

"And we would like to borrow a room, as well."

Reicher smacked his forehead and smiled.

"Oh, oh right. You can't relax if you drink still wearing your traveling clothes."

He laughed, but then under the deep wrinkles of his eyelids, he shot a glance with a surprisingly alert glint at Myuri.

"By the way, I'm sure you've heard the rules of the church from the guard at the gate, am I right?"

"We did. He said girls stay in a separate room."

Myuri stared back at Reicher, grinning while she spoke. It was rather courageous of her, or perhaps insolent. Reicher stared blankly at her, but after blinking sleepily, he sneezed again.

"*Hic.* Pardon me. Then, let me take you to your room. There are few people here at the moment, so there are good rooms open."

He slipped by them to head outside.

"Ooh, it's cold!"

The cool air must have felt good to a body warmed by liquor.

He spoke with good cheer, with Col and Myuri following after him as he walked off.

When the people working in the courtyard saw Reicher, they called out to him and waved, even the ones far away. Though he was drunk during the daytime, all evidence indicated he was a beloved priest.

Not to mention that, barring the Black-Mother, his prayers of safety were the only thing that offered the people solace when they anticipated a journey at sea.

"Well, to start where I left off…"

Reicher began to speak as he walked around, checking the dried fish hanging from branches instead of fruit in what must have originally been the vegetable garden.

"Like I was saying, huge uproars. And they don't come back after leaving in a small boat. Sometimes they fall into the sea; other times it's shipwrecks that drift away."

There are those who expect a certain holiness in the severe northern seas, hemmed in by snow, permeated with cold and clear air. Reicher must have seen off so many people with that attitude in the past; he now shrugged his shoulders in defeat.

"Most of those nobles don't know anything about this land… The closest are from Winfiel and Ploania. The farthest come all the way from countries in the south. At any rate, when those people who come burdened with responsibilities but wind up dying, we are always the ones regarded with suspicion."

How had Hyland represented the people who controlled this land?

"I heard that pirates are the ones in charge of this area."

Col's comment made Reicher look back at him gloomily over his shoulder before sighing.

"I can't really say much to that, because they are pirates, no matter how you look at it. But they're also not pirates of any sort."

Reicher continued as he fixed the knot in the string of one of the dried fish.

"They typically protect trading ships and watch to make sure real pirates don't plunder fishing boats or ravage any of the islands. Well, it's easy to understand if I say we're responsible for how difficult they are to reason with through talking."

To put it in more familiar words, they were a self-defense force.

"Without them, we would not be able to keep these wayward waters in line. Our resources are limited, so if everyone acted as they pleased, we soon wouldn't be able to maintain our livelihoods. The threat of violence is like the hoop that keeps barrels together. Without it, we wouldn't even be able to collect taxes from those who come to work here each season. Our land would be carved up by outsiders and soon vanish. They exist out of necessity."

The crunching snow echoed beneath their feet. Every couple of steps, a puff of white appeared and hung by Reicher's left shoulder, then disappeared into the air.

Col could tell by his posture that while the priest considered the pirates his ally, he was also resigned to their presence.

"But those who only hear about them through stories make a lot of noise, claiming *Oh! The pirates killed folks from the south in secret because they don't like them!* Those who don't know how truly terrifying the seas are here don't heed the locals' warnings, leading to accident after accident."

As Reicher finished speaking, he stopped in front of a spectacularly large building.

"Here we are."

The entrance was up several stone steps, likely as a way to keep the door from being snowed in.

The foundation of the lodging house was made of stone as well, but everything above was wood. Col had spent many winters sleeping on stone floors, but he had only been able to stand that until his healthy teenage years. Already past twenty, he was relieved to see he would not have to relive those days.

"Go down the hall and you'll find the assistant priest who runs the house—you'll get your sheets and blankets from him. He'll also tell you what room you'll be staying in. Feel free to leave a donation when you do."

He smiled at them pointedly.

He then spoke again, maintaining his expression.

"An empty island is ideal for building a monastery on, but if people don't live on those islands in this sea, then I think it's best to consider them uninhabitable. They are too dangerous because the currents around them are too complicated or there are too many rocks just underneath the surface of the water. Well, you wouldn't be able to tell by only looking. A lot like faith, isn't it?"

Reicher smiled and bumped one of his shoes against Col's, shaking the snow from it. Though Col could appreciate how unassuming the old priest acted, he could not find the heart to laugh along with the joke.

"And so, the people around these parts aren't very welcoming to those who are clearly southern priests. Just sniffing around so much is enough of a nuisance, but then they wind up dying in accidents, which brings down suspicion that no one needs again. Of course, the people who interfere with trade by straining their relationships with the locals are just as much as a nuisance."

Reicher was clearly telling them to behave themselves, keep their distance, stay for a few days, then go home.

A positive way of thinking about it was to take it as a kind warning from a resident of this sanctuary.

"I cannot, however, go home empty-handed."

Col tried resisting, and the elderly priest suddenly shrugged in a drunken manner, giving up.

"Either take on a local as your guide, or if you're on your own, then you must ask a local before doing anything. Especially if you plan to go out to sea."

Reicher recited his advice, still standing in the doorway, facing them as they stood inside.

"That will keep you safe."

Then, without any chance for them to respond, he shut the door on them.

After the distancing sound of crunching snow completely vanished, only silence remained.

Myuri readjusted the luggage on her back and looked toward Col.

"He doesn't like us."

Col looked down at her, and she was smiling.

"Travelers are always treated like this. There are few places that welcome them."

"Really? But everyone has so much fun eating together in Nyohhira."

Col adjusted his packs as well before he urged Myuri along as the two of them walked down the hall.

"Nyohhira is rather unusual. Most places in the world do not welcome outsiders. The ones who disrupt the common people's quiet lives are often outsiders."

Myuri did not seem to really understand straight away, but she would come to do so in time as they continued to travel.

"That is why we must go about our business quietly at our destinations, especially in places with few people."

Myuri knit her brows and looked up at him with a frown, as though saying, "You're lecturing me again?"

But this was not about the teachings of God or consideration for others. It was more about telling someone how to stay alive if they became lost deep in the mountain woods.

With Col silently staring back at her, she seemed to understand immediately.

Myuri made an appropriate expression and nodded, gulping.

He wanted her to take this moment to understand that traveling was not all fun and excitement and that there was nothing better than living peacefully at home.

While he thought about this, Myuri suddenly spoke with a grave expression.

"It's the same as when the king pretends to be a commoner, right? I hear about that a lot in stories."

"..."

Myuri grinned—*It's all right, I know.*

He thought that she really did not understand at all, but what he did know very well was her optimism.

Their room was small, and the bed was just two wooden trunks pushed together with a blanket laid over them.

But a room was still better than the large rooms and storage areas on the other floors—the facility was definitely constructed as a base for merchants' trade.

He could imagine that comfort was a secondary concern at a base made for commerce, so he was right to have donated when they borrowed the sheets. It was a time in which even sins could be forgiven if the appropriate amount of money was offered to the Church.

And since the two of them managed to borrow a good number of blankets, they would be able to sleep in warmth and comfort.

Then, they had to put lunch together after dropping off their belongings, so they went back outside soon after. They decided to see the miraculous remains that Yosef had mentioned, so they asked the soldier at the gate. It turned out they were close enough to reach the site on foot. It was also in the opposite direction of the port, so they decided to go there first.

However, the snow on the roads was deep, and the guard recommended they wear woven straw boots over their shoes. Just as Col thought about how kind he was, the guard proceeded to ask for money. It seemed he was angling to make some pocket money on the side, but it was not a bad price so Col properly paid. There was also the wisdom of his merchant benefactor to consider. It was important to gain the favor of anyone possible when visiting a place. No one could say who might be able to help on another day.

There was no proper road leading to the miraculous ruins, so they traveled along the river and worked their way upstream. As they walked on what would be a field in the summer but was currently covered in snow, it did not take long before Col could feel himself sweating. His traveling shoes were already heavy, but he wore straw coverings over them. He had never found it so difficult to walk. But without the covering, the inside of his shoes would have become soaked; then, if he was lucky, his feet would be swollen from the chill, and if not, frostbite would settle in. The straw boots were indispensable during Nyohhira's winter as well.

He was soon short of breath, but Myuri kept pushing forward with a bounce in her step, like a snow hare.

"Hurry up, Brother!"

Unlike the mountains, there were no cornices or streams on the island and Col was not worried they would lose their way since they walked along the river, but he grew irritated thinking about the path back. He wished they had brought a sled of some sort, but he shook his head, reminding himself they could not indulge themselves in luxury.

"Come on already, Brother!!"

Myuri had gotten so far ahead he could no longer make out her expression when she impatiently turned back to him and yelled.

Though the island looked small from the ship, with just a mountain and its foothills, Col was coming to realize that it was more than large enough for wide, flat fields. In summer, he could imagine how the endless snowfields became grass, producing a year's worth of feed for the livestock.

A forest finally came into view, lying at the foot of the mountain. The miraculous ruins were apparently at the end of the road in the forest.

"You're too fast!"

That was all he managed to say. A puff of white rose from where Myuri stood, perhaps because she sighed. She, of course, would not wait for him and rushed ahead.

But he did not hold a grudge against her apparent heartlessness. Instead, he was impressed with her youth and the strength to forge a path forward on her own. He thought about how he would be able to see this again when she got married, and he considered it a rehearsal.

He smiled dryly and continued to put one foot in front of the other.

When Col finally caught up to her footprints, he also reached the entrance to the forest. Myuri was sitting on a large, bulky rock and eating a large icicle. There were several hanging from a nearby tree, resembling so many spears.

He could tell she had waited quite a while because there were three round snow sculptures at her feet, some large enough to have needed an armful of snow. She had even given them faces made out of twigs.

"Brother, you almost remind me of Father."

She was implying that he had no strength, but he did not even have the energy to reply to her that she had too much.

His shoulders heaved, and Myuri watched him in exasperation before breaking the icicle in two and handing him a piece.

"Don't eat too much or you'll get cold."

Even though Col was usually the one to caution her, it was Myuri that did so to him.

And it did not seem that Myuri had simply walked in a random direction, as she sat at the mouth of the road leading up to the mountain. Under the evergreens, whose needles never fell even in winter, there was a snowy path, hardened by footfalls.

He expected nothing less from a girl with wolf's blood, raised in the mountains.

"But the ground here is kind of weird. Are all islands like this?"

The hardened snow did not seem like it was on a steep incline uphill, instead forming more of a gentle slope. Myuri had raised her question as Col followed after her, managing to keep up this time.

"What do you mean by weird?"

"That river's weird, too."

She stopped, turned back, and pointed. There was no undergrowth in this season, and they could see quite far even from the forest.

There were the footsteps they had left behind and the nearby river.

He wondered what was strange about it, then suddenly realized.

"...The color of the river is the same as the sea."

Drawn in the snowy fields, there was a long, thin, dark-blue line.

"Yeah. That's probably not a river but the sea."

"The sea? But..."

They had come rather far inland from the mouth of the river. It could hardly be called an inlet, nor was it a canal. He could only think of it as a river when he saw how it snaked along.

But a river should have been much more active. The water was silent in the snowy fields.

"It certainly does look like a dead, blue snake, doesn't it?"

As though it had stopped what it was doing and just lay there.

"And look."

Myuri returned her gaze to the forest and pointed off to the side ahead of them.

"It ends there."

The river ended suddenly. The blue water from the sea turned green at the water's edge, washing the white snow. It was not pouring in, nor was it flowing.

"Maybe it was a river a long time ago," he said, and Myuri looked back at him.

"Huh?"

She looked as though she had seen a mountain move.

"Is it that unusual? Mountains fall, forests dry up; it's not odd for a river to dry up and die. Even more spectacular things happen regularly in your adventure stories, don't they?"

Myuri's face went red as she pursed her lips.

"...I—I don't think what happens in books are real! You're teasing me, right?"

This girl had only spent ten-odd years on this earth.

She had been raised in a hot spring village that seemed to stand on the boundary between dreams and reality, which muddled her perception of things even more.

"Even scenery can change a great deal with the passage of time. There are things such as cataclysms, which can be nothing but punishment from God, and even small things can trigger them. This world is not eternal. Eternity is reserved for God's kingdom in heaven."

Almost everything in this world was like a house of cards, destined to fall someday. That was why he wished to support people amid such uncertainty and cruelty.

He wished he could tell Myuri more about this, but she likely would not listen.

At least that was what he thought, but she was silent and wore a rather grave expression on her face.

Perhaps to her, the rivers and mountains would always and forever be as they were. Though she had never met a dragon or a wizard, the rivers and mountains had always been by her side.

"You learned something today."

He approached her and placed his hand on her head.

"Everything fades with time. Dust will return to dust, ashes to ashes. That is why we must spend the time that God has given us fruitfully."

He added that was why sleeping in was unreasonable, and she finally huffed, like her normal self.

"You always lecture me!"

"I wish I did not have to."

"Sheesh!"

Though she was offended, her gaze returned to the end of the river and her cheeks also quickly deflated.

Then, she spoke, still facing away from him.

"But Mother said the same thing. I guess it's true."

He gulped unwittingly.

Myuri's mother was a wolf and wheat spirit who either lived for hundreds of years or perhaps never aged—a being known as the wisewolf.

That was why, even though the wisewolf Holo traveled with a merchant she met in a village and fell deeply in love with him, she continually hesitated to cross that one line. Her partner was human, and his life would vanish in the blink of an eye. The passage of time could not be stopped.

But they rejected the natural laws of the world to grasp the happiness before them. Though it was destined to slip from their hands like sand, they believed their memories of taking hold of it would last forever.

How sad and how painful it must be.

And there was a chance that Myuri, blood child of Holo, would share the same fate.

Myuri was not human.

Col had vowed that he would always be her friend, but there were some things he could do nothing about.

Like her father Lawrence who, no matter how hard he worked, would one day without a doubt no longer be able to lift up and embrace his eternally young wife, no one could win against destiny.

"That's why I…"

Myuri suddenly looked back at him, smiling.

"Like Mother taught me to do, I'm living every day to the fullest that I can."

"Myuri…"

Her innocent smile was strength itself. She had the courage to keep walking forward, even if the road ahead of her was dark.

It could have been attributed to youthful ignorance, but it was more probably that she chose to live this way. Hers was a smile that told him he could believe that.

"…"

He grinned awkwardly, and she nodded, satisfied.

"That's why I'll eat any food I think looks good and sleep when I want to. There's even a reason why I play when I want to, you know? You're always talking about moderation, Brother, but there's no time to be moderate!"

She puffed out her chest and spoke confidently.

He was almost touched by her speech. Then he dropped his fist onto her head.

"All that has nothing to do with a life of debauchery."

"Aww!"

Myuri raised her voice in a whine, and she puffed out her cheeks.

"Brother, you dummy!"

"I am not a dummy. You need to stop trying to talk your way around people at some point. You can never be too careful."

"I'm not trying to talk my way around anything!"

They walked along while arguing.

It looked like Myuri was throwing the usual childish tantrum, but he could somehow tell that she was doing it on purpose.

And there was still something she had not mentioned. Since she had the blood of the wisewolf in her, there was the possibility that she, too, would live for eternity—so it was possible that she was reaching out toward anything that caught her attention. However, what had caught her attention was not food, nor was it an amusing toy.

It was Col himself.

He had a sense that he understood why she did not mention that.

Had she said that she reached out to him because he, too, would eventually be gone, that would mean recognizing that he truly would no longer be around someday. The superstitious elderly often spoke of it: That which is said aloud soon becomes reality.

Myuri relentlessly complained that he was hardheaded, inconsiderate, a bully, but she clasped his hand as they walked side by side. He could even feel the strength of her grip through his thick gloves, like a little girl who could not go to the privy by herself in the middle of the night.

He could not reciprocate her feelings, but as an older brother, he did not consider it problematic to stand by his little sister's side until she no longer feared the dark. Fate was something to be feared, and the only way to stand up to it was to pray, as miracles virtually never happened.

God was great because he was the one who could overturn everything.

As they continued up the snowy mountain path, black cliffs suddenly appeared out of nowhere. The pitch-black stones were so jagged they seemed evil, though not too tall, only reaching around Col's height. The rock formations stretched forward on either side of the pair.

The path wound along the cliffs, heading for the river. Myuri peered curiously at the odd scenery, and she drew closer to sniff at the exposed stone of the cliffside.

"This is where the king's clothes begin."

Col had suddenly realized where they were, causing Myuri to look up as well.

"Wow, it is. The color of the leaves is different."

The line they had seen from the water where the plant life changed seemed to be right where they stood.

"It changes so quickly, doesn't it?"

"Hmm, I don't know. It feels like there may be another reason why..."

"Another reason?"

"Like an earthquake, for example."

Myuri did not ask what an earthquake was. It was perhaps the first time she had heard the word.

"There are times when the earth shakes violently, like a giant stomping around. When that happens, the ground sometimes breaks and can shift like this."

He had been in lands like that when he was a wandering student much farther to the south, and so he occasionally experienced earthquakes. People often said that it was because God was angry with the evil deeds of humans, but since the northern pagan lands never knew anything about earthquakes, the wrath of God and other such explanations seemed far-fetched.

"Huh."

Myuri's response was dull.

"You believe some weird stories sometimes, Brother."

And then, she went and said that.

"You don't believe me? I have, numerous times, exp—"

"Are you sure you weren't drunk? If the ground was moving like you say."

Though she had no doubts about stories of pirates with daggers in their mouths, raising wild war cries, she was skeptical of the strangest things.

Exasperated, he followed after her, but the lay of the land, strangely, did not change.

As the cliffs consistently appeared to the right where the river was, they got closer and closer to the higher parts of the mountain. If it were a king pulling up his drooping pants to around his belly button, then they were walking on where his belt would be.

The black face of the cliffs was such a stark contrast to the snow, but there were several places that were covered in thick roots. If an earthquake really had happened, then it had been a long time ago. If he asked to hear the stories from the island elders, then they would certainly know of remaining legends.

As these thoughts whirled in his mind, Myuri had stopped ahead of him. She seemed brighter perhaps because the sunlight illuminated her. The glow could only be seen here, where trees did not grow, creating a clearing. The road, too, had been hardened and well-traveled, so it could have been used as a place for prayer.

In the sunshine, Myuri stood with her mouth agape, staring up at the mountain.

Wondering what was enshrined in the place, Col walked into the clearing.

Immediately after, a violent shiver ran down his spine.

"Wha...?"

An unbelievably giant serpent raised its head, as though it would strike at any moment.

"Wh-wha...?"

Col stared upward at the beast but had forgotten they were on a slope, so his posture crumpled and he fell squarely on his behind.

No, there was no time for this. He needed to get up, take Myuri's hand, and run back into the forest—quickly!

The more he struggled, the farther his feet buried themselves into the snow, and the harder it became to get up.

When he finally stood and looked up, the serpent was in the same place with its mouth opened, unchanged.

He calmed his screaming heart, panting, then gazed up at it again.

What he saw was not the jaws of a giant serpent.

"...A cavern?"

The ceiling was high and wide. A great building of a large commercial firm could easily fit inside. What looked like fangs were overhanging stones, roots and ivy wrapped around them. The snow had the look of a white snake's skin, and when Col examined the whole once more, he could see nothing but the giant serpent.

It appeared to be a rather deep cavern at first glance, but as his eyes adjusted, he could tell that it was actually quite shallow. The surface of the rock was the same pitch-black as the cliffs, and the unique roughness of its texture made him think of aberrant beings.

"Brother, are you okay?"

He had been so involved in what was in front of him that he had not noticed Myuri at all.

She brushed off the snow that covered him, and she helped him get up.

There was no mischievous smile on her face, perhaps because of how agitated he had become.

"Th-thank you. But what is…?"

"Someone's offered flowers here, so this must be where they pray."

Myuri pointed to where the serpent's tongue would be if the opening was a mouth. Farther inside the cave, where the snow did not reach, there was a pile of rocks along with an unusual winter offering of flowers, just as Myuri had described.

Then, sitting quietly there at the top, was a figure of the Black-Mother.

"I wonder why her back is to us. Maybe someone's idea of a prank?"

As Myuri had pointed out, the figure of the Holy Mother was facing the inside of the cave. Figures and statues in places of prayer typically faced the people praying, so it left a rather odd impression.

"Maybe there's a monster inside."

If the figure of the Holy Mother's protection, which had the power to create miracles, was necessary, then it was possible.

"Should I turn into a wolf?" Myuri asked while she fished out the pouch full of wheat from her shirt.

As a person with the blood of a wolf spirit running in her veins, she could use the wheat her mother had passed down to become a wolf herself.

Col did not entertain the possibility that she could win against any towering serpent that came slithering out, but she could throw him on her back and quickly escape.

"There might be trouble if someone saw you, so…," Col explained as he peered inside the cave, though it did not seem like anything was hidden inside.

And as he approached, he could clearly see that the cave was not deep enough to hide anything.

"I wonder what she's looking at."

Myuri stood by his side, examining the figure of the Black-Mother as it stared silently into the cave, and then she tilted her head. Though she had mentioned someone placing it backward as a joke, it did not seem to be an adequate explanation.

"Do you think they found the jewels here?"

"What?"

Her words were sudden, and he looked back at her.

"You know, the little doll here is made out of whatever that weird stuff was, right?"

Without a drop of respect in her, Myuri pointed and waved her finger at the figure of the Black-Mother.

"...You mean jet? But..."

He had seen mines in the past before, but this felt different compared to every other mine he had ever known. Mining operations always angled downward. The ground in this hole was flat, and the ceiling was extremely high. It should have been much easier to mine starting from the top rather than going upward. More importantly, it was hard to imagine that the figure was placed here in a hope that jewels would appear from this hole.

And he felt like he had seen this somewhere before. Where was it?

"Do you want to try and dig? Mother dug a hole and found water when Father asked her back when they were opening the bathhouse, right?"

As though Myuri's inner seven-year-old boy was tingling, Col could see the ends of silver hair from the hem of her coat. Her wolf ears were likely sticking out already under her hood. On an island surrounded by a frozen sea, in such an intriguing place, a black figurine of the Holy Mother was being worshipped in an incomprehensible manner. Her curiosity was like a wasp's nest that someone poked with a stick.

"Or maybe there'll be water for that dead river if we dig."

"What?"

As she spoke, Myuri headed farther into the cave, moving about the rocks at her feet.

Col watched her, holding his breath, and looked up toward the ceiling, then at the Black-Mother.

His body leaned backward, like he was reeling, because he began to move in reverse; he stepped behind himself because he had a certain hunch.

What had he first thought when they entered the clearing from the mountain path?

It was almost like a serpent was jumping out to attack them.

In that case, it was clear as to why the Black-Mother had her back to the outside.

He had seen this sight before. He had not been able to piece it together well because *it was frozen in time.*

The ground at his feet changed from black gravel to white snow. He took two, three steps back, looking at the whole image. The mouth of the serpent, which seemed as though it would attack him at any moment, started to look like something else.

"..."

What flowed along the river might not have been water. He looked back, and it became perfectly obvious as to where it was flowing. And then *the Black-Mother.*

"Brother, what's wrong?"

Myuri emerged from the cave, her eyes screwed nearly shut due to the reflection of light on the snow.

"Hey, Brother?"

She pulled on his sleeve, and he finally came to.

"No..."

He shook his head and looked back into the cave once more.

Once he became obsessed with the idea, he could not shake it off. He was wrong in thinking that he had seen it somewhere before. He had heard a similar story before, and he knew it well.

"Brooooootheeeeer?"

Myuri mischievously waved her hands around before his face but jumped when he finally looked at her.

He took her hand as she flinched, and he began to walk off.

"Huh? What?"

"There's something we need to confirm."

He pulled the confounded Myuri along, taking the road they had originally come from. It at first seemed like she would trip over herself, but the girl raised in the mountains did not stumble.

"Sheesh, Brother!"

He ignored her complaint as his head was already full of things he had to think about.

The Black-Mother faith was not a sham or a superstition. But *as a faith, it still might be false.*

His job was to judge whether or not the northern seas would make suitable allies for the just cause of the Kingdom of Winfiel in their fight against the Church.

From the gaps between the trees, he could see the port town of Caeson.

The dead river that split the island in two drew an azure line in the field of snow.

CHAPTER THREE

Col could only run at full speed until he reached the edge of the forest, and once they exited onto the snowy fields beyond, he began to pant. Soon he could lift his feet no longer. Reality never went the way he imagined. Myuri could only roll her eyes at him, but his legs propelled them forward, fueled by a sense of duty.

Myuri had thought they were going to take a rest at the church, but they passed through it and headed straight to the port.

It was just after noon so the main streets they passed were mostly empty. After searching around the docks, Col quickly found what he was looking for: a boat bound for the monastery.

Considering what Reicher had told them, Col thought such a sudden request to be ferried over would be refused, but when he called out to the men at the port, the tips of all their noses bright red, laughing together merrily, every man clamored to be the one to take them. He ended up deciding with the flip of a coin, then paid the fare, which cost about the same amount as a whole loaf of rye bread in Atiph. It was not an easy proposition to cross the water in springtime, but rather one that would mean the end of his life if he fell in, so he did not consider the cost to be excessive.

It also accounted for the fact that the captain himself would be taking a risk.

It was a small vessel, one that would be full after seating four adults, and thanks to the rowing skills of the man who claimed to be a fisherman, they glided across the dark sea.

The harbor soon grew small in the distance, and the captain's friends waved their hands wildly toward them.

Though it was barely noticeable from the port, they could clearly feel the waves shifting under them as they got farther and farther away from land. The boat was small; even inside, they were close enough to the water that if he reached out, he could touch it.

He thought Myuri might crouch on the bottom of the boat for the duration of the crossing, but she sat silently beside him. She must have been angry at him because when they had crossed through the main street, they went right by a restaurant with good smells wafting from it. But she seemed a much more committed helper to his job this way.

"An apprenticeship, eh?" The captain suddenly spoke to him.

"…I beg your pardon. What?"

"You aiming for an apprenticeship? With the brother."

The compact captain already had sweat dripping from his forehead. His breath was also pure white, while his smile was strained.

"You were running around the island so frantically with that little friend of yours there."

Since it was such a small place, they had likely been watched ever since they arrived before noon. Reicher's warning had certainly not been a joke.

"Or if you're planning on building a new monastery, I suggest you don't."

There was no malice in the man's words as he continued to smile at Col.

"I've heard that many times on the way here. Are there really that many people who come to do that?" Col asked.

The captain responded without so much as a pause in the motion of the oars.

"Even if we're only counting the most obvious-looking guys, there's at least one every year or two, without fail. Sometimes merchants even come to take a gander around the islands. Their noble friends tell 'em to come build a monastery, and they're hoping to make some shiny coin for themselves. Most of them are southerners coming up here to gather herring and cod."

Construction, ordering daily supplies, transporting visitors, plus other odds and ends. The merchant who had taken Col in when he was a child had told him there was not much money to be made trading with monasteries, but perhaps these business-men had intended to work themselves to the bone for the monas-tery in service of God.

The boat had come rather far from the port, and likely due to how small the vessel was, the lake in the sea seemed unusually large.

There was something peculiar about the loneliness at sea. Any-one could find faith here.

"Mr. Reicher at the church hammered that story into us."

"Ah, Father Reicher the drunkard."

The captain laughed.

"Though it is true that my lord and employer ordered me to investigate the region, right now I simply wish to meet the monk who oversees the faith in this land."

"It looks like you visited the shrine up at the foot of the moun-tain and everything, too."

"Wha—?"

Col was shocked, wondering how he knew. The boat captain's face wore a mysterious expression.

"You can clearly see anyone walking over the snowfields from the port, and you have a good view of the sea from the shrine, right? *Look to God and he shall watch over you, too*—that's one of his teachings, isn't it?"

The man was right. Now that he thought about it, Col turned back, and behind the captain, he could see the island and the mountain. The tiny, ant-like white dots must have been the clearing before the shrine in the serpent's mouth.

How perfect it was that he mentioned the shrine. There was something he wanted to ask before going to the monastery and meeting the monk there.

"Is there a reason why the black Holy Mother is facing away from us?"

There was no doubt that the line dividing plants on the mountain was that distinct because of those cliffs. Besides, the withering river had changed into a spindly sea, and in the middle of its flow sat that cave. That being the case, it certainly gave the impression that she was praying for it to come back to life.

"Ha-ha, a studious priest you are. Not something you see every day."

Col was not a priest, but it did not seem that the captain really thought he was one, either. The sense he got was that was just how the captain termed anyone who looked like a man of the Church.

"Most of the guys from the south don't pay any attention to this land. So that makes me happy. I'll gladly tell you."

As he worked the oars, he cleared his throat.

"This is a story from back when my gramps was a kid. When a dragon still lived at the bottom of the sea."

As they got farther out onto the open water, the wind grew

132

stronger and the waves grew higher. Col squinted his eyes as the water sprayed him, and the captain stared off distantly, vigorously pulling the oars.

"We've been fishermen for generations, and our boats have always been made from wood. But it's cold up here, you know. Trees take a long time to grow; people generally cut them down faster. The islands around here lost their woods quickly, and soon there was nothing but grassland. Now, the only trees left standing are in Caeson, and it's been like that for a long time."

Even if they considered the entire journey by ship from Atiph, there was no doubt that Caeson was the only island that held any trees.

"We live with the sea, and we need to use wood to cross it. We had no choice but to rely on the trees in Caeson. It's like the candle of our life, allowing us to hold on as long as the flame is still lit. But…"

Then the boat rocked and nearly tilted over, and Col hurriedly clung to the side. He held out a hand to Myuri, who had collapsed, and when he looked back to the port, he could nearly no longer see it through the haze. He could only see the fuzzy blackness of the mountain.

"We don't know why, but God had become angry."

Col held Myuri with one hand, gripping the side of the boat with the other; then he looked at the captain, who took a deep breath, then exhaled deeply.

"The mountain spit out fire."

The goats, who were typically unfazed by anything, had apparently been agitated all day, and something strange had caused the birds to all take flight as well. The captain said that though it was currently the snowy season, the air was warm as if it were spring.

Then, the ground groaned, the mountain shook, and the snow that fell was not cool and white but instead hot and black. Rather than snowmelt, molten stone traveled down the river toward the town, burning everything in its path.

"There weren't enough ships. Gramps, who was just a kid at the time, somehow got on a ship, but it was crammed with people and there was no way it could get out to sea. They only went out far enough that they could still see the faces of the people stuck in the port, and there was nothing else they could do but watch the burning mountain and wait as hell itself approached them. The place he lived burned; the bread of their life that was the forest burned; his parents and brothers and sisters still in the port were about to meet the same fate, but at the very least, he was on the water. The frigid waters would be able to cool and harden even molten rock. His heart felt like it would be torn from the feelings of both despair and relief."

If there was a ship that would save people's lives, then it was only natural for them to climb aboard. But accepting that would do nothing to lighten the pangs of guilt. Even during the commotion in Atiph, when Hyland put her life on the line and went to the Church, the most logical choice for Col and Myuri was to escape by themselves. Though Hyland had also strongly encouraged them to do so, Col had still almost been crushed by his own powerlessness and guilt.

"But when almost the entire top half of the mountain was covered in fire, my gramps could see someone walking on the snowfields toward the mountain. Silhouetted by the flames was a woman. The guys watching from the port and the water thought it was someone who'd completely given in to despair. Then, the moment that figure stood in the river, that road of the flames, a miracle happened."

The captain spoke as though he had seen it himself, likely because he had heard the story countless times, and the images had ingrained themselves into his mind like he had seen the event himself.

Even Col could imagine what the people on the ships had seen when he turned around to look.

"The hellfire pouring down the mountainside dammed up in the middle of the river. It was split in two and began to die down. Maybe it was a lucky thing that the snow had been so deep. The molten rock, split in two, rolled slowly down the hill; then, cooled by the snow, it hardened. The cooled rock became an embankment, preventing anything flowing after it."

That was what those sudden cliffs were. To be able to stop such a flow of molten rock, it must have been huge—something that would leave behind a giant cavern.

"The top half of the mountain had been razed, but the bottom half was fine. While smoke still rose from the stones, people ran to where the miracle happened. Beyond the strange rock face, still smoking and red from the heat in places, was a big cavern. It looked like the entrance to hell itself, smoke billowing from it. Apparently, molten rock dripped from the ceiling, like the stomach acid of a great beast. And then, in the entrance—sitting there was a pitch-black lump of charcoal."

When Col saw the shrine, he had the unshakable feeling that he had seen it somewhere before.

And that had not just been his imagination. It was almost identical to an old legend from the village he was born in. Once, when a flash flood came crashing down the mountain toward the village, a large frog god appeared and bravely offered itself to save the village—there were such tales in any region.

That being said, it was one thing for a frog to stand against water, but the woman who appeared in Caeson halted the burning flow of molten rocks.

"And so, the Black-Mother…"

The captain glanced at Col when he murmured.

"She was the one who saved us from danger."

As the man spoke, he lightly tapped his waistcloth. Col thought for a moment that the captain had a dagger stored underneath, but it was most likely where he kept his figure of the Black-Mother.

"Half the trees that supported our livelihood were lost, but after that, our people had terrific fishing season after terrific fishing season. Then, maybe as a reminder of the Black-Mother, we even found veins of coal. Everyone, including my gramps, worked hard and saved money and bought lumber from faraway lands. They wouldn't touch the trees on the island. Thanks to that, though, now it looks a bit more like a proper forest. And that's why the colors are different, as you see them."

The stark difference in colors of the forest was not because the plants were different species but because the ages of the trees.

"And that was when the monastery was…?"

"Yeah."

Col turned to face forward again, and the mass of earth he had seen in the distance had now come into view.

He could see a stone building squatting between two rock formations that extended out like horns.

A small boat was docked at the shabby pier.

Removed from all the impurities of the mortal world, there was no place more perfect than this to concentrate on prayer.

"I've heard that my gramps' gramps, the ones who built the monastery, had a political reason for building it at the time. Because unlike now, the war against the pagans was truly raging during his time."

For generations, the Church had been obsessed with subduing the pagans in the northlands. Even in the current day, there were many who regarded the region with suspicious eyes, but it must have been truly terrible years back.

"They realized that if they built a church, then people would come here from the mainland, asking for tax and jurisdiction and whatnot. So they only erected a building in a place that was completely uninhabitable. And so, it implied that even though our people may have converted to the teachings of God, we wouldn't accept a ruler."

Of course, without a supervisor, it was difficult to put them under the Church's jurisdiction. Hyland had also said that the Church tried countless times to put this region into its sphere of influence but had given up due to the endless problems.

These people lived their lives constantly balanced on the edge, and there was no way they could afford to pay tithes and other Church taxes.

Even so, they were a hardy people.

"As for the teachings of the Church themselves, well, we were taught by the priests that the merchants brought along to pray for safe passage. The monastery stood empty for a long time, but... then, the brother who's there now, appeared. That was almost twenty years ago."

His words were unexpected.

"This was back during those good fishing seasons, when you could stab a sword haphazardly into the water from a boat and pull out a whole skewer of fish, which was around the time the coal mining started to empty out. The old men argued and argued if they should cut down the trees to build more houses, create more families, and continue mining for coal or build more boats to go fishing or else fall into bankruptcy before long. One day, the fisherman found a battered boat on those rocks and a person sitting inside it."

They were now close enough that they could see inside the windows of the monastery.

"Everyone was surprised. Of course they were! How reckless would you have to be to come alone in a tiny boat to these waters? Then, he spoke. He had been sold into slavery somewhere to the south, and when he touched the jet his master held, images of this land spread in his mind. He said the jet was a fragment of the Holy Mother. Then he climbed aboard a tiny boat as he was told and drifted all the way here. He said he was sent to carry the heavy burden of this land upon his shoulders."

The captain stopped rowing the boat and began preparing rope in order to dock at the pier.

"He wore a lone set of rags. He didn't have food but instead had a mountain of black figures of the Holy Mother. The old men believed that he was sent by the Holy Mother and left him to solve their argument."

Their boat approached the pier, blown by the wind, and the captain tossed the rope around a stake, then pulled them in.

"Surely, what led him to this land was the fragment of the Holy Mother's body."

"A relic," Col murmured subconsciously.

Relics—items that were associated with miracles, like cloth that a saint would have worn or the body of a saint itself. They were believed to work miracles, bringing prosperity and able to fight off demons or sickness. There were many people who prayed for miracles, and there were merchants who specialized in them.

Col had only ever heard about them in stories, and most were shams.

Of course, he would not say that about the Black-Mother, but the captain gave him a troubled smile.

"What Gramps and the elders had were pieces of the Holy Mother. But what I and the other young fishermen have is jet found on other islands besides Caeson. We can claim that if it came from the mines of Caeson, then it's a piece of her body, but the mines are practically all dried up now. There's no doubt it's the brother's hand carving, but it's not a piece of the Holy Mother. But, well, it's good enough. My kids and their kids might have to order jet from other countries. It's the Holy Mother, so I don't think we'll lose profit, but…it makes me a bit sad."

Yosef had also sighed over the decline of the mines.

However, with a strength that belied his current dour mood, the captain fastened the boat down.

The dinghy jetty, washed by the waves, stretched up onto a rocky island that hardly seemed habitable.

"Well, we're here."

The captain kept one foot the boat and put one foot on the boards to pull on the anchoring rope because the waves relentlessly rocked the small vessel. As Col thanked him for his consideration, they hopped onto the pier.

"Thank you very much."

"Oh, don't mention it. We can't just waltz over here without good reason, either. I'm happy to have an excuse." ·

He smiled and produced a small figure of the Holy Mother from beneath his belt.

"Pray here, and you'll be in sound health for the decade to come."

It sounded like he was joking, but it did not feel like one.

It became clear that the reason the men clamored when Col asked for passage was not for the money but for the chance to come to this important place. It may have been that everyone was so fervent in their faith that if left unchecked, the island would overflow with people.

"Well, when you're finished, come show yourself at the pier. It's the rule that I have to leave here now. The guys back at the island will think I've outsmarted them!"

The man was grinning mischievously.

"I understand."

The captain pressed the figure of the Black-Mother to his chest once more and bowed toward the monastery, released the rope, hopped into his boat, then glided off.

The wind and the waves crashed against the rocks without pause as the cold crept in through Col's feet, stealing his warmth.

The story of the Holy Mother who saved the island was almost exactly how he imagined it. He felt the people of the island had several practical reasons for respecting the Black-Mother as the Holy Mother.

The only remaining problem was the monk.

"...So you noticed, Brother."

Myuri's gaze was sharp, perhaps due to passing up a break at the church and the restaurant back in the port town.

Or she may have been angry because he should be talking to her about those who were not human.

"I told you about the village I was born in, didn't I? But I was not confident about it back there."

"It didn't smell like grilled meat, either."

Col was startled, and Myuri cackled mischievously. For a moment, he thought about lecturing her about respecting the dead, but her expression soon became serious.

"She was probably the same as Mother."

Perhaps Myuri did not say "the same as me" because when she changed into her wolf form, she was not that big. Her mother, Holo, became large enough to swallow a man whole.

"But even Mother wouldn't be enough."

Certainly, not even a wisewolf would have been able to fill that cavern.

"Maybe if it was the Moon-Hunting Bear?" Myuri spoke, making no attempt to hide her excitement.

The Moon-Hunting Bear was the incarnation of destruction, a being that occasionally appeared in myths from ancient times throughout the mainland. It may have been a spirit that truly did exist once, and it was said that it was large enough to sit on the ridgelines of mountains, and it could reach out and touch the moon. Many spirits died by its claws, and it ripped the earth itself in half. The story goes that after a violent rampage, the bear disappeared into the western sea.

It would make sense that the woman's whereabouts were unknown if, after saving the people of the island, she turned to ash.

That being said, what he wanted to know was not what happened to her.

It seemed like Myuri knew that.

"So, why did we come here in such a hurry?"

"If the Black-Mother is not human, then there are four possibilities in this region's faith."

Beyond the unstable jetty that seemed like it could crumble at any minute was a bare stone building, where calling it "simple" would be better than it deserved, built on a reef to keep people away.

"The islanders either know she is not human and worship her as the Holy Mother anyway, or they truly believe it was a miracle of the Holy Mother wrought by God."

Had he whispered, he would not have been able to hear his own voice over the sound of the waves and the wind.

"Then, there is the possibility that the monk making the figures of the Black-Mother knows about the miracle, or he doesn't."

As she finished listening, Myuri shrugged her shoulders and looked at him, amazed.

"You're really picky with the weirdest things, Brother."

Myuri had made a comment, but that was not the case.

If the islanders and the monk both truly believed in the miracle

141

of the Holy Mother, then that was fine. There was no way to prove what happened in the past, and they had already converted to the teachings of the Church, so they could be trusted. However, it would be a different story if the islanders and the monk believed that the miracle was actually caused by someone who was not human and did not actually consider it an act of God.

If they simply wore the teachings of the Church as a cover, then Col and Myuri would need to overlook that deception should they become their allies in their fight with the Church. And judging by how the captain spoke, while the people of this region looked at the Church's authority with suspicious eyes, they were still earnest in their faith.

And so, he needed to see the monk who was making the Holy Mother figures that served as the basis for their faith.

While lacking in other areas, when it came to matters of faith, Col had the confidence he could see through the fabrications of others. Monastic life was to fight with oneself, so any deception would be readily visible. There was no way someone with clean nails and spaces between the fingers would be devoting themselves to unforgiving moderation, no matter how tattered their clothes were.

"But, Brother, they won't like inquisition."

Myuri, born and raised in Nyohhira, a gathering place for travelers, spoke as though she understood.

"I must check to see that the faith in this land is righteous."

There was a sudden strong gust of wind, and for a moment, his body had almost been blown away. Myuri closed her eyes under her hood and brushed her bangs away.

"Well, I guess that's your job."

Myuri shrugged and pressed a gloved hand to her nose.

"But it's cold. I feel like I'm going to get sick. Let's at least hide behind a rock."

Though she was used to the snowy mountains of Nyohhira, this was a place where the sea wind blew. They walked up the pier, supporting each other, and landed on the reef. It was too small to be called an island, and in addition to the shedlike building, it would have felt crowded with four or five adults huddled around a fire.

The waves almost reached their feet, perhaps because it was high tide, and they were splashed with water whenever the wind blew. If something happened, it seemed impossible to swim to a port with people, and no one would notice yells or a raised flag.

Were someone to truly be living here day to day, there was no way they would be of ordinary sensibilities.

It was like the legendary recluse living in a hermitage in the desert from the scripture.

"Myuri, please wait for me in that hollow."

Col lowered his voice but not because he was going over some secret plan. Monasteries were silent as a rule.

"Why? I want to see the inside, too."

Myuri objected, of course, and spoke frankly.

"Women cannot enter monasteries. This is a matter of respect for the faith."

She began to say something, but she seemed to tell by his expression whether he would give in if she argued some more. She pursed her lips, disappointed, and looked away in a huff.

"It will be over quickly."

He patted her shoulders lightly before taking a deep breath. He watched her sit down before making his way to the monastery, but when he glanced back, she was dramatically hugging her knees and making herself smaller. He sighed, returned to her again, and wrapped his own scarf around her neck. The wool scarf covered her red nose, and she looked up at him as though to say, "Oh well, I suppose I'll forgive you."

And once again, he neared the stone building. There was not a scrap of luxury about it, and it felt more like a storage shed in the backyard of a company building that could be found in a large town. It looked like it could fit, at the most, two rooms, and one just barely big enough to fit an adult lying down. It was a place completely unrelated to the comforts of living, in various senses of the word, and it was strange how someone could truly reside here.

However, candlelight poured from a window—a square simply cut out from the walls, not even any oiled paper to cover the holes.

There was no door, and hanging in front of the entrance was the skin of a shark or something of the sort.

He pushed aside the hard, cold, rough skin and found a place of prayer.

There was a shelf on the opposite wall of the entrance with lit candlestands on either side of it. In the middle sat a figure of the Black-Mother. This was a substitute for an altar.

There was nothing else in the dreary room, but something odd suddenly caught his eye. Beneath the altar was the sea.

Perhaps due to the outside light, the color of the water had changed from blue to green. There were no waves since the walls cut it off, but it was still clearly connected to the sea outside in some fashion. It was possible that the monk bathed there as he prayed, but Col shivered when he imagined it. If he dipped his body in there, there was a chance the icy seas would drag him right out.

"Do you need something?"

Col jumped at the sudden voice.

Flustered, he turned around, and from the other room, a man as thin as a twig with a beard that had never been cut was standing, studying him. If he had seen him in town, Col would have certainly assumed he was a beggar.

144

But his hands looked like they had been painted pitch-black, signifying that this person was the monk on this island.

"P-pardon my intrusion."

Col straightened his posture, placed his hand on his chest, and bowed his head.

"I am called Tote Col. I aspire to be a man of the faith."

When he saw the man's arms as he bowed his head, he winced. The skin had become like leather from the salt and dirt, and it looked more like a wood carving than human arms. When he raised his head, the eyes peeking out from behind those eyelids looked fake to Col, who could not detect any emotion residing in them, almost like a deer in the mountains.

"For my studies, I wished to hear more about the story of the Black-Mother."

His legs were shaking not only due to the cold. The monk wore tattered rags, and his legs were dreadfully bare. Col felt embarrassed for how warmly he dressed. He cowered before this man.

Then the monk opened his mouth.

"Pious servant of God. I am nothing but a fleck of dust that offers prayer. God orders us to give what we have, but I have nothing. I cannot even produce hot water."

The monk, nearly every feature but his eyes mostly hidden between his hair and his beard, looked troubled, even compassionate as he considered Col.

"State my name to the harbor. Those of kind hearts will welcome you warmly."

The monk called himself Autumn.

He could not find it in himself to question the righteousness of faith to this Autumn.

What made him think that was inside of Autumn.

"There is nothing but prayer to be found here, traveler from the south."

He lingered sadly, and perhaps because they were growing numb from the cold, he quietly closed and opened his pitch-black hands once. Behind him, Col could see a figure of the Holy Mother he was working on as well as his few tools.

Yosef had said that this man made all the Black-Mother figures by himself. He could not imagine how much perseverance was needed to create such detail in this cold, drafty stone structure. Even when Col occasionally warmed his hands while he transcribed, it was indescribable hardship to work during the winter.

He imagined Autumn carving the figures of the Holy Mother and thought—

He was simply carving away his very soul.

His voice slowly rose from his throat not out of respect.

It was something that was more similar to fear.

"May..."

He managed to rouse his wavering voice and asked.

"May I ask just one thing?"

Autumn looked at him with the eyes of a grazing deer, then closed them, signifying he was listening.

"What is it...that supports your faith?"

There were those who had tremendous theological knowledge, whose sermons touched the hearts of people, yet drank in the hot springs and ogled naked dancers. There were others who, once they donned the robes, suddenly became self-restrained, austere servants of God. He deemed that irresponsible enough, but God never denied the occasional episode of self-care.

But Autumn was different.

He had the eyes of a deer that ate nothing but grass or one that even refused to eat that grass.

Col wanted to know so badly what had caused him to be that way.

"What will you do with that information?"

It sounded like a question from a demon, because this man had no interest in Col himself.

And yet, he squeezed out the courage to ask.

"I wish to know what your faith is like."

Even Col was aware of how insolent the query sounded coming from a young man in nice, warm clothes. He saw now how he had stood in the shoals and assumed he knew the depths of the ocean. Such faith was actually possible in this world.

But he felt like he had to ask now. He could not feel any attachment that Autumn might have had on life, and if he did not reach out now, the man might disappear forever into the heights where Col could not reach.

"What faith is…?" Autumn murmured from behind his beard. His shoulders shook.

It took Col a while to notice that he was laughing.

Autumn opened his eyes slowly. Perhaps he was not looking at Col out of astonishment?

"Faith, to me, is salvation. So it is obvious what it is that supports me."

What slowly came to look at Col were the eyes of a martyr.

"The awareness of my sins."

At that moment, Autumn seemed to change. The more he thought about that, the air around him transformed. From the depths of his being, which had been like a plant just before, gushed out anger, deeper than the seas itself.

His trembling legs were no longer his imagination, and he found it hard to breathe.

If this anger was what Autumn directed at his own sin, then it was too late for the word *repentance*. He loathed himself. He was a lion—running wild, baring its fangs, claws digging deep, drowning.

As Col simply stood there, overwhelmed by the man's presence, it was as though Autumn had shut the door to his heart. Winter changed to spring in an instant, and he returned to his previous self, speaking softly.

"Of course, I will not say that is what makes up faith in its entirety. There may be faith that gives thanks for a happy life under God's will."

As though to show that his words were neither lie nor merely concern for Col, Autumn softened his eyes for a moment.

But he soon sighed, and his eyes returned to the color of the deep sea.

"I am a sinner. Thus..."

He gave a dry cough.

"...I shall not side with Winfiel, nor the Church."

Col did not dare raise his voice in a cry, but he was so startled he almost made a noise.

As he recoiled, Autumn closed and opened his hands again.

"This island cannot exist without trade. There are many quick-eared merchants. News of the commotion in Atiph has already reached us. Besides, it has been almost three years since both sides began fighting. It is about time something happened."

He spoke like a sage, stepping down from his pedestal just to speak to him.

"You say you are with the Debau Company, so perhaps a messenger from Winfiel? Maybe not."

A chill went down Col's spine—he knew that much. He had assumed this man was a monk, removed from all worldly affairs. He assumed that this man, of all people, was unconcerned with the mortal world, surrounded by the walls of a house of God, living by prayer all day, every day.

"Well, I understand if you do not wish to answer. But..."

It was just as he was about to continue speaking.

"Stop, stop!"

Col could hear Myuri's voice coming from outside.

"Let go, I said. Let me go!"

He wondered what was happening and looked at Autumn, but the monk gazed out the entrance, as though he might comment on how strong the wind was.

Aware of how rude it was, Col turned on his heel to go outside, and he reeled. There was a group of people who looked like their very livelihood was ruffianism, and Myuri, her arm gripped by one of them, had been strung up like captured game.

Then, behind them, floating on the water, was a sword-shaped boat.

"Y-you people—!"

Col was about to speak, but it occurred to him that it was rather himself and Myuri who were the intruders.

This was a sanctuary of the islands, and not even the islanders could approach casually.

"Leave her be. These are my guests."

Col heard a voice from behind him. Autumn showed himself, and the men immediately let go of Myuri and dropped to their knees. It was the bow of a servant.

Myuri, now freed, scrambled over to Col and clung to him.

"What is this?"

One man answered the monk's short question.

"We beg you to come with us."

After he spoke, Col could hear a long, deep inhale from Autumn.

"Very well."

At his response, the men rose and created a path for him.

No matter how he looked at it, they appeared to be pirates, and they served Autumn.

And so the answer was simple.

This was the center of faith for the northern islands, and—

"You said you were called Tote Col."

Before he took his first step, Autumn spoke.

"Why don't you come see the depths of my sins for yourself?"

The thing made him aware of the sins that supported this boulder-like faith.

"And then leave, for the sake of this island."

He did not wait for Col's response and walked down the path the pirates had made for him.

Though he was as skinny as a dried branch, he did not budge in the gusts of wind.

The pirates on standby at the pier began their preparations for Autumn to come aboard. The rest of them stared at the intruders from the south.

It was different from hostility. This was a gaze reserved for outsiders.

"Lord Autumn has commanded it."

One of them spoke. Refusing now would lead to an even worse outcome, and Col wondered what Autumn was up to, of course. A monk led pirates, and he prayed because of his awareness of his sins. His hands were pitch-black from making the figures of the Holy Mother, but it could also mean his hands were dirtied with sin.

Col was searching for allies for the Kingdom of Winfiel in their fight against a corrupted Church.

He needed to know what was happening in this land, where a sinful monk spread his teachings.

"Oh, God be willing…" he managed to reply, and without showing any emotion, they headed for the boat.

Beside the pier sat a small vessel with several oars. After some people climbed in, it made its way to a larger ship waiting a bit farther out. The boat captain who had brought them to the island in the first place was watching on from a distance, a worried expression on his face.

"I wish I was a bird." Myuri mumbled.

Of course, if she were, they might be able to escape.

"But there are certain things we cannot run from."

"…?"

Myuri looked at him with a puzzled expression, and one pirate pointed silently to the empty boat.

Col took her hand and jumped aboard.

Then, as she put her hand to her chest, she said, "Just say the word, Brother."

And I will become a wolf, is no doubt what she meant.

He appreciated her spirit but did not imagine that would solve any of their problems now.

The pirates, who existed to resolve issues that could not be dealt with using talk, had come to call on the monk to iron out a problem that could not be tackled with violence.

What would he show them?

The numerous long oars poking out from the ship on the contour of its slim body made it look like a skeleton.

The ship they boarded was called a galley, one that was known for how slaves and prisoners worked the oars to propel the vessel at high speeds.

It was quite late afternoon; clouds began to cover the sky, and the sea was dark as night came early in the winter.

The wind was strong, and white, foamy waves appeared here and there. There was no shouting or singing on deck, and the pirates rowed silently. Autumn sat at the bow of the ship with his head bowed, like a criminal about to be sent to the gallows.

Col and Myuri had been left in the back of the deck. They were not being watched over, nor were their hands tied. In any case, the crew held no interest in them.

It could have been said the seafarers were dedicated to their work, but even passionate craftsmen sang songs about their craft.

"It's like a ghost ship." Myuri murmured.

She must have heard that word from a guest in Nyohhira, but that was exactly what it was. They hushed themselves, making it feel like only the dead rode on this ship. That was all he could see.

The ship passed straight across the lake in the sea and entered the cluster of islands that surrounded the lake. As they did so, the waves quieted and the wind died down. How they lifted the oars, brought them back down into the water, paddled, then raised them again all in a line began to look like a pagan ritual.

The ship slipped between the islands. The ship they had come on from Atiph could not compare to its speed. He now understood that when war finally broke out between the Kingdom of Winfiel and the Church, this power would become a crucial element to whomever it sided with. But at the same time, because he knew that they would be counted among military powers, Autumn listened for sounds of the outside from his stone shed.

However, Autumn had said he would not side with either power.

Perhaps it was due to faith, or maybe there was another reason.

Next to Myuri, who touched the pouch of wheat at her chest and whose eyes glinted on guard, Col gripped the Church's crest at his chest in anxiousness.

The only sound on the boat was that of the oars hitting the water as they passed several islands. Each was impressively bare of trees. Had the forest burned in the eruption at Caeson, then the entire region would have perished.

Their gratitude toward the Holy Mother was certainly not an exaggeration.

But to be conscious of one's sins? To continue to regret giving one's entirety to the Holy Mother? What sin was Autumn repenting for to continue carving figures of the Black-Mother?

Then, there was movement on deck. At some point, two pirates stood on either side of Autumn at the bow—one held a big shield, and the other a large wooden mallet. The pirates stopped rowing and the boat glided across the water by energy alone.

Before long, the mallet hit the shield, and a loud *dong, dong* echoed throughout.

"It's the signal to attack." Myuri said, having probably heard stories of pirates before.

As the sound of the shield continued to echo, everyone else grabbed their weapons. There was a *thud* and a shock that ran through the ship, perhaps because it had hit the seafloor. The water must have been rather shallow, as the pirates simply jumped off the ship and into the sea.

They were not instructed to get off or to stay. They were being treated as though they were not there at all, and Col started to feel as though he was having a nightmare.

Under the dim, leaden skies, he looked at Myuri beside him.

"I doubt anything fun to watch will happen."

The girl, her nose flushed, narrowed her red, forest spirit–like eyes.

"It's okay. I'm here with you, Brother."

"…Aren't you worried about yourself?"

Myuri smiled, to which Col responded with a dry smile of his own before getting up. Even in Atiph, when he had fallen despondent in face of the vulgar and violent darkness, it was Myuri who had been the one to support him.

Most of the pirates were on the beach. There was a lonely village that looked like it might get blown away by the wind, and there were only a few run-down shacks. Boats perhaps used for fishing sat on the beach, exposed and on the verge of decay even now, with seaweed and shells clinging to them.

In the solemn atmosphere, roaming goats plodded along wearily, but their calm made them seem as though they had given up hope in all things.

When Col dropped into the water, it was so cold it felt as though he had been bit; he then helped Myuri down into the water, then pulled her up onto the beach.

Right after that, a piercing voice echoed around them.

"Please, forgiveness! Mercy!"

It was a shock, like suddenly seeing the red of blood in a colorless dream. Nyohhira was a hot spring village, so though there were a few disturbances caused by drunks, he never heard the desperate screams of someone truly afraid.

They were rare, even at the executions on the street corners that he had witnessed several times on his travels.

He could hear the voice from one of the sheds.

"Mercy! There must be—there must be a mistake!"

Had one of the pirates bellowed in anger, it would have been much better. That would at least signal a conversation between two people.

But no one there opened their mouths; only one middle-aged man continued to cry.

Myuri stood still in shock, even forgetting to blink.

Were she to speak, she might say that they should not have come here.

"Mercy...Lord Autumn..."

With a moan, the owner of the voice was pulled out from a shed. Pirates held him up on either side, as though he could not even walk on his own legs. It was too much—Col's body began to move to stop it, but when he looked again, he saw a wooden brace along his right leg.

154

It was violent to be sure, but it did not inherently seem that way.

Yet, when Col saw the honest-looking man being pulled outside and falling face-first onto the ground, crying, his heart ached.

And the hand the man clung to belonged to the monk, Autumn.

"I exist to fulfill my duty." He spoke shortly, and he directed his gaze into the shed.

Who came out next was a pretty young girl, even younger than Myuri.

"The number of resources is limited. You cannot fish with that leg anymore. Someone must leave this island."

"Oooh...Sheila, Sheila!"

The man called the girl's name. They seemed to be father and daughter. Though her face twisted at her father's cries, she did not take his outstretched hand.

"Lord Autumn, Sheila is my only daughter, my only family! Mercy, mercy!"

Autumn did not even shake his head. One pirate urged the girl on, and she hesitantly walked forward, taking care not to look at her father on the ground.

"My leg will heal! I will be able to fish again! I can mine charcoal! I will even gather amber for you!"

His appeal was weaker than the embers left over in the furnace at dawn.

Productivity of the mines had worsened, and searching for amber involved wading waist-deep in water to scour the beach floor. In this cold, that was enough to knock out even the strongest.

It was clear there was not much he could do with such a severe leg injury.

But what were the pirates planning to do with the girl?

"So, please, please...don't make Sheila a slave...!"

Col gulped, and his body tensed.

This was the darkness in half of half of the world.

This was the whole story of the slave trade. In resource-poor regions, there was a strict limit to the number of people who could work and the number of people who had to be provided for. And so, due to the father's injury, he went from a provider to one who was provided for.

If there were only so many chairs, then one person would have to stand.

It would have to be someone weak, a young girl.

Col's breathing had become shallow, hot. There was nothing he could do about the customs of the islands.

That being said, was this something he could forgive? Was it okay for someone who called himself a monk to command this?

Sheila followed the pirates and stepped into the sea as though she was being led into the jaws of death. Once she was sold as a slave, she would no longer be able to live and walk on this ground.

Col's heart was beating so fast it pained him. He could not interrupt. He knew that. It would only make him an enemy of the pirates, and in a worst-case scenario, it would even cause trouble for the Kingdom of Winfiel. A dark shadow would fall across his great goal of protecting righteous faith for his own small sense of justice.

But he could not overlook this. He had to recall why he left Nyohhira for the outside world. Did he not resolve to point out injustices for what they were, so that the world would be a better place, even if he was up against a giant?

There were things that servants of God with true faith had to say.

He knew, however, that a sound argument would not make the situation any better. The fisherman's leg would not heal, the islands would not grow any richer in resources, nor could he make the gold from selling the girl into slavery any less dirty. Before him was a situation in which praying showed its true powerlessness.

All that was left was faith. Autumn might be planning to preach to the fisherman about the nobility of endurance. Even Col froze at the rashness of such an action. He had just lost his daughter, and how would the very man who made that happen preach to him about it?

Or perhaps it was possible if the man believed in Autumn, and by extent, the Black-Mother.

Col had even forgotten to swallow in this tense atmosphere, and then Autumn spoke.

"Hate me."

He said it again. "Hate me. I pray to repent for this sin. I pray so that the islands may continue to prosper. I pray to God for your health and the happiness of your daughter."

Autumn fell to his knees and folded his hands in front of his chest. The man, who had lost both his tears and voice from astonishment, instantly changed his expression to that of rage.

"How dare you!"

There was an awful *thud*. The man used to be a fisherman, and though his leg was bad, the strength in his arms was in good shape. He grabbed the kneeling monk's beard, punched his cheek, and when the beard slipped out of his hand, he grabbed his hair and punched him again.

Unlike the sound of hitting a tree or a rock, the terrible noises echoed in the dim, empty village.

The man straddled Autumn, beating him black-and-blue.

No one tried to stop it. The pirates stood around them, and the villagers watched from the doors of their sheds, frightened.

Then, after he had hit him multiple times, the man was out of breath, and he stopped, fist still raised.

"I…"

Autumn spoke as he lay on the sand.

"Let us pray for the girl and your happiness…It is my duty to burden myself with this sin and pray to God that it may be forgiven."

There was a dull *thud* sound as the man punched the sand next to Autumn's face.

"…Urgh…"

The man collapsed onto Autumn's chest and began to cry, and the pirates finally pulled him off.

Autumn did not take anyone's hand, standing up by himself. It was difficult to see due to his beard and hair, but when the wind blew, visible ribbons of blood streamed down his face. This was a creature who suffered sin. An old goat who consumed the sins that someone reaped, digested them, then ate them again.

It did say in the scripture that God would forgive the sins of sinners, but Col had not imagined it to be like this. Autumn's rationale was so logical that it seemed as though he was using what was written in the scripture arbitrarily.

But there was a spirit with an overwhelming sense of self-sacrifice. An undeniable torrent of faith.

Autumn watched as the man was returned to his shed, and then he spoke quietly.

"Let us go."

The pirates obeyed, filing back toward the boat.

As this all happened before him, Col could not budge from his spot. The silent footsteps of the pirates walking on the beach was like a march of dead soldiers that are sometimes said to appear in the snowy mountains.

After the pirates passed them, Autumn was last in line, halting to stand before them. His eyes were not critical, nor did they ridicule or hold any excuses.

He looked at them with sad, forlorn eyes.

"I will do this until my sins have saved the islands."

His lips were cut in several places and were bright red.

"These islands are balanced on a dangerous scale. There are times when one must wield a sword in order to keep the balance. The Holy Mother preserved these islands with a miracle. No matter what, I must protect these islands."

There was no way a boy who only ever read books in his hot spring village should stand before this.

When Col turned to the side, he was simply glad he had not collapsed to his knees.

Autumn looked at the young man with a distant expression and continued to speak.

"I am lucky. God forgives many sins."

Then he walked off. Though his steps were unsteady, he did not fall, nor did he take anyone's hand.

Autumn harbored as much sin as he could carry on his back and did nothing but pray. The islanders revered him because, in place of the Holy Mother, he sacrificed himself to support the islands.

"Guests."

As Col continued to stand in place, one pirate called out to them.

"We will be sending you to the port by a separate ship."

They had no choice. He did not even have the strength to talk back.

He concentrated on nothing but pulling Myuri along, who had also lost all speech. They climbed aboard the small boat before they were shipped off to Caeson.

By the time they arrived, it was nighttime.

Luckily, there were no clouds and the moon was out. They walked along the pale-blue, glittering snow and arrived at the church.

The island was filled with poverty and guilt.

But this place, a base for merchants from the south, was filled with the warm glow of candlelight.

When Col awoke, he still felt like he was in the middle of a nightmare. He felt like he had just repeated the scene from the dim beach over and over instead of sleeping.

When he woke up, his head was heavy and in pain, similar the morning he awoke after being sick in bed for three days.

He could not forget the look in Autumn's eyes then, and he wanted to scream.

Would he have sacrificed himself for his faith so readily? Had he pretended he knew everything about the world, just by reading books?

Autumn was still staring at him. Col closed his eyes, but he felt Autumn chasing him. Those eyes, deserted by everything in the world, frozen like the bottom of the sea, bored into a silly boy who hailed from a hot spring village.

Forgive me. I didn't know. I was only looking at half of half of the world.

Forgive me, forgive me…

Those words and the sound of Autumn being punched rang in his ears.

The ground wavered beneath him, and he could hear another voice from far away. The moment he thought the world would end, he could hear it clearly.

"Brother? Are you okay?"

His heart beat so fast it was painful, and his face was damp with sweat.

"Brother?"

He felt his shoulders being shaken again, and he finally understood that Myuri had woken him up.

But was he really awake this time?

He breathed in through his nose to calm himself down, and he could smell fresh water. It was a familiar smell, one that let him know it was snowing outside. The room was unusually dark, likely because thick clouds were covering the sky.

Myuri, who had shaken his shoulders to wake him up, was sitting on the corner of the bed. She held a comb in her hand; she had been diligently brushing her hair.

"You look terrible, Brother."

She showed him a troubled smile, then reached over to grab the waterskin from their luggage placed by the wall.

"Have some water."

Col accepted the skin and drank from it, finding the water had chilled well. It was then he first realized that his throat was parched.

"You..."

"Hmm?"

He gave the skin back to her and asked.

"Did you get enough sleep?"

Myuri had taken the skin and was about to drink from it, but she stopped.

She smiled dryly, drank some water, then answered.

"You're always worried about other people."

She bent forward and placed the skin and her comb on top of their things, then hopped backward and sat on the bed with a *thump*.

"Auff—!"

Myuri's silver tail collided with his face with great force.

He could smell her sweet scent, a hint of sulfur mixed in with it.

"Myuri, you are always, always—"

The continuation of his words was interrupted when he saw the expression on her face as she turned back to look at him over her shoulder.

It was a sad, mature smile.

"Hey, Brother?"

She faced forward again, stretching her legs and placing her heels on the floor.

"I think we should just go back to Nyohhira."

She looked back at him again when she finished talking.

"You don't look happy, Brother."

She reached out to him and placed her hand gently on his forehead. Her small hands were cool.

"You were having nightmares all night long. You calmed down a little bit when I patted your head, though."

Her slender fingers ran through his hair, and for a moment, he was almost satisfied knowing that, but she began to chuckle. It must have been a joke.

But in his faint memories of the night, he did feel like someone had run their fingers through his hair like she was doing now. Perhaps it was a memory from when he was sick in Atiph?

Myuri watched her hand as she slipped her fingers through his hair over and over.

As though satisfied after doing that for a while, she pulled away from the top of Col's head and then poked his cheek.

"Let's go back to the village."

She had said the same thing during the commotion in Atiph. It was their escape from an ugly reality.

"I would be completely in agreement if you were the one returning."

He forced his body up, but the moment he did so, a terrible lethargy as well as a headache assaulted him, but the cold helped to keep him collected.

"But I must fight for righteous faith."

"Even when you look like that?" she said.

His words caught in his throat. He did not know what he looked like.

What made him uneasy was that he knew there were things inside of his heart that he had to hide.

"It's the same thing as what happened in that other port town before. I don't think you were meant for this."

Myuri placed her hands on the side of the bed and mischievously pulled both legs up.

He thought she might stomp after reaching a certain height, but her body fell backward as though a string had been cut, and her legs fell, too.

Her weight pressed on his thighs through the blanket as she lay on the bed.

"You're kind and honest."

She then rolled over to lie on her stomach.

"When you see the old beardy guy, you immediately start thinking that's the right way. And then you put so much pressure on yourself. It was the same when you were with that blondie in Atiph, too."

It was as though she had peeked in on his nightmare from the outside.

"I think you do best working hard in places with bubbling hot springs, reading books, sometimes talking about complicated things with guests, and sticking your nose in my business."

The last part of that sentence sounded a bit like a joke.

"If Mother would let me leave the village by myself, what I would do is explore a little bit, then come home. Lively towns, calm fields, severe climates, desolate lands, or endless pastures...I'd look around at the scenery and the people who live there; think, *Wow, there sure is a lot in this world. Well, that was fun*; and come home."

Col could easily imagine her doing that. He could see her alone, carrying a beaten rucksack on her back, sometimes turning into a wolf as she roamed around the world.

"But you're different, Brother."

The only part of her that smiled was her mouth. Perhaps she was growing irritated.

"Wherever we go, you think it's your house, you consider everyone you meet there your best friend, then somehow end up believing that you have to accept everything you find there, and then you can't move on to the next town. You always worry so, *so* much over it. After leaving Nyohhira, watching you while we're outside the village made me realize why Mother didn't mind me leaving home, especially with what happened yesterday."

Myuri got up on all fours and drew closer to him, then plopped her head onto his chest. Her wolf ears, covered in the same color of fur as her hair, tickled the tip of his chin.

"I can't leave you alone, Brother. You're more softhearted and honest than Father is."

Myuri wrapped her arms around him and squeezed, clinging to him.

"You're not meant for the world beyond the mountains. If you keep following that blondie, there will just be more and more awful things. I don't want to see you have nightmares every time that happens. One day, you'll just break. Brother? Let's just stay Nyohhira, where it's warm and exciting. It's a small village filled with song and dance, where the last year is the same as this year, and this year will be the same as next year. I always thought it was cramped and boring, but leaving made me realize that it isn't at all. There are so many good things about it. So, please?"

As she clung to Col, she rubbed the base of her ears against his neck, fawning on him.

In that place, where he was treated as a competent priest, he went about his daily work, living comfortably.

In that place, there was the master, an intelligent and understanding former merchant; his wife, the maternal wisewolf who saw through everything but kindly accepted him; and their daughter, who was like the midsummer sun as well as a person who admired him.

Was there anything he could want more than that? It was unimaginable.

But he looked down at Myuri as she clung to him, holding his breath. He gazed at the beautiful hair she got from her father, a strange color combination of silver flecks in ash, and her expressive wolf ears.

Was he sure this was not a continuation of his nightmare?

Was a demon trying to pull him to the depths of the sea?

Did such a restful place truly exist in this world?

But they were so far away from all that in this place where a frigid sea surrounded them on all sides!

"I can't." He answered, grabbing Myuri's thin shoulders and pulling her away from him.

Her body was slender, as light as an angel.

"I believe in the teachings of God. It's my wish to spread those teachings, which will become a support for those living in this world. I knew that the world would be an ugly place. Knowing this, I came down the mountain. That is why...I must protect these righteous teachings."

He desperately recited his mantra, as though repeating it for himself. Even despite how Autumn's eyes, on that dark-blue-colored beach, had seen just how empty those words were.

As he gripped her shoulders, Myuri looked at his hands and sighed.

"What does 'righteous teachings' mean to you anyway?"

The knowledge written in the scripture became a lump and gradually rose in his throat. There was much he could explain.

Though that is what he thought, he froze when he heard Myuri's next words.

"If righteous faith is support and guidance to live, then I think me liking you is righteous faith."

Though they belonged to a young child, her eyes peered at him quite discerningly.

"And even though the god you pray to doesn't give you miracles, you've given me plenty."

She lay her cheek on his hand gripping her shoulder and nipped it.

"The one who saved the island gave them a miracle, so wouldn't any way the islanders chose to show their gratitude to her be righteous? It doesn't matter what the Church says."

His hand was now caught between her shoulder and cheek, and she spoke nonchalantly. "And even if someone who's not human did something right, it's wrong because they're not human?"

"That's—" Col began, but when their eyes met he lost any ability to speak.

When he noticed the presence of a nonhuman entity at the shrine, was that not what he had so naturally thought?

He had explained it so calmly to her.

He had said that if they were faithful to the Black-Mother even if they knew she was not human, then it was wrong. Even though Myuri's mother was not human.

He was at a loss when he came to realize his own shortsightedness, and Myuri grasped both of the hands on her shoulders and began to play with them, putting them together and pulling them apart before his chest. She finally placed them on her own small cheeks, closed her eyes, and spoke.

"Mother talked about that. She said people like Brother and Father have two perfectly good eyeballs but only look at one thing, so look around for him. She was completely right."

She gripped his hands again and moved them about, rubbing them against her cheeks and giving a ticklish giggle.

And then, she suddenly placed both onto the blanket.

"For you, I would even be a guard dog, but I hate watching you walk in a direction that doesn't make you happy. So..."

We'll go home.

To paradise on earth, filled with warmth, endless song, dance, and laughter—to the hot spring village, Nyohhira.

"Okay, Brother?"

She climbed onto him and clung to him again. She was warm, and he could smell the sweet scent of fruit. If he hugged her back, her silver tail would wave happily and she would wiggle about. And that was how they would lead a drowsy life together.

And if he were to simply give up on the path of God and hug Myuri back, he would at least be making one girl happy. Was that not his part? His dreams were too outrageous. His mind had simply been stewing too long in the hot baths.

There was also still a part of him that fought back— *But.*

He hesitated to wrap his arms around her back because even she had made the decision to go through hardship in Atiph. Even though she did not want to, in the end she changed into a wolf for him in order to save Hyland, who had also resolved to sacrifice her life if need be.

The only one who hadn't risked anything was Col. Standing on the boat as the mountain spat all-consuming fire while most of the people were left behind was none other than himself.

Of course, he did not want to fruitlessly put himself in danger.

Rather, he was afraid that if he did return the embrace of the ball of warmth that was Myuri, then he would no longer be able to feel the cold of ice, the heat of fire, or even certainty itself. He was afraid that if he lost his ideals for the world, then he would never be able to feel the true joy of this world ever again.

It was certainly terrifying and painful to look at Autumn's dark faith.

But if he looked away, however, he was worried he might never feel the light of the sun again.

Should he close his eyes and ears to the world, he would never be able appreciate the sights and sounds of its majesty.

"Myuri..."

He murmured her name, and her tail moved lazily.

She had surely thought over things for her helpless brother, finally finding a way that would hurt him the least.

But that was an unnatural way to live, like subsisting solely on honey. He was aware that he indulged her too much, and she, too, was trying to indulge her spineless brother in the same way.

If he bit her neck, the bittersweet taste of an unripe fruit would let him forget everything.

But the sweetness of honey could only be enhanced by bitter rye bread.

"Myuri, what you say is indeed correct."

"So—"

"But think about it more. I...Even if I misjudge, in order to save the neglected, like I once was, I want to show people the path to God. I must think seriously now about how I wish to associate with the world."

When Autumn had shown him the sin he was burdened with, there was no admonishment for the young man. It was not anger but eyes that housed sadness of indescribable depth.

As Myuri had said, it was not possible to keep moving forward, accepting everything from all the people he met as his own. It was impossible to save one village, one town. Not to mention that wanting to reform the Church and spreading the correct teachings of God throughout the world was just a delusion of grandeur.

However, should he choose to live a life where he turned his back on the things before him, then there would have been no reason for him to leave the village he was born in in the first place. Then, he would have never met Lawrence, a merchant at the time, and he never would have met Myuri. They were doing all this because he believed the world could be changed, no matter how insignificantly or meaningfully.

Though both good and bad, Col could not imagine himself now without faith. Even if he was able to cover his eyes and plug his ears and run away to the mountains from all the hardships of the world, he did not want to reject his present—a series of past moments in which he so boldly stood up.

Of course, what Myuri had said was correct. She truly meant what she said. He would often become too engrossed in whatever lay in front of him; his legs would not move, and his mind would be thrown into chaos. But even if the faith residing within him was not yet ripe, he had the confidence that it was not false, either.

He had to ask himself again how he wished to interact with the world. Would he act like Autumn in the face of misery and poverty that he could do nothing about? Would he pretend like he never saw it in the first place? Or would he choose a third path?

Col had to look around himself carefully. He could either return to Nyohhira or commit himself to Hyland.

He was old enough already; it irritated him to know how he acted without thinking, how he grew flustered after clashing with things. He always had to thank the silver wolf, who kept watch in all directions for him.

So he looked at Myuri, who pouted because she had failed in persuading him in the end, and belatedly wrapped his arms around her in a hug, then kissed her lightly on the forehead.

"I am truly thankful that you worry about me from the bottom of your heart," he whispered into her wolf ears and rubbed his cheek against them.

Myuri looked up and stared at him, eyes wide.

Then, her face flushed red in an instant.

"Wh-wh-why now...?"

"Why now, indeed. My eyes and head have grown clouded and dull from steam, and I was not thinking seriously about anything."

He said and sighed.

"I was not chasing my ideals; I naively wished that the world would be as I wanted it to be."

Myuri clung to him again, as though trying to hide her expression, and her tail moved busily back and forth.

"You're so much more of a dreamer than I am, Brother!"

Col smiled wryly, and as he patted her back lightly to calm her, he laughed at himself because she was exactly right. Since he was only ever dreaming, it was natural that he found himself at a loss when he woke up to reality.

Autumn had been much too real for him. If Col could properly face the monk and the circumstances surrounding him, then surely it would be a source of growth.

Moreover, he had his very own cute guardian spirit, so now was not the time to be frightened of nightmares.

"Well then, Myuri—"

It was just as he was about to speak.

There was a loud *thunk, thud* and then a groan outside of their door.

Someone had fallen down the stairs. It was snowing outside, so they must have slipped on their wet shoes.

Col tried to get up to see what the matter was, but Myuri still clung to him and did not let go.

"Myuri, please move. Someone needs help right outside our door."

The person who had fallen at the end of the hall shouted curses, perhaps having dropped something. Or perhaps they had injured themselves and were groaning in pain.

Yet Myuri still clung to Col silently, and when she finally let go, she sighed.

"I trust you, Brother."

Don't get your promise wrong is what she meant.

"Of course," he said, taking that responsibility. As he got up from the bed, he draped his coat over his shoulders before adding, "But it does not mean we will be going back to Nyohhira."

Sitting on the bed, Myuri bared her teeth at him before burying herself into the blanket.

He smiled slightly, then opened the door and entered the corridor. He looked left and right, spotting someone sitting by the staircase. What surprised him was the sight of Reicher, cradling a small cask of alcohol.

"Mr. Reicher. So it was you. Are you hurt?"

Col entered the corridor, closed the door, and as he approached, body shivering from the cold, Reicher looked up at him with dull eyes and smiled weakly.

"Three flights of stairs are rough for me at this age. My leg got caught and I fell."

Col did not point out that he was clearly drunk.

"I spilled some of my drink, too. What a waste."

It was possible the man yelled not because of the pain but because he spilled his liquor.

"Can you stand?"

"Yes, of course. By God's protection, I'm not hurt."

Col knew how to treat drunks. Whatever they said, simply nod in agreement. There was no point in spouting logic to them, as they would only grow angry. He only checked to see if any injuries were visible.

"You seem all right."

"Yes, but perfect timing. I came to call on you."

"Me?"

He held out his hand and pulled Reicher up when Myuri came out from the room. As always, she was pouting, but she helped him stand, too.

"You met Lord Autumn, didn't you?" he spoke when Col placed the man's arm around his own shoulder to support him.

Reicher looked at him with breath reeking of alcohol and a tearful smile.

"We concluded a meeting together just now."

"A meeting?"

Reicher tried to remove the cork from the cask in his hand, but since he only had one hand free, he could not. He fumbled about before it finally fell from his hand, but Myuri caught it.

"A meeting for selling the island girl to a slaver. All the southern merchants are here, you know."

When he said that, he was no longer looking at Col. His eyes were open, but they did not look at anything.

"I prayed for the girl's future. But I carry no sins with me. I live an easy life here, surrounded by stone walls. Did my prayer have any meaning?"

As Reicher spoke, he reached out to the cask in Myuri's hands.

And that is when Col finally understood.

Reicher did not enjoy booze—he found need to drink it.

"And I'm not brave enough to run from here. Oh God…"

The old priest began to bawl, and he covered his face with the hands that had reached out to his drink.

Col was not the only one who froze in place in Autumn's presence.

When he thought this, he readjusted his grip on Reicher and spoke.

"Let's go somewhere warm."

Myuri looked at him, annoyed, but she did not try to stop him, and she dutifully helped Reicher down the stairs.

No one was at fault.

But the open pit in the earth was terribly deep and cold.

If they could not fill it up, then they needed to know its depth and remember its cold.

The problem was figuring out how to avoid being swallowed up by it.

"I was once the chaplain of a church that belonged to a landlord and his family. I only prayed for the safety of him and his family, and if I could lend an ear to the woes of their retainers, then it was a good day."

In the office of an assistant priest who had various jobs on the first floor of the residences, Reicher began to tell his story.

He slouched at the edge of the chair, wrapping the cask with both of his hands.

But only his words were clear. It was as though the still-living parts of his heart were telling him they must be so.

"Even in such a safe, large territory, three generations of strategic marriages will create knots like the eyes of demons. It was no one's fault, but everyone had started hating one another. Once someone lights a spark out of self-interest, everything catches fire in an instant. Well, it was quite tragic."

Reicher cradled and caressed the cask, but he did not drink. Just having it in his hands seemed relief enough for him.

"Children killed their parents, younger brothers murdered older brothers. Brides killed by their mothers-in-law, and mothers who threw their children into rivers. The mercenaries we hired did not do their duty, wreaking havoc in the villages throughout the domain instead, and honest farmers who sued for damages were hung in the gallows."

The window in the office was simply a square cut into the wall, and the snowfall was clearly visible from inside.

The peat in the furnace crackled nervously as it burned.

"I couldn't take it anymore and left, so I wandered. Where would I find salvation? Then I overheard men talking about the miracle on this island. I came, thinking the Holy Mother could provide me with what I wished for, but that is when I met Lord Autumn."

Reicher sighed deeply and closed his eyes.

"If misery is soot that has seeped into the world, then Lord Autumn is *a dustpan*. He dirties himself black and receives everything. Then God rinses him. I was shattered—I didn't know that could be an answer."

Autumn's actions were frightfully rational, using the logic written directly in the scripture. What was difficult to believe was that he had kept his good heart as he did so, and he was truly praying for forgiveness of his sins.

"I heard Lord Autumn was originally from the islands."

Reicher quietly answered Col's remark.

"He said he was born here, then sold off as a slave when he was still young. There are many of those like him here. There are lots of tough, hardworking folks here, after all."

The guard who had looked at Myuri had also assumed she was a slave.

"Long ago, when ships with sails weren't as common as they are now, they also sold off adults, or so I've heard. As rowers for ships. I've heard they played a major part in wars on the seas."

It was cruel work, and most of them would be completely wrung out, finally leaving the ships after three years.

"Leave" did not necessarily mean they were let off kindly at a port, though.

"Ever since I've come here, I've tried all I can to make sure we sell to respectable slavers, but there's no way to find out where they are all sold to."

"Are there those who buy their freedom and come back?"

When Col asked this, Reicher smiled with a coughing fit.

"There may be people here and there who buy back their freedom after all their hardships. But they know that there is no place for them here if they came back. There's no wood to build houses to live in or materials to build boats for fishing."

He sighed deeply, as though a fragment of his soul had escaped through his mouth.

"We can only keep so many sheep and goats, and there's only so much fertile land for cultivation. We're somehow pulling through with the taxes we collect from those who come out to sieve for amber and those who mine for charcoal in the summer. I know how the southern merchants do things, and so in order to make sure they're not forcing unfavorable trade agreements upon the people of this land, I keep an eye on things with divine punishment as my shield. Everyone wants his protection for their journey at sea...But I don't know how much even that helps."

In his own way, Reicher was pouring his all into this land he had washed up on.

If that was the case, then the merchants in the courtyard who had waved to him so congenially must not have had the friendliest of relationships with him. It was more likely they thought of Reicher as a traitor, while considering the people of the island to be friends of the merchants. This man had lost all his spirit, except that which could be found in alcohol.

"What's more, the Ruvik Alliance, an important pillar in the

176

support of this church, is discussing the possibility of reducing the number of the islanders' boats even more. Our savings will diminish, too."

Praying would not fill an empty stomach, nor would it free anyone from the shackles of monetary transactions.

What this land needed was money.

And what did not add up in the balance books, Autumn took upon himself as his personal sin.

Reicher was drinking likely because he felt like his guilt would crush him even now.

Had Col and Myuri not been there, it would have ended up the same. Col looked at the girl beside him, and her beautiful red eyes stared back at him questioningly.

While they were in their exchange, Reicher adjusted himself in the chair, removed the cork from the cask, and took a swig.

"...*Pahh.* This is unacceptable as a clergyman, but..."

The man certainly drank like a bandit.

That was what Col was imagining, but Reicher's next words were painful.

"I wish war would break out soon."

"...War?"

Autumn stood at the head of seafaring pirates. Those aboard ships gathered information, allowing him to know right away that Col and Myuri, who had so shamelessly wandered in, were working for Winfiel.

Col thought that Reicher might be the same, but the priest took another swig from his cask and exhaled painfully.

"...*Guh.* W-war. Winfiel has risen in revolt against the pope's tyranny, and the fire has finally been kindled in Atiph. Now, it's just talk about when it might all go up in flames. When it does, I just know that the islanders' manpower and fishing industry will play a crucial role."

Reicher was about to drink more, but Col, of course, stopped him. He was drinking like he was trying to end himself.

"Mr. Reicher."

"…Who will weep for me if I die? I know even God has already forgotten my name."

He smiled in bitter irony, but he did not try to force himself to imbibe again. Perhaps he had wanted someone to stop him.

He placed the cask on his lap limply, then looked up to the heavens and closed his eyes.

"If war broke out…then the price of fish would rise. Many of the islanders might become distinguished soldiers. The kingdom, the pope, whoever we work with, the reward will be the same."

Reicher talked as though to himself. He knew that even if they earned some money that way, they would only be comfortable for but a moment. And while it was almost certain some would thrive in the war, there were many who would die and others still who would come home with wounds they would carry for the rest of their lives.

"Oh God. This land only perseveres on the sacrifice of others. May God have mercy on Lord Autumn, as he continues to burden himself with sin…"

He prayed deliriously as the energy slowly drained from his head down, and soon he fell asleep right then and there. They retrieved the cask before it fell and placed it on a nearby shelf.

The way Reicher was slumped in the chair made it appear less like restful sleep and more like he had completely exhausted himself.

Col had Myuri fetch the assistant priest to ask what should be done, but he simply shrugged and told them to leave him be, that this was nothing unusual.

He could not bring himself to do that, but he knew all too well how difficult it was to carry a passed-out drunk. Then the assistant priest added peat to the furnace and draped a blanket over Reicher, so he would not be risk catching a cold.

Seeing that, they thanked the assistant priest and left the office. Col wished to have a breath of fresh air, so they exited into the snowfall.

"Brother?"

As he reached the bottom of the steps, Myuri called out to him from the top.

"What is it?"

"Are you okay?"

Standing under the dim, snowy sky, Myuri's silver hair looked like threads of ice.

"I'm all right."

Then the expression on her face changed to that of slight surprise before she came down the steps.

"What is it?"

"I was just thinking how cool you've gotten. To think you were so sniveling just before that!"

He simply could not shake the somber expression from his face, which likely made him seem calm.

"It doesn't matter how cool I am, but thanks to talking with you, I feel as though I've been able to steel myself."

"Hmm?"

"Let's bring Mr. Reicher along when we board the ship back to Atiph."

Myuri was not surprised, but her rounded, reddish-amber eyes looked at him.

"He's someone who can't escape. I don't really think we could convince him to, either."

That was correct, and he understood how Reicher felt as well. Had Col himself come here alone and met Autumn, he would have surely ended up the same way.

"But luckily, he cannot hold his liquor as well as Ms. Holo."

They would simply bring him on board after he passed out. He was not attached to this island—he was a prisoner of it. Once he left, chances were good that he would never come back.

Then Myuri widened her eyes at such a rough plan, and her lips slowly changed to that of a smile.

"Brother, that's bad."

"A true solution would be to find a way to make everyone on this island happy, though."

"That doesn't exist."

She declared her conclusion without hesitation, even though she knew nothing about how big and complicated the world was.

That would be what a girl's realistic intellect was.

"I cannot agree with that. But we lack the time and numbers to do so at the moment. So we can only think about what we can do right now."

Myuri openly stared at him before suddenly looking away.

It was like a master who watched his apprentice finally grow to realize their full potential.

"Then can you reconsider this crazy 'fix the world' thing? And stop working with that blondie?"

"I have, for now, given up on sending my very young little sister home."

"I'm only *like* your little sister!" She protested as she stomped her foot.

As they talked in the falling snow, whiteness covered their heads and shoulders before they knew it.

As Col brushed some off Myuri, he spoke.

"Why don't we eat at the port for now?"

It seemed he had spent quite a long time having nightmares, and it must be noon around now.

Myuri squinted as he brushed the snow off, and with narrowed eyes, she opened her mouth.

"...Can I have meat?"

"Do you remember what Mr. Yosef said? The fish should be good here."

"Then I want fried fish. With lots of salt on it!"

Though she seemed frail when her mouth was closed, her tastes were that of a drunk.

"Don't eat too much."

"Okay."

It was their typical, clear-cut conversation, but there was something definitively different.

He was holding on to Myuri's hand just a bit tighter than usual. She must have noticed as well.

In his hands was an extraordinarily precious jewel.

He had learned the depth of the darkness in the world, and now finally, he also knew the light.

Myuri sat dissatisfied at the table in the canteen because there was no fried fish to be had.

Towns and villages that did not butcher a number of pigs every day could not keep a daily pot of fat. Herrings and sardines did give off some fat, but those who did heat them in a pan would likely not want to eat what was fried in it.

So in the end, she had a hodgepodge of fish stew, which was a bit of an exciting-looking dish for a girl raised in the mountains. The fish heads that floated in it, clearly a departure from the animals of the mountains, were mashed in half, their mouths crowded with eerie-looking teeth. It was only natural that even Myuri hesitated. However, once she started eating, she found that every bit of fish was delicious, and the soup had the perfect amount of saltiness for dipping bread. Her meal left her no room to concentrate on anything else.

The bread they ate was not made of wheat but of chestnuts. There was a peculiar hardness and harsh bitterness about it; this was not something one ate for fun. Col had not thought there was anything particularly luxurious about Nyohhira, but despite it being so snowy and deep in the mountains, the village was rich in food, likely due to its popularity as a place of healing, receiving its fair share of imports. He was once again made painfully aware of how blessed they had been.

"What are we going to do next, Brother?" Myuri inquired as she bit into a rather slim fish head, sharp teeth poking out from the corners of its mouth.

Her voice was low, maybe because she was busy biting the meat from the head, but it was more likely that it was her own way of being respectful in the quiet canteen.

"Preparations for a ship to go home...I would also like to investigate the island just a little more."

"...You're not giving up?"

When she looked at him with irritated eyes, he could not help but smile wryly.

"I do not think that saving the island is such an outrageous idea. I may be able to help somehow, and it may even be of benefit to Heir Hyland, as well."

When she heard Hyland's name, Myuri made the uninterested face she always did.

"By giving the island what they need, they may side with the Kingdom of Winfiel if war breaks out, even if not openly."

"What about money? Isn't that blondie rich?"

Myuri dunked her bread into the salty broth and bit into it.

"Money is powerful and will certainly help us. But it's easy."

"Easy?"

Her mouth was full of bread as she sloppily asked a follow-up question.

"Its appeal may as well be the same as violence. However, if we take the time to learn about the land and give the people what they truly need, they will understand our sincerity, even if it was worth the same amount of money. You see?"

Then she chewed loudly and swallowed with a *glug*. Myuri studied the rest of the bread, then nodded.

"I guess, if someone gave me my favorite kind of bread, I think I would do all I could for them."

Though she typically preferred quantity over quality, it seemed the chestnut bread was not very good.

"So, in the meanwhile..."

She spoke vaguely up to that point and waved for him to come closer.

Col leaned over, wary that she may be planning some sort of trick, and she spoke to him.

"Can I look into who the little doll really was?"

Col stared back in surprise, but she was surprisingly serious.

"Mother won't tell me the details, but she doesn't know where her old friend that I'm named after and her other friends are, right?"

Myuri was implying that the Black-Mother may be one of them.

Myuri's mother, the wisewolf Holo, once ruled over a forest in a land called Yoitsu, so it was hard to imagine that a much bigger wolf worked under her. There was a vague sense, though, that in the bygone age of spirits, size meant justice.

But knowing that this young girl was often bothered by the blood flowing through her and other nonhumans, his feelings were complicated. Though she seemed to not mind, at the end of the day that feigned indifference extended no further than the expression on her face.

"If the legend is a clue, then I have no idea why the fishing became really good after she stopped the lava."

That was a good point. If the Black-Mother was not human, then what was she an avatar of?

"We'll search for that together. It's dangerous alone."

Col sat back down in his seat.

"I'd be fine even if I came across a bear."

"You may come across painful truths that are more frightening than any bear."

He ripped off a piece of the chestnut bread and put it in his mouth. As he chewed quietly, Myuri sat across from him and stared off into space, perhaps deep in thought.

Then she suddenly looked back at him, and this time closed her eyes and tilted her head slightly, worried about something.

"What's wrong?"

She groaned, answering as she furrowed her brows.

"Which do you like better—coddling me or being reduced to tears when a painful moment takes us by surprise?"

Col could not say he "liked" anything about the latter.

He looked at her in exasperation, and she suddenly opened her eyes in realization.

"Oh, you should just coddle me before and after something bad happens. That way, I'll get the most out of it if you come with me." She said with a satisfied smile.

"You should not be thinking in terms of profit."

"Mother told me; she said that girls shan't cry without accounting for it first."

He was not sure if he would say he did not expect it from a mother and daughter of wolves, but she only seemed to be receiving precise instruction on the way of the hunt.

"I would prefer if you did not cry," he said with a pained smile, when Myuri's expression suddenly turned serious.

"The same goes for you."

He could not believe a girl half his age said such a thing to him.

But simply because she was half his age did not mean that he was not happy to have someone worry about him.

"Thank you."

He thanked her earnestly, and she looked at him dubiously for a while before grinning and returning to her food. He gazed at her for a while, and his mouth naturally began to smile.

It was often said to let one's beloved child go on a journey, but when he looked at Myuri's growth, he could only react with surprise. Or perhaps it was he who had not grown up, and he was only now realizing how amazing she was.

When a child became an adult, it was an important rite of passage to learn how wide the world was and how tall the sky was. If Col could learn the cold of ice and the depths of the sea, then perhaps he would grow more as a person as well. It was possible he could even find a different angle to look at his ideas for creating a new institution from the war between the Kingdom of Winfiel and the Church. Since faith took forms even he could not imagine, there was no single shape for the key to the gates of heaven. God's house took many forms.

And he now knew that even the actions of nonhumans, like the one on this island, could help spread the teachings of God. Which meant the size of the gates needed to be made a bit larger as well.

He had been so shocked by Autumn that he had lost his head, but that, too, was a significant problem. To live among the world of humans, it was a problem they would have to seriously face one day. It seemed that Hyland had already realized the truth about Myuri and was vaguely aware that there were people like her throughout the world. Therefore, even in the smallest of possibilities, there was a chance that Caeson could become the precedent to open a new path.

Then, those like Myuri, who had stood before the world map at the trading house in Atiph, might not have to lament that there was no place in the world for them. There were many besides humans who possessed beautiful souls.

Col could not save the girl from being sold into slavery, nor could he offer any words of comfort to that lonely gaze of Autumn's, who had no choice but to do what he did—but he could save Myuri.

When he reached that conclusion, something occurred to him.

"Myuri, I want to ask you something."

"Hmm?"

Myuri sat satisfied before her bowl, which had turned into a boneyard, and she looked at him.

"Was Lord Autumn human?"

If the Black-Mother was not human, and the one who had spread her teachings was Autumn, then this possibility was the first thought that naturally came to mind.

But Myuri closed her eyes, as though searching her memory, and cocked her head.

"It was cold and my nose was a little stuffed, but I would have known if he smelled like beast. I could only smell the sea. It was like he hadn't taken a bath for a really long time."

Which meant Autumn was human.

Had he not been, though, then many things in his report to Hyland would have changed, and in the case that they did become enemies, she needed to know how disastrous that could be.

But it seemed well that he did not need to think about that.

"Are you full, by the way?"

"Yep. Thaaank you for the food."

Then, with Myuri in tow, they walked around the port a bit.

It was a small town with no walls that could be crossed from one end to the other in a very short amount of time. Standing outside of town, the only thing to see once the buildings had disappeared were the snow paths extending in various directions, hardened by repeated footsteps. Their presence was only enough to guess that somewhere ahead there was a place where people gathered.

On the main street, there was a collection of buildings, a sign hanging from each of their eaves denoting different artisans, but it did not seem that they typically had goods out for display. Nor did it seem likely that any of these places were currently at work, as silence lay over them.

The only places open were a rope makers' workshop that handled nets, and a blacksmith with a harpoon and a hatchet on display in the front. No matter what, it seemed that these two workshops were indispensable.

However, the net looked like something that had simply been re-braided whenever it became torn, while the bladed goods seemed more suitable for smashing instead of cutting. Without materials, craftsmen could not braid new rope, and without fuel, smiths likely could not refine their tools how they wanted.

What would make the people of this land happy seemed to be, without a doubt, fishing tools. It would become the pillar that would support their daily lives.

It is written in the scripture that to help others with ulterior motives was hypocrisy, but Autumn had shown them that virtuously doing nothing carried no weight on these islands.

Such a thing may become a seed of deceitful faith, but one could also nip it in the bud if there was a chance it would bloom. At the very least, it was much better than the misshapen rigidity of the current Church.

Col had to recognize that simple prayer would be of no help in reality.

And as he thought about all this, walking around the town, he realized that it was not quiet because of the hard times but simply because it was the snowy, cold season. Yosef's trading house, too, just happened to be uneventful during the middle of the quiet season.

What made him notice this was that when they occasionally passed someone on the path, they would stare up at him, eyes wide. It was as though they could not believe someone was walking there.

In truth, he had almost had it with the cold. They should return to the church.

They had just returned to the path along the dead river.

"It's different from Nyohhira, isn't it?"

He had not felt like opening his mouth in the cold, and it was his first time speaking since the canteen.

"Have you been someplace like this before?"

"When I sailed to the Kingdom of Winfiel, it was a bit livelier than this. And I traveled mostly in areas where it didn't snow in the winter."

"Places where it doesn't snow in the winter, huh? I can't imagine anything like that."

Myuri gazed out to the sea, her breath white. As they stood still, the snow piled higher and higher on them, as though urging them to return to their room.

"Let's go one day. The color of the sea is completely different; it's an incredibly exhilarating sight."

"The color of the sea can change?"

"There are some waters that aren't blue, but I've never seen such a bright green before today."

"If you've seen it before, then it can't be a color that you've never seen."

Myuri turned around and revealed the mischievous grin on her face.

"Now is not the time for jokes. Let's head back to the church."

"Okay," she replied obediently and followed behind him.

Then she suddenly stopped walking and looked out to sea again.

"Is something wrong?"

"I thought I was imagining things but...I wasn't. A ship is coming."

"A ship? I suppose there are still people who go out fishing on snowy days like this," he said, but he only noticed it when he turned to look at the port.

It was quiet, and even the smallest of boats had been pulled up on land and turned over. Maybe it was not a fishing boat.

Then Myuri continued.

"I think I saw that ship in Atiph."

"Are there differences in ships?"

He did not really think before asking, and Myuri met him with a cool stare.

"Every shipwright has its own style. Duh, that's so obvious!"

She knew odd bits of information as she had experience working as an errand boy unloading cargo in the Atiph port for the Debau Company.

He took her word for granted, but he did not think it particularly strange that a ship from Atiph would be coming to this port.

"It must be a trade ship. That's how we came here, remember?"

"Yeah, but...Yep, I knew it."

Myuri spoke as she created a visor with her hands to keep the fluttering snow out of her eyes and stared out across the water.

"It's a company boat."

"From the Debau Company?"

That was certainly odd.

The ship that Hyland had arranged for them had belonged to a different company. That was why Yosef had not known they would be coming. The reason they had not used a ship from the Debau Company was simply because there were none scheduled to travel to this region then.

But when Col stood next to Myuri and looked out over the water, he could see another ship behind it.

Though it was far and just barely visible over the horizon, they could tell how large it was even from where they stood.

It made it seem like the one in front was being chased, fleeing in their direction.

And it really did seem strange that a whole two ships would arrive together on such a snowy day.

He realized that fishermen had emerged from their houses in the port to stare out over the water.

"I wonder why?" Myuri asked quietly.

She spoke as though she had just watched her prey in the mountains act strangely.

"Aren't you cold?" he asked because, before he knew it, the snow on Myuri's hood and shoulders had piled up into quite a thick layer.

When he reached out to brush it off, white clumps fell from his own body.

Though he was clearing the debris from her, she did not even glance at him. Her attention was focused at the port.

The ship from the Debau Company hurriedly slipped into the docks, ignoring the island fishermen as they watched on in astonishment. Soon, a ramp was placed onto the pier.

Down from the deck came a man wearing plenty of clothes, his figure perfectly round.

The hand brushing Myuri came to a stop.

At the same time, she sucked in air through her clenched teeth.

"I'm not cold." She smiled fearlessly. "I'm excited."

The one who had alighted from the ship was Yosef. As he propelled his pudgy body forward at an unsteady run, he kept glancing out over the water. With displeasure, he swiped off the snow that clung to his frame while he ran straight toward them. But it did not seem like he noticed they were there. He had not raised his head once, concentrating only on running along the path.

Even when he was close enough that they could hear his heavy breathing, Yosef still had not sensed their presence. When he finally did look up all of a sudden, he was dangerously close to running into them.

"O-oh?!"

Yosef, flustered, stopped in his tracks, his expression plainly saying, "What are you doing here?"

Of course, that was what Col wanted to ask as well.

"Is something the matter?"

Yosef, completely out of breath, opened his mouth twice but could only bring himself to cough instead of speak. After placing his hands on his knees and taking several deep breaths, he stood up.

"Th-this must be the will of God. I have an urgent message for you."

White billowing clouds came forth as he kept panting.

Nervousness raised a shiver that ran through Col's body—*did something happen to Hyland?*

"A message came from Atiph for me. Then I came as fast as

I could in my ship, but I was mainly concentrated on staying ahead of that thing behind me."

He made it clear that both vessels arriving at the same time was no coincidence.

"And what was the news from Atiph?"

Yosef coughed painfully once more, then managed to string some words together.

"I don't know from what country, but a high-ranking clergyman from the south is bringing a very important merchant with him to the north."

"High-ranking? With an important merchant?"

Col could not quite grasp the situation.

Then, behind the coughing Yosef, the giant ship's silhouette was becoming clearer.

The men gathered at the port all began clamoring incoherently, pointing. It was a bit of an exaggeration to say that he could not believe his eyes.

"It's...huge..." Myuri murmured in a low voice.

The ship looked like a mountain gliding over the water.

It would not be surprising if there were five or even six decks. From each side of its giant hull sprouted a surprising amount of oars extending into the water. Befitting for a giant, they slowly steered the ship across the water with great force. The sight of it evoked images of God's own ship, soaring across the sky.

But if this were a divine vessel, then there must have been a religious conversion of some sort. On the sail fluttering above the giant ship was a painted crest that Col knew very well.

"The Ruvik Alliance?"

They were the world's largest mercantile group. Due to a focus on conducting long-distance trade, they controlled the largest number of seafaring vessels by far. The Ruvik Alliance was somewhat legendary among merchants. It was often said they once went to war with a king for disputed special privileges and emerged as the overwhelming victors.

In the northlands, most people thought the spectacular rise of the Debau Company had lessened the Ruvik Alliance's power, but Col knew people only entertained that sort of talk in the north.

The giant vessel that had appeared in the port town of Caeson possessed an overwhelming, coercive force.

"They're not here for trade," Yosef continued to explain. "That ship did not stop off at any port on the way here. They must have enough crew for full shifts and enough food on board. Such a big ship can't sail in the narrow passages between islands, so they must have taken quite the long way around, but our boat still struggled to keep ahead of it on the sea routes."

The ship was too large to dock in Caeson, so it dropped anchor off the coast. Smaller boats were lowered from the side of the ship, and the men from the port sent out their boats, too. They were likely going to ask what their purpose was.

"Oh, the guard dogs have arrived."

Among it all, Myuri pointed out to the water. There was the pirate ship.

"I wonder what will happen?"

It was eerie enough that such a giant ship would stop at such a small port town.

Col understood for the first time that authority could be visible.

"I don't know…However, if those oars coming out from the side of that massive ship so much as hit the pirate's vessel, they will undoubtedly sink. The Ruvik Alliance has a reason behind this display, why they brought out that ship. If they're planning to trade, then the hold will have to be filled with mountains of gold and silver in order to pay. We merchants would never embark on any pointless ventures."

Col understood the reasoning from traveling with a respectable merchant. It was clear the travelers had come to this land in order to obtain something, but what?

What could they hope to trade for in this land of ice, where everything had been swallowed by poverty?

"Oh God, please protect us."

Yosef prayed, then pulled out a small bundle from his bosom.

"Oh, Holy Mother, please give us protection."

Snow continued to fall.

The painted crest of the Ruvik Alliance flying eerily above them, visible amid the drifting specks of white.

CHAPTER FOUR

As a rule, outsiders who stepped foot on the island stayed at the church.

The visitors from the Ruvik Alliance were not excepted from this rule.

They proceeded toward the fortresslike church in a showy manner, as though it were a royal visit.

The people who disembarked from the gigantic vessel matched the information that Yosef had passed on to Col.

In the lead were four flag bearers, each hoisting up the banner of the Church. Walking along the path they left in the snow were four knights of the Church carrying a palanquin, where a majestic, kingly man was seated.

A drape embroidered with gold thread hung around his shoulders, rings with jewels the size of eyeballs decorated his fingers, and on his head sat the pointed hat that symbolized the pedestal of the pope. Col did not know where he was from, but he came from a church in a town that was host to a cathedral, where he held the position of archbishop.

As someone who wished to become a clergyman, Col had no

choice but to show the utmost respect. He bowed his head when they entered the courtyard, but when he stole a glance at the seat of the palanquin, there he saw an energetic man in the prime of his life, rather young for his rank. Col surmised there was something extraordinary that made up for his age. Perhaps it was the ambition that the man could not completely keep from showing on his face.

A great number of knights followed in after, but in this cold, with metal armor wrapping their bodies, the single piece of cloth draped over their shoulders was a token defense. Snow immediately blew over them, and soon they began to look like the snowmen on the side of the road after a while. Their faces were strained not for the sake of their dignity but because they were worried about frostbite.

"That's a lot of boxes of gold."

Horse-drawn carriages followed behind. Yosef whispered his comment to Col, almost unintentionally. There were four of the sturdy draft animals, lowering their heads out of necessity as they pulled their burdens along.

Behind that was another guest on a separate palanquin whose outfit made him look like a ball of fur. He must have been the merchant from the Ruvik Alliance. His subordinates followed in droves, clerical staff carefully carrying packages that likely contained parchment, as well as hired mercenaries bringing up the rear.

Reicher was the one who came out to greet the procession. His face was twitching, but it probably wasn't an affliction of his usual drunken state. Undoubtedly, he was sober at the moment.

It was as though a wolf had suddenly appeared among the rabbits.

"What do you think? The letter said to return immediately if there might be any danger to you two. With signatures from

Master Stefan in Atiph, as well as a Lord Hyland. A noble of the kingdom?"

No matter how anyone looked at it, the only conceivable reason this many people would come calling during this time of year was the fight between the kingdom and the pope. Hyland's fears were not groundless.

Hyland had only told him to investigate the situation. Nothing more.

On the other hand, it would be unthinkable to leave the island before learning what the other party's goal was.

Col had hesitated momentarily, but after finally making up his mind, he began to speak.

"We are to find land for a monastery, but we also have one other goal as well."

Yosef blinked in surprise, then showed him a troubled smile.

"Of course you do. That's to be expected if Master Stefan personally takes to pen and paper. I am aware of the situation."

He shrugged his own big shoulders before placing his hand on Col's.

"Please let me know if I can do anything to help."

Col wavered for a moment on whether he could trust this man but decided to do so in the end. He could not imagine that Yosef had run so earnestly to greet them after they came from the boat if he was insincere. Just in case, he looked toward Myuri, a literal wolf among men. When she noticed his pointed stare, she grinned back. Her instincts also indicated it was safe.

"I wish to know what they want."

Yosef gave him the thoughtful gaze that those who lived in harsh environments shared.

He peered into Col's eyes for a few moments. Perhaps he saw something there, because he slowly closed his eyes, then placed his hand over his chest in a salute.

At the same time, the regal archbishop descended from his palanquin and folded Reicher into an exaggerated embrace. While that was happening, the assistant priests stood at the front of the procession, raising their voices, doing their best to make the way for the honored guests.

"We might be chased out of our room at this rate."

They had been given a private room far beyond their means, but that had been because the hall was empty.

"My relatives have a house here. Why not stay with them? The other townspeople don't think too highly of them, but they may not say anything in this situation."

The people here were mostly of the opinion that nothing good could come of having deep ties with merchants from the south who came to do business. This alone was a clear indication of the disparity in power.

The Ruvik Alliance and the archbishop who came by ship certainly knew about this, so Col suspected that they were deliberately displaying their position of strength. Whatever their purpose may be, it definitely involved driving a wedge into the region because of the anticipated war with the Kingdom of Winfiel. Those boxes of gold, piled as high as the mountains, were none other than flexed muscle.

This region was certainly wanting for money. If they had enough gold and silver coins, there were any number of unfortunate hardships they could avoid. Even Col had considered offering them money to win them over.

There were several strange things about all this, however.

These islands were lands the Church tried to win over many times but had always failed to in the end. Going on that, he thought such obvious tactics would only bring resistance. And he could think of even worse things than that.

For example, if the islanders used the money they received to arm themselves and build new ships, it would actually become more difficult to control them with the threat of force. The Ruvik Alliance was a mercantile coalition that was mainly based in areas even farther south than the Debau Company. No matter how many massive vessels they owned, it would be virtually impossible to indefinitely deter the northern islands from betrayal. It was inconceivable for anyone to deploy an armada for surveillance when there was a war to fight.

If the islanders acted rationally, then the inner circle of the pirates, including the island of Caeson, would first wring money from the Ruvik Alliance, and after straightening out their systemic issues, they would send words of friendship to the Kingdom of Winfiel. Or perhaps they would threaten to intervene during the war itself. By constantly adjusting the scales of who they sided with at the moment, they would be able to have their cake and eat it, too. It was possible they could continue to squeeze out money from both parties. Autumn had no reason not to refrain from such an opportunity.

Squeezing money from a rich country and Church would not pain the good-hearted nearly as much as selling the daughter of a fisherman with a broken leg into slavery.

So the question was this: If Col was able to think it through this far, then why did the Ruvik Alliance and archbishop not realize it?

Or perhaps the grand merchants were inciting the archbishop to make irresponsible decisions? Perhaps they had convinced him that this land was a poverty-stricken region deserving of pity, and that by granting them lots of much-needed money, the inhabitants would even side with them in their war against Winfiel. If that happened, the merchants would obtain a market to sell various kinds of goods, giving them an opportunity to earn money.

However, the core issue with that plan was still the distinct possibility of betrayal. If the people of the islands did not ally with them in the war against the kingdom as expected, the people held responsible would be whoever planted the false information.

Moreover, there was also the problem that Yosef had pointed out.

Merchants never did things pointlessly. If they brought boxes of gold, then they were aiming to return home with something worth their while.

It was highly unlikely that they would be buying an equivalent amount of fish.

What were they planning to take home?

Even if the archbishop planned to exchange the money in return for certain special privileges, for a merchant to bring only money to leave here was much too wasteful.

The scales did not balance out.

The entire situation was peculiar.

"Are you thinking again, Brother?"

When Myuri called out to him, Col snapped back to reality.

The procession into the church had calmed for now, and they were all beginning to find their places. The ones remaining in the courtyard, standing around and chatting, were merchants unrelated to the Ruvik Alliance or porters. The snow that had been falling all day was growing stronger, but it seemed everyone had completely forgotten about the cold after witnessing such a sudden event.

"Yes, there's something I just don't understand…," Col wondered aloud, bringing Myuri and Yosef to exchange glances.

Then they heard a loud voice coming from beyond the courtyard.

"The Ruvik Alliance is using all accommodations in the church! To those staying in the church, please move to the port town! If you cannot find alternate accommodations, then please come to us with a proposal! The Ruvik Alliance is using all accommodations in the church!"

The first thing the archbishop and the wealthy Ruvik Alliance merchant did was stuff gold into this church's pockets.

Those who lacked the money were kicked out into the cold.

"Oh dear, such extravagance for such an empty time of the year."

As Yosef stroked his beard, he smiled absently.

"Well then, shall I introduce you to my relatives' house?"

"Yes, please. Thank you."

"No worries. After all, Master Stefan has written me many times, too, so that I remember to mind my manners."

When he heard that, Col imagined Stefan, frantically writing the letter.

At the very least, his conscience ached terribly.

Then they retrieved their things from the room and left the church.

The Ruvik Alliance and the archbishop.

What a shady pair.

The inside of the tall building with sharp corners seemed more like a cavern.

The floor was packed dirt, and a stone, waist-high hearth lay in the middle of an arrangement of furniture.

There were stairs in this house leading to a higher level, but the second floor was only so big. The rest opened up to the ceiling, where the underside of the roof was visible. Crossbeams ran lengthwise and breadthwise across the ceiling, where a great number of fish and vegetables hung off them. It seemed they were being smoked in the fumes emanating from the hearth in the center of the house.

Myuri's mouth was drooping open, as though looking up at bats that hung from the ceiling of a cave, as she gazed at the preserves of a cold land.

"Find anything interesting?"

The shrill, amused voice belonged to an old woman with wrinkles on her face so deep it was uncertain whether her eyes were opened or closed.

Yosef's relatives' home only housed this old woman and her son's wife. Her son and grandson had both gone to work in Atiph.

"If I sleep on my back, I think I'd only dream about food."

"Heh-heh-heh."

Myuri had said something similar when she slept under the wool blanket. Col shot her a sideways glance before giving thanks for allowing them to stay, even handing the wife several silver coins. The wife, who kept the house while her husband and son were gone, had more muscle in her arms and width in her waist than he did. Her faith, too, was abundant, as she was so grateful to him that it almost flustered Col. He felt rather guilty that he was not actually a priest.

When they finished exchanging greetings, Yosef rushed outside to the gathering in town. It was not Autumn, but the elders who took care of the day-to-day on the island, and so he left, saying that a meeting was likely about to be held to deal with the situation. The people of Caeson must have been reeling from the giant ship that appeared so suddenly.

On the other hand, the two women in the house were enthusiastic to treat these two odd guests who had come to stay with them. Even the old woman had her sleeves rolled up as she began preparing supper.

With nothing to do, Col and Myuri sat by the hearth fire. Finding himself unable to calmly watch the peat fire, Col went outside instead.

There was still a bit of time before the sun set, but thick clouds blotted the sky, laying a gloom over the land. The dismal color in the air was the same as that time on the beach.

He circled around the house to the back garden and found a shed. He took shelter under the eaves while the snow still continued to fall.

"Brother, you'll get sick if you keep coming outside."

Myuri had followed him outside, squishing his cheeks together with her hide-gloved hands as she spoke reproachfully.

"I'm anxious."

"…"

She simply looked up at him silently as they stood beside each other. She seemed slightly irritated—there was a strong sense of *Again?* coming from Myuri.

"That was a lot of boxes of gold. They may demand conditions, whether they like it or not."

"But isn't it a good thing, though? The islanders need the money."

She was right, and that was exactly what made him worry.

"I doubt they are doing this out of the goodness of their hearts."

"Well, those noble-looking people in the palanquins didn't look very nice."

She chuckled.

"And I must investigate what conditions they might force upon the islanders. If I cannot, then I will be unable to complete the mission that Heir Hyland has given me. If their talks settle quickly, then I need to report my findings correctly, as quickly as possible."

"Well, I guess I don't really care about that."

Myuri crouched down, gathered some snow in her hand, and pressed it together.

"Then, what should we do? Do you want me to eavesdrop behind the walls?"

She threw the snowball, then waved her hands before bobbing them up and down above her head.

It seemed like she was imitating a rabbit, though she was actually a wolf who fed on them.

"If they've occupied every room in the church, then that also means they want to keep people away. That means to listen in, you'd have to go around outside the walls. But no matter how good your ears are, you won't be able to hear the voices inside the building, no?"

"Then I can just be a wolf and sneak in. I don't think they'll notice me if it's night and the snow is falling."

The color of Myuri's fur was flecks of silver mixed in with ash. Even a master hunter would have trouble finding her on a snowy night.

"Well, if you did that for me, then sure...No, but..."

Myuri could not change into a wolf as easily as her mother could. Plus, he had just learned that she was much more bothered about her wolf heritage than she appeared to be.

He did not want to force her to do anything she would object to.

These thoughts in his head, Myuri folded her hands behind her back and took two, three steps forward.

He wondered what she was up to when she spun around and stuck her face in his.

"Yep. It's hard for me to become a wolf, and I might get into trouble," she said with a smile as she turned her face away from him.

He could see her cheeks and how red they had become from the cold.

"But I think there is a way to give me some courage..."

Her words were pointed, her eyes expectant. When he flinched, she pointed to her cheek, just to drive the point home.

Everything had a price, but Myuri seemed to be enjoying how troubled he looked. These kinds of actions were typically not used in situations like this.

"...It is dangerous, so let's think of a different plan."

"What? Aww, come on, Brother!"

Myuri showed her crushing disappointment with all her being.

"And it would be serious on the off chance that someone sees you. When word gets out that a wolf was spotted on such a small island, then everyone will fly into a panic."

"Blehhh!"

Myuri puffed out her cheeks and kicked the snow at her feet.

If it was possible, their best option was to get information from Yosef via an intermediary.

While Col was weighing their options, Myuri's head suddenly rose. Like a beast that had heard the footsteps of its prey on the snowy fields, she instantly stood up straight.

"Is something wrong?"

"I hear footsteps."

"Footsteps?"

Myuri lifted her hood slightly, and Col noticed her wolf ears moving underneath.

"There are a lot of people walking together. I think they're going to the church. They're on the big street."

"The townspeople are heading to the church...which means the negotiations are already starting."

Merchants believed that time was money. And since these particular merchants were racing against the Kingdom of Winfiel, it was more important than ever.

Myuri strained her ears to listen for a while, and then she lowered her hood back into place. Before long, Col, too, began to hear the sound of footsteps on the snow, but it was only one person. The *crunch, crunch* came closer to the front of the house, then the sound of a door opening and closing soon after.

"It's the round man."

"...Mr. Yosef."

There was an odd similarity between her and her mother, Holo, who also rarely called people by their name.

Col and Myuri circled back to the front and entered the house, where they found Yosef was in the middle of talking to the two preparing dinner.

"But, Auntie, it's what we decided on at the meeting."

"Heh-heh. Giving hospitality despite our poverty is the heart of Caeson. If we abandon our guests, our dead grandfathers will come creeping out from the bottom of the sea."

As he argued with the old woman, the wife noticed Col and Myuri and called out to Yosef and the old woman.

"Oh, Mr. Col."

"Did something happen?"

"Well, see…"

Yosef's expression was troubled as he spoke.

"His Grace, the archbishop, wishes to hold a banquet of friendship and has invited all the leaders of the island, but we don't have enough people. So we're looking to get the women's help, but…"

The church did allow women to stay, but there were a great many rules about various things, and there were likely very few with idle curiosities who would come so far to this frontier. As Col thought, he could feel someone looking at him. When he turned to look, Myuri's eyes were oddly bright. It was his failure as a brother that he did not know what this girl, who fancied adventure stories, was thinking.

"No, no. We'll take care of the guests in our house. They are servants of God! We can't make any excuses, not even to our Black-Mother." The old woman insisted stubbornly, holding a thin carrot in her hand.

The wife did not know who to side with, and Yosef was distressed.

As they stood before them, Myuri reached around behind Col and tugged on the hem of his clothes.

You know what to do.

This may have been exactly the opportunity they were looking for, and the plan she was thinking about could be a much better alternative than turning into a wolf and sneaking in.

It was only for a few seconds that he hesitated.

"There's something I wish to talk to you about."

"Oh!"

Col spoke to a dazed Yosef.

"If possible, we wish to learn the visitors' purpose as soon as possible and return to Atiph."

Myuri nudged him from behind to push him forward as he spoke.

The considerate man nodded in understanding.

"I see. Very well. Then...All right, I will tell them I will be sending four people from my house. Will there be a problem with that, then, Auntie?"

"With what?" The old woman asked doubtfully, and Yosef responded.

"We'll all go to the church together. Then there will be no guests to take care of."

"Mmm? What, are they going to stay at the church instead?"

The old woman looked at them, a disappointed look on her face. But four people?

The church was asking for women's help. The old woman, the wife, Myuri...He counted them all, and that was when he finally realized what he meant.

"Er, ah—"

"Aw, you should."

Myuri was the one who said that. He turned to her, and she wore a mischievous smile on her face.

Col could not let this happen. He desperately tried to make excuses.

"Mr. Reicher and the guards have already taken a good look at my face, and I will arouse suspicion no matter what kind of a disguise I wear."

His argument just made Yoesf's shoulders shake with laughter. It seemed he was joking.

"Forgive me."

He dropped his shoulders in disappointment and Yosef continued.

"Sir Col and I will remain on the boat. We can send help in an emergency, and there is lots of strong drink on the boat."

"Thank you so much."

Yosef nodded, then told the old woman and the wife this and that and then went outside for a bit.

Myuri sighed, disappointed.

"I was so close."

"That's not funny."

"I've always wanted a big sister."

It seemed pointless to respond, so he merely sighed as Myuri shrugged, smiling.

"Well then, I'll go prepare your clothes. You won't look like an islander girl dressed like that," the portly wife called out to them with a dry smile.

On the other hand, the old woman had started collecting pots, pans, and other cooking utensils, wrapping them all together with a straw rope. Though she was small, her back hunched over, she was also dexterous and moved without faltering. There was no doubt that she had been just as hard a worker in her youth.

"Okay!" Myuri responded enthusiastically and made her way to where the trunk was.

She was clever; she could certainly play the part of a server while looking for a chance to get close to the archbishop and company to hear what they were discussing. Even if Reicher questioned her, she could get out of it by saying she was helping.

"Well, I think this will fit the little miss."

The wife took this and that out of the chests stacked in the corner of the house, before finally pulling out a wrapped package. Myuri also looked on in great interest, wondering what she would be wearing. It seemed the outfit had been in the chest for quite a while, as it was completely covered in dust that gave the wife a coughing fit, and Myuri cackled.

Col sat by the fire in the hearth as he watched them, but there was something strange about it all.

He could not put his finger on it, but when he did, he realized it was the structure of the family.

The old woman, her son, the son's wife, and then their son. The men had all gone off to work in Atiph, so it was an all-women household. Then why did they have clothes for a young girl?

She unwrapped the package, and there was a simple yet warm-looking outfit. Myuri held it up to herself, and it was miraculously the perfect size. The make of the clothes gave them a childlike air, and they were obviously not the kind that belonged to a wife or an old woman.

The wife watched Myuri as she quickly changed. There was a gentle smile on her face as she dabbed the edges of her eyes.

"I just couldn't let it go. I did not think it would come in handy one day," she murmured and sighed.

By how she spoke, it was clear that the owner of these clothes was no longer around. Myuri noticed as well, and the color drained from her face.

"…Sickness?"

"Yes. She was always resilient and a hard worker. She was the kind of child who would always keep on smiling, even after falling into the sea in the middle of winter."

211

"Really? We wear the same size, but I guess we have more in common than I thought."

"Oh my."

She was first surprised at Myuri's words, but this was soon followed by a happy smile.

"The sleeves might be a bit long, but the length is perfect. Truly, thank you for wearing it."

"The sleeves are fine. Right, Brother?"

Myuri changed quickly and spun around, skirt fluttering. The clothes were pale in color, made using only plant dyes; a bit plain for a girl, but they suited her well. There was almost a sense that if Myuri wore things like this on a normal basis, she would become more ladylike.

"Yes," he agreed, but the wife did seem a bit bothered by the sleeves.

She went to retrieve a needle and began quickly stitching. Or perhaps, she simply wanted to dote on her young visitor.

"It's been...five years since she left us. Time goes by so quickly."

Myuri behaved and sat still as the wife sewed her clothes. The old woman had immediately headed off to the church after she finished putting away the pots and pans.

The crackling fire in the hearth was awfully loud.

"It was a day just like this."

She shortened the sleeves just a bit and measured the length as Myuri raised her arm. It seemed perfect. She nodded, satisfied, and began work on the other sleeve.

"It was so sudden. That day, we ate together as normal, and we were just about to go to sleep."

She finished stitching the other side, and it was perfect once more. Myuri did not say anything in thanks and could only stare at the wife.

The wife continued to smile as she talked about her memories and dabbed the edge of her eyes again. She sniffled, and Myuri placed her hand on her shoulder, as though it was natural for her to do so. Though she was surprised at first, the wife thanked her and placed her hand on top of Myuri's.

It was clear what happened to her daughter.

He already knew that such a thing was a common occurrence.

"She must be working her hardest in a distant town now. Knowing that is enough for me to be happy."

She had been sold as a slave.

And it would have been just as the wife doubled over and suffered in sadness. Like an arrow had been shot through his head, a flash lit up in his mind.

Of course, that is why he never noticed.

It was not that the island had enough goods for all the money the large company had rushed over.

And it would solve both the island's and the company's problems.

Regular goods would be sold, and that was that. But slavery was different.

Families would worry about their loved ones even after they were taken far away and they would pray for their happiness.

Therefore, by buying slaves, the Ruvik Alliance was, in a way, taking the islanders hostage. That was because if the islanders angered the slavers, then their friends and family who were sold off might meet terrible ends.

On the other hand, it was worth paying mountains of gold as the workers, even merchants, on the island could be bought.

If that were the case, then where did the archbishop fit into all of this?

A bitter taste filled his mouth as he felt nauseous from something sour swelling up inside of him.

Perhaps the archbishop had gotten wind of Autumn, learning that the islands were very serious about their faith. So he had come along to bestow the proceedings with the authorization of an archbishop, in order to make sure that nothing would obstruct the buying of slaves—and securing them as hostages.

The merchants would obtain goods, the islanders would receive money, and the archbishop would secure power on the cusp of war breaking out.

It was brilliant—three birds with one stone. Whoever thought it up was an evil genius.

Col felt nauseous because it was nothing more than the logic of the powerful—entirely bereft of mercy, no compassion. The rulers' arrogance was obvious: They must be satisfied if we give them money, right?

The Church, which was meant to be the house of peace for the people, had already fallen too far to be saved.

That much was clear to Col after he had seen the archbishop riding in the palanquin. That was the behavior of nothing less than a king.

This could not be forgiven. It could not be overlooked.

It was not simply for the Kingdom of Winfiel.

Even more fundamentally than flaunting the teachings of the Church, it went against his own conscience.

"If she lives in a town far away, we'll let you know if we come across her on our travels," Myuri said to the wife, who kept wiping at the tears while continually thanking her.

Being sold as a slave and departing on a journey were two completely different things. A thousand flowery words and purple prose could not justify something that brought about so much unhappiness in households like this or the house of that fisherman at the beach.

Then, what was there to do? he pondered, and the first thing that came to mind was Autumn.

Because he was the one solely responsible for the faith on the islands, they had no choice but to persuade him in order to have a realistic chance in stopping this revolting scheme. As he reached that conclusion, Yosef returned.

"Oof, it's cold. The snow is coming down even harder."

The wife suddenly grew embarrassed, seeing that he had returned. She hurriedly released Myuri from her embrace and smiled reassuringly.

"Oh dear, I'm getting old."

"I think you're still pretty young!"

Yosef stared blankly at the two, who had grown so close in such a short time.

Col approached him.

"Mr. Yosef, there's something I wish to ask."

"Oh? What is it?"

"Before you said that you would be able to put out a boat immediately."

Tension crept into the man's bearded face.

"Yes, I can. Is something wrong?"

"I wish to go see Lord Autumn."

He had to reject the archbishop's intentions. This scheme would deal a heavy blow to the Kingdom of Winfiel if it came to pass, so once the kingdom learned of the situation, they would undoubtedly think up their own offer. It would not be as terrible as buying a large amount of slaves. Once there was a viable alternative, Autumn should be more receptive of what they had to say.

He recalled Autumn's solitude on that gray-colored beach. There was an air about him that made it seem he would make destructive decisions on a whim, even though he should have been searching for salvation.

After the archbishop stuffed his ship full of slaves, what would be left on this island besides unhappiness?

215

"I have my mission, and there is something that I must discuss with Lord Autumn."

"That's…No, I won't ask. You are someone that Master Stefan took the time to write about. But there is no need to send out a boat."

"Huh?"

"Lord Autumn is already in the church. His Grace and the others must have stopped by the monastery before coming into port."

A feeling that stole away the strength in his knees overcame him. They were prepared.

But that did not mean everything had been decided.

And they had a way.

"I see."

He took a deep breath, then turned his gaze to the corner of the room.

"Myuri."

The prank-loving girl, whose silver hair had been braided in pigtails by the wife, looked over to him like a puppy.

"I have a favor to ask of you."

On the way to the church, they met up with the other women who all carried pots and pans and food on their back. It seemed that not only would they receive an allowance for cooking but they would also be buying ingredients with the great amount of money they had, so Col could hear their excited voices as they walked.

The women stepped lightly as the snow danced around them in the wind, even though it was dark and they did not particularly pay any attention to where their feet landed.

Only the church was hazily visible in the darkness, perhaps because they had lit a large fire in the courtyard.

"Will this really be all right?"

Col dropped his voice as low as he could and asked Myuri, and she, carrying a hatchet-like blade wrapped in cloth on her back, looked at him with a mischievous smile.

"It's fiiine. See, there are plenty of people the same height as you."

The women walking along the path all certainly seemed the kind who could beat him in any test of strength.

"But I'm a bit sad."

"About what?"

As Myuri brushed the snow off her hood, she spoke.

"I finally have a *big sister*, but she doesn't smile very much."

"..."

Yosef's joke had become reality, and though Myuri seemed like she could just run about in happiness, something was still awkward about her. Perhaps she was being considerate toward him in her own way.

Col had only told Myuri about what he realized of the archbishop's plan and what they would be doing after. Though irritated that he never knew when to give up, Myuri had grabbed a comb and smiled for him.

She even told him to call her name if he got lost because she would come find him.

"If the plan goes well, I'll smile as much as you like."

"Really? Then will you spend a day in town in Atiph dressed like that?"

She had loosened his hair, brushed it out well, then fixed it up with the oil she brought from Nyohhira. She lightly powdered his rough skin with a mixture of shell and zinc powder.

217

He wore clothes borrowed from the wife, paired with gloves and a kerchief. It was perfect.

"I'll think about it," he responded with a wry smile, and Myuri smiled, too.

The church seemed a bit like it was a festival. Or perhaps it was shelter in a castle for the townspeople to escape from war.

There was no particular examination at the gates, but the guard did indeed notice Col immediately.

There, the wife whispered something to him. They exchanged a couple of words, after which the guard drew his mouth taut and withdrew slightly; he must owe her something. It was a small island after all.

As the guard let him through, Col lowered his head in apology. But Myuri, skirt fluttering, looked at the guard and grinned.

"Didn't I say there were perks to dressing as a girl?"

The guard smiled wryly and shrugged.

After passing through the gate, they found a large bonfire lit in the courtyard, and it was as bright as day. It seemed that the dining hall kitchen was not enough to make food for everyone, so there were pots here and there, cooking. It seemed that the Ruvik Alliance had the foresight to bring enough wood for fuel, and the smell of burning firewood comforted him.

"Please quickly take whatever is finished inside!"

Worn-out assistant priests walked among the boiling pots and heated griddles.

But they still seemed rather skilled, and maybe it was just as lively and busy during the peak fishing season.

All the women around them seemed to know one another, but perhaps because the inside of the church felt like a different world in their own land, no one seemed to notice that there were two strangers among them.

"See? No one can tell."

She sounded proud for some reason, and Col simply shrugged before he lowered the luggage on his back.

Next, they had to find out where Autumn was. The courtyard was filled with women cooking and men who had not eaten enough warm food on their long voyage at sea.

He likely would not arouse suspicion wandering around here, but it would be different inside the building.

Just as he wished he had some sort of tool, he noticed that Myuri had disappeared from his side.

He looked around in a panic when someone poked him in the back.

"Sister?"

There stood Myuri, holding a draining basket. He was surprised to see two large shrimps, boiled to a bright red and still billowing steam, inside of it.

"We can just bring these in and say, *Hello, we've brought these for Sir Beard*, right?"

She loved pranks, and she even surpassed her mother, once called the wisewolf, in telling plausible lies.

He took the basket gratefully and began to walk off, Myuri in tow.

"Sister, people won't move out of the way for you if you talk in such a quiet voice."

She winked mischievously.

"That's the liveliest building."

What she pointed to as they walked was the building in which they first met Reicher. It seemed there was a large hall and furnace there—ideal for a banquet.

He realized how odd it was for him to wonder if Reicher was having a good time drinking. And when Col imagined what anguish the troubled priest would feel when he learned of the archbishop's plans, his chest ached. At the entrance of the building, there was a young knight of the Church, walking in place in an attempt to ward off the cold, so this must be where all the high-ranking members were. Myuri jogged over to the knight, who was looking out at the fires in the courtyard with round, wanting eyes.

"Excuse me, we've been told to deliver the village's specialty shrimp."

"Shrimp? Ooh, that looks excellent."

"We were told to deliver it to Lord Autumn in thanks. Do you happen to know where he might be?"

"Autumn...Sorry, I don't know who that is."

"A really old brother with an insane beard?"

"Oh yes, he went into the chapel. The smell of grilling meat must be painful for him. He must be an amazing person who does nothing but severe training, so I'm sure he'll be happy to have some shrimp."

It sounded like the banquet had not quite started yet.

Just as they were about to head off to the chapel in a rush, the knight stopped them.

"Wait a minute."

His voice was hard. The sword hanging at his waist rang with a *kachink* sound.

Facing away from the knight, Myuri and Col exchanged glances.

Had they been found out?

Myuri was much more decisive in times like these. She twirled around.

"Yes?"

"That woman."

He had ignored Myuri and looked straight at Col as he talked.

At that moment, she bit her bottom lip and brought her hands to her chest.

If he snuck in dressed as a woman, then there was no helping it if he were to be deemed a spy.

There was no one to help them here, on this island surrounded by freezing seas.

It was just when she was about to pull out her pouch of wheat.

"I have a favor to ask."

Huh? had almost escaped his lips. He coughed it off and looked at Myuri.

"My sister is ill and can't talk very well. What is it?"

"Um, right. Uh, well…"

The knight looked around, then spoke with a guilty expression.

"Could I have some of that? Please? Even if it's just the legs."

Begging for food was unbecoming for a knight of the Church.

But no one could win against the icy cold and an empty stomach.

Col and Myuri exchanged glances again before she reached into the basket and handed the knight an entire shrimp.

"'We must give all that we can.'"

Though she never seemed to be listening to his lecturing, she always was.

"These are going to get cold, so we'll be off."

Myuri shoved Col's back and walked off. The knight glanced back and forth between them and the shrimp, and his expression finally softened. The only ones who indulged in luxury and drowned themselves in the logic of the powerful were their masters. The ones serving under them were simple and endured poverty like the rest of the masses of the world.

Overturning the archbishop's plot would save people like them.

Newfound resolve bubbled in him as the knight suddenly waved to them. Col could not help but wave back to the happy and somewhat shy man.

Myuri laughed at him, and Col regained his usual senses.

"You're a nice lady."

She was hoping he'd snap back, so he said nothing.

The chapel was next to the library, in front of the garden that now housed rows of dried fish.

No one would come to a bastion of abstinence and silence at a time of singing and drinking and celebration.

When they opened the door and entered the chapel, they were greeted with air colder than the outside.

"...He's here."

Myuri sniffed and wiggled her wolf ears and whispered as quietly as the snow falling to the ground. Col nodded silently and entered, then closed the door. It was pitch-dark for only a few moments, and once his eyes adjusted, he could faintly see the outline of the building.

They passed through the corridor, ascended a short staircase, and there was an open door. There was one long aisle in the middle of rows of long pews that faced the altar.

And there he was.

There was Autumn, crouching down like a black beast.

"This is a place of prayer."

He did not speak particularly loudly, but his voice reached Col's ears in a way that made it sound like he was right next to him.

Col passed the basket of shrimp to Myuri and walked forward, unafraid.

"Lord Autumn."

Autumn did not move, but it seemed he knew immediately who it was, and he may have even guessed what his business was. Col stopped in the middle of the aisle and spoke.

"I need to talk to you."

"Did I not say this is a place of prayer?"

"I apologize. *I pray thee.*"

Autumn did not answer or turn around, but he did straighten his rounded back.

"It may be just my misunderstanding. I shall accept if you laugh, grow irritated, or censure me. However, there is a chance my conjectures might sadly be true, Lord Autumn. As a servant of God, I must speak on it."

Autumn's shadow seemed to swell, perhaps because he was angry they interrupted his prayer or perhaps because he had inhaled to sigh deeply.

Regardless, he turned around and met Col's gaze straight on.

"That archbishop and merchant have come to this island to buy slaves. Is that not correct?"

His eyes must have fully adjusted to the darkness as he could see Autumn clearly.

It seemed there was a window of treated glass on the ceiling of the chapel. The light reflected faintly off the snow and filtered inside.

"I thought you were a foolish spy."

There was no happiness in being right. He only made clear that there were a great number of worthless people in the world that occupied seats of power.

"Then, Lord Autumn, you understand what I wish to say."

Col leaned forward, hoping his words would reach further inward.

But not a single hair on Autumn's beard moved. As though bound by the rule of silence, he did not speak. Col understood then that the holy man was well aware of the archbishop's plan and had already made up his mind.

Even though he should have known it was a destructive choice, those emotionless eyes were like those of a hopeless goat.

"God will understand our words."

That was all he said in response. Those words stung all the more for those serious about prayer.

Col used the moment to take a deep breath and then replied.

"We live in the world of mortals. The words of mortals would be enough."

"Hmm."

It was the first time some emotion appeared in Autumn's eyes. That encouraged Col, and he gripped his fist tightly.

"Please do not clasp the dirtied hand of the Church as they continue to cling to rotting power. If you let the Kingdom of Winfiel know of the islands' plight, they will surely give you some aid."

Col did not have the right to make such promises nor any guarantee.

But at the very least, he believed in Hyland. He believed that God's true teachings were still here. He wanted Autumn to believe that, too.

"And what would come of that?"

That was his only response.

"To receive any sort of charity is a mistake."

Autumn slowly began to move toward him. It felt like the darkness was closing in.

"I only believe in the Black-Mother's protection."

She who had sacrificed herself for the island and may have not been human.

Not only was that the root of Autumn's fanaticism, it normalized the act of sacrifice.

Which meant there was no reason for Autumn to refuse talks with the Ruvik Alliance, who owned mountains of gold in real life.

To choose what was certain into one's hands was an invariable principle for those who lived in unforgiving circumstances. Even if it was burning metal, the need was overwhelming. It was necessary to calmly take a hold even if hands burned or flesh charred.

"Pray," Autumn murmured as he slipped by them and exited the chapel.

Col could not bring himself to turn around to watch him go, let alone chase after him. Standing before the elegantly arranged place of worship, he could not move.

What was God doing? Why did he not appear from his altar? Even if he glared at the Church's banner, spread out wide above the altar and lit dimly from the snow, the only response he received was silence.

He turned around and felt like running. His legs could not move forward because there, standing in the middle of the aisle, was Myuri, holding the basket.

"Brother, your promise."

Her gaze pressured him. He was honest and good-natured, and once he left the dreamland of his hot spring village, the claws of reality tore into him.

Maybe what Myuri had said was right.

But was it really just? Were both Autumn and Myuri both saying that the correct way to deal with a cold reality was to have a cold heart? Was it right to simply shrug one's shoulders and accept that this was reality with a cool head, in cold blood, even?

Those impertinent words had led to dozens of people being sold as slaves.

Suddenly, he was filled with raging fury.

There were things that even he could do.

Should he show it?

"Myuri, lend me your power."

"Huh?" she asked back, bewildered.

With a wide gait, he drew closer to the girl standing in the middle of the aisle and gripped both of her slim shoulders.

"Brother, what? Ow, hey, that hurts!"

Myuri twisted herself and tried to run, but the basket dropped from her hands and the beautiful shrimp fell to the floor.

Right as she looked down at the wasted food, with the side of her face in front of him—

"…"

This was how he could get her to act. He knew what she wanted and how simple it was to bend her toward his conviction. Feeling like he had gotten his revenge, his lips left her cheek.

"Myuri, become a wolf and jump into the banquet, pretend to be a servant of the Black-Mother, and then their plans—"

He only made it that far.

As Myuri continued to stare at the floor, tears rolled from her eyes and made a small *tap* when they hit the floor.

"…"

There were no words. She looked at him, glaring. Her reddish-amber eyes wavered in anger and contempt.

It was only then that Col understood what he had done.

He hurt Myuri.

Truly, deeply hurt her.

"M-Myuri…I…"

"Don't touch me!"

Her voice tore through him, and his hand stopped. She collapsed to the floor and stared at the shrimp—cold, legs broken. It was almost as though something precious of hers had died with it.

"You always treated me so well only because you wanted to use me?"

She bared her fangs and her claws as he stood there in shock.

"No, you didn't. I know that much."

Her words sounded gentle, but her mouth was twisted in scorn. She crouched, retrieved the shrimp, and placed it in the basket.

It was only moments earlier that it looked so delicious, but now it was nothing but a cold corpse.

Myuri stood, still staring at the basket.

Then, as though a string had been cut, she spoke.

"You were nice to me even when I got in your way. No matter how spoiled I acted you were still kind to me. There is no way such a nice boy could stand up against *that*."

When she looked up, he had never seen her face so filled with anger.

"But I wanted you to be cool, so I thought that maybe you could manage. You're stupid and never look around you, but your honesty is your strength. I thought you could somehow accept this island and move on in your own way. I was going to help you because I knew you would keep working hard even if you kept obeying whatever orders that blondie gave you. But—"

She sniffled and furiously rubbed her eyes with her arm. This was not the girl who would walk around all day with bread crumbs on her mouth unless her older brother looked after her.

"All you ever do is just run around like an idiot. And to top it all off...you—you..."

Thinking that she would do whatever he asked of her if he gave her a kiss was exactly the same species of arrogance the archbishop possessed. There was no love, no compassion—only what was most convenient for his egotistical self.

Myuri sniffled one more time and said, "I'm going home. Sorry for getting in the way of your trip."

She whirled around, and there was no chance for him to call out to her. But had there been a chance, what would he have even said? He understood nothing.

And the most wretched part was that somewhere in his heart, he accepted it all calmly like it was the obvious conclusion. Or perhaps, he was trying to deceive himself from the scale of his own sin by acting brash.

He did not really understand. What he did realize was that he had just lost something precious.

That was Myuri herself, of course, but also the enthusiasm he had to be someone who lived in good faith following the teachings of God.

Though blood had rushed to his head, he still acted so selfishly toward the girl who had always looked up to him. There had not been the slightest glimmer of righteous faith in his mind.

He looked away from the darkness Myuri disappeared into and stared up silently at the banner of the Church. Up until now, it had always seemed like a strong crest that he could rely on when things were rough, but now it simply showed him how small a man he really was.

For the first time in his life, Col wished to disappear.

Then came the sound of the door creeping open. Perhaps Myuri had left, or maybe she was already on her way back? He hoped for the best, and for a brief moment his pain eased slightly, but it was a number of men who poured in. They wore armor on their bodies and several of them held shields.

It did not take long for him to realize that was only because it was proper etiquette to keep blades sheathed in the chapel.

"So you're the rat from Winfiel."

From between the knights emerged the wealthy merchant, who had been on the palanquin and wearing clothes that made him look like a ball of fur.

He signaled the closest knights, and the ones with shields surrounded Col. There was no point in fighting back, and beyond the crowd, he could see knights flanking Myuri, holding her in place, though she had not been tied.

Autumn had likely been the one to inform them, but Col did not feel anger nor despair.

"If you behave, we won't hurt you. We wish to proceed peacefully."

Col had not inherited the blood of wolves like Myuri; he had no fangs and claws with which to fight nor the will to use them. Really, he thought if he could trade his life in return for a chance to send Myuri back to Nyohhira safely, then he was fine with that.

He turned around, and the merchant nodded, satisfied.

"Good to see you're reasonable. We'll let you go if you stay put here for a while. Details of our negotiations will pass through word of mouth among the fishermen regardless. If anything, letting you go will be a display of our leniency."

The knights pulled him up by the arms.

The merchant studied him from head to toe before snorting.

"Winfiel's people have many talents. Bring him," he commanded the knights, then turned on his heel and exited the chapel.

Myuri did not so much as glance at him, nor did she reach for the pouch of wheat around her neck.

If they let her go safely, Col would be happy.

Myuri would return to Nyohhira. And sometimes, she would venture outside the village by herself.

Then, what about himself?

What should he believe in? What should he live for?

The snowfall grew stronger and stronger.

A knight murmured to himself, "It'll be a blizzard."

As they had promised, they did not treat him roughly. Col was thrown into the treasure repository within the chapel, then locked inside with plenty of blankets and water. Without any windows, the room was pitch-black, and once the knight who locked the door had left, silence enveloped him.

It probably would not be until the next morning that Yosef would know what had transpired. When he did not return to the house, Yosef would understand that something had happened in the church. But even then, Yosef had no power to free Col from this place, and it would likely be difficult to leave by boat.

In the meanwhile, the archbishop and Autumn would finalize their talks, collect people from the various islands, then put them on that massive ship as slaves. In exchange, the islands would earn gold and a brief period of relief.

But what would peace for the islands be like if earned with such methods?

Did Autumn consider this a good thing? Was it another form faith could take?

As Col pondered that, he laughed to himself inside. No matter how many times he thought about this, it was never anything more than playing pretend.

There was no trace of Myuri, who should have been with him, as though she had melted away into the darkness.

He wondered if this was another kind of dream, and he was sinking deep into its depths.

That, however, was nothing more than wallowing in self-pity. It was merely an attempt to escape how horribly he had treated Myuri and all his wretchedness. That was no different from hoping to wake up and find her sitting at the edge of the bed, combing his hair.

What he should be doing now is trying to search for any form of her in the darkness.

If not, he felt like he would never be able to see her again.

"..."

But he had no idea how he should call out to her. Though the scripture was filled with the words of God, he could not think of a single one that he could use.

He wanted to devour himself in his misery. Embracing the darkness, he felt like he was about to cry uncontrollably, but then no tears came.

He did not know how much time had passed, but he suddenly heard footsteps. They were not metallic but that of soft leather shoes that walked listlessly and somewhat uncertainly. They stopped several times and sometimes turned back. But the noise did eventually draw near to the repository, and there was the sound of a key in the lock.

"Are you all right?"

It was Reicher.

"The knights were talking about an agent from the kingdom who had been caught, so I thought perhaps..."

Reicher spoke quickly as he continued glancing back at the chapel entrance.

"I have no way to know for what reason you are working for the kingdom. But if you pity me, then please hear my plea."

Col was confused for a moment because it was none other than Reicher who opened the door to the treasure repository, where he was being kept. So then why was Reicher practically begging him? Shouldn't it be the other way around?

But he then realized what Reicher had unlocked was really his own heart.

"Please report to the kingdom about the negotiations with the archbishop. The snow will swell with the coming wind and become a blizzard. It will be difficult to get to the open waters off the shores of Caeson for a few days. But if you send out a boat tonight and sneak among the narrow passages between islands, then the islands will block the wind and you may be able to get south somehow. If it goes well, then you will have a week's head start on the archbishop's ship. You can gather reinforcements and wait for them in the southern sea routes."

As Reicher rambled on, Col could see that he, too, clung to his hopeful imagination.

He was met with an ugly reality that could not be erased by drink every day, so he had no choice.

"So please save the people on the ship."

Col could not see it going so well, unfortunately. If a kingdom ship attacked one the archbishop rode on, then it would be an unquestionable act of war. This was not something to be carried out lightly.

But the reality was that Reicher had opened the door for him. And Yosef had said earlier he might be able to send out a boat. Nothing would happen if he stayed here. So he nodded and took Reicher's hand.

"Come with me. We will leave this island."

They were the same. Both trapped by the island, a shadow that could not move.

Reicher, however, suddenly smiled and shook his head.

"It would be quite a mess if I left. I pardoned myself from the banquet by saying I was headed for the privy. Go quickly."

Reicher looked at him and gave him a troubled smile.

"I've always wanted to try saving someone."

As grief welled up in his heart, Col embraced Reicher and patted the priest's back.

He turned around and found Myuri standing there, staring at her feet.

"May God watch over you."

It was not meant for anyone in particular, nor did he know if the prayer would help at all.

They left the treasure repository and hid among the commotion of the banquet.

Reicher quickly vanished, and Col could not call out for him.

That was what traveling was all about. He knew that.

"Let's go."

He knew she would not respond, but he said so anyway and walked off. Myuri followed him obediently. No matter how much it bothered her, she would have to take Yosef's boat to return to Nyohhira.

They wove through the drunk men and the women who danced with them, eventually reaching the gate. The guard was drinking alone, greeting them with a look of mild surprise, but did not say anything in particular.

The snow beneath their feet was unstable like sand. They slipped and slid as they walked through it, almost like the snow was ridiculing their hurried steps. His breath quickly grew short, but he did not fall behind Myuri the way he did when they descended the mountain. They had to keep moving forward. There was no point in living otherwise. He endured his regret and sadness and stepped forward with all his strength.

They arrived at the port, where the wind howled at them even if they stood still. The snow stung their faces like flying stones. Waves crashing in from the sea echoed loudly, though he could hear the creaking of the wood on the ships and pier. They headed toward Yosef's relatives' house, where they found him by the hearth, warming his hands. When he looked at them, the tiredness in his eyes was replaced by a glinting light.

"We need a boat."

"Leave it to me."

He did not hesitate. He dumped some liquor into the fire, and it blazed strongly like a beacon.

Col undressed and quickly changed. He gathered their things and hefted the pack onto his back. For a moment, he wondered how much silver he should leave them, but it might only cause the women trouble if there was evidence that they had significant ties to these outsiders. So in the end, he left nothing as he exited the house.

They headed to the port in the wind and snow, and Yosef, who had left before them, was standing at the pier, beckoning to them.

The ramp had been set up to the boat, and there was a wavering light on deck.

"Heh-heh, this reminds me of when the Church attacked long ago," Yosef reminisced and put them on board before he himself jumped on, then removed the ramp. He then stuck his head down the stairs leading below deck and yelled.

"All right you bastards! Show them the spirit of the island people!!"

According to the common sense Col had gained during his travels, setting sail at night was an act of suicide. Even in an emergency, boats would not set out without at least the light of the moon.

But not only was the moon nowhere to be seen, they were trying to set out in heavy snowfall and howling winds. The waves rose high, and the boat was already rocking even in port. Their confidence was not based solely on the fact that everything would be fine simply because these were familiar seas they lived in. With their courage, they were indomitable sailors.

Col finally understood why the kingdom and Church were serious in their considerations about whether they should ally with the islanders. They were survivors and warriors who fought with the overpowering being that was the sea. Like jumping behind enemy lines under a rain of arrows, it was not an easy task to set sail at night on white-crested waves.

By giving money, the people could prepare ships.

But bravery was different.

"Sail!" someone yelled, and the oars slithered out from below.

They struck the dock violently—it seemed they all pushed off at once. The boat slowly parted from the pier, and this time it was the pier that made the ominous creaking noise.

After they had gone a certain distance, the oars on either side of the boat rose up into the air, then lowered into the sea in perfect unison. The boat began to move vigorously and parted from the docks.

On deck, without any cargo to serve as a barrier, they were exposed to the full brunt of the snow and wind. Yet Col did not feel the least bit cold as he gazed toward Caeson, the brightly lit church in the distance.

What had he come here to do?

That dizzying question seized his chest, and he could not breathe.

"It's all right to throw up on deck if you get seasick, by the way."

As the boat suddenly began to rock back and forth, Yosef spoke with a smile.

"If you lean over the edge, you'll get sucked into the water. There are beasts that hide in the sea at night."

Col did not take that as superstition or assumption; he believed it was real.

The sea on a moonless night was as dark as any nightmare. The occasional white waves reminded him that this was reality. Like a shivering child, the boat wavered back and forth and rocked wildly on occasion. The thumping impacts from below may have been the waves or a monster trying to pull its prey underwater.

Before long, the light in the church was a distant glow.

"Did you manage to talk to him?" Yosef asked, relaxed, thinking that if they had come this far, then they were all right.

At some point, he had produced a small wine cask in his hands.

"Well, yes..."

Col gave a vague reply, but it was glossed over in the darkness on the water.

"Good. That means Master Stefan will save face, too."

He smiled and handed Col the cask. He took a sip, and it was bitter distilled liquor.

"Once we pass through this and slip into the waterways that lie between islands, the wind and waves will die down like magic. We just need to be patient."

Reicher had said the same thing.

"Thank you so much."

Col was grateful, wishing they would reach that point quicker.

"Leave it to me," Yosef replied, puffing out his chest.

With brief pauses every time the boat rocked, the captain slowly made his way to the stern. Col looked around and found Myuri sitting at the base of the sail yard, wrapped in a blanket with her eyes closed. He only needed to take a few steps for his voice to reach her, but it felt like an eternity away.

Like turning away from his own wounds, he looked away from Myuri and out to sea. However, that did nothing to calm him. The sea had grown more fearsome since they left the port and reached the open water.

He had no idea if the growing wind was due to the speed of the boat or a signal that the blizzard had drawn near. The breaking waves disappeared with raging force behind them, and it was almost like they were hurtling down a river. He could no longer tell the flickering of light in his eyes from the glow of the church. *How very much like faith that is*, he thought.

As though his core had been spirited away, he could no longer feel the cold. He simply stared out over the water.

The boat would continue south, reach Atiph, then he would report what he had seen to Hyland. That was all Col could imagine. He could not see what would come after that.

He could not return to Nyohhira. Myuri would hate that. But

he felt that staying by Hyland's side would be too much for him. Whatever had resided within him was now gone.

Because he could not even believe in himself.

His mind empty, he watched the shapes of the foam on the waves as they broke on the sea. They looked like white birds soaring through the darkness while snakes slithered along the surface of the water. He saw a particularly large wave and thought it looked like an angel. Its wings were spread out on either side, ready to take flight.

He was annoyed with himself at first—that he would think such a thing—but he noticed something odd about it. Though the shape of the wave itself wavered, it did not disappear. Rather, it instead looked like it was growing bigger and bigger.

No, it *was* getting bigger.

That was no wave.

It was a boat!

"Mr. Yosef!"

He shouted as loud as he could, but that was when he finally realized that they were sailing on rough, wild seas. His voice barely reached his own ears, and the drops of ice felt like stones as they hit his face.

The boat rocked back and forth, and it shook feverishly whenever a wave struck them from below.

Col made his way to the stern of the boat with the other sailors, firmly planting his feet as he went, where Yosef stood gripping the helm, and raised his voice again.

"Mr. Yosef! A ship!"

Yosef grimaced—either from the cold, or from snow in his eyes, or because he had heard his foolish report. But there was no mistake. Col turned around again, and the angelic white ship's trail was growing bigger.

"A ship! It's coming closer!"

The boat rocked again, and after a brief sensation of floating, Col smashed into the deck. He desperately pulled himself up, and though Yosef and the others had of course managed to stay standing, they stared in shock at where he had pointed.

"Pirates!" Yosef yelled and let go of the helm, then jumped down the stairs leading below deck.

The speed of the oars immediately grew faster, but there was no way to tell how much faster they were going in the featureless darkness. And the pirate ship was tapered like a spear, prioritizing mobility.

On the other hand, they were aboard a mercantile boat—wide and stout.

He recalled how it felt when Autumn led him onto that sword-like boat.

It was catching up.

He could almost see the face of the angel of death.

"Mr. Col!"

He turned around when he heard Yosef yell. He was at the base of the sail yard, gripping Myuri's arm.

Then he lost all sound again.

Following Yosef's gestures, he turned back to the sea.

There it was—like a monster suddenly appearing out of the mist.

Like the long fish they had in the dining hall in Caeson, a pointed end closed in on them.

He recalled his leisurely conversation with Myuri:

"What we'll do is crash into our bounty from the side; then, with our swords in our mouths, we'll raise a battle cry and leap onto the other boat, right?"

He vaguely remembered his response as being *"How would you be able to raise a war cry with a sword in your mouth?"*

The tip of the pirate ship pierced the left side of their boat from below.

"_____"

He did not know if someone had yelled something to someone else or if it was his own cry.

When he realized it, he was in the darkness.

He could not tell up from down, and he had the sensation of struggling with his arms and legs, but it may have been his imagination. The smell of the oil she put in her hair gave him the sense that Myuri was nearby. Perhaps it was his own desires that made him hear, "Brother!"

Myuri.

The moment he thought that, he was greeted with an intense shock and could no longer breathe.

He had only realized he fell into the water when his body floated to the surface.

"Geugh, agh! Goch..."

He coughed, only for a wave to envelop his entire body with water again.

He found himself brimming with fear of not being able to breathe more than being afraid of the freezing cold.

His body was heavy, like he had fallen in mud, as the clothes that were meant to keep him warm soaked up water.

Desperately he moved his body and pulled his face from the water, inhaling deeply. Then he opened his eyes to see the side of the boat. It had not capsized, but some oars were missing. It was possible they had been thrown into the water on impact.

He looked up to the railing on deck, and he could not help but smile.

No matter how far up he stretched, he would never reach it.

And pushed by the waves, the boat was heartlessly drifting

. away. There was nothing around him; he would be left behind in the black seas.

That was when Col realized he would die here.

The cold began to drain the strength from his body. He had been taught what to do when someone fell into the river while hunting during the winters back in Nyohhira. It was simple: Warm the body by any means. Otherwise, they would lose feeling in their arms and legs within a hundred breaths, lose consciousness before the next hundred, and reach death without finishing the last one hundred. If he found someone in the river...He did not finish the thought because he understood there was no need for the rest.

That was because the sea was colder than any of the rivers in Nyohhira, and there was no way to pull himself up out of the water.

Not waiting for the next one hundred breaths, Col sank into the water. All the choices he had in life began to disappear.

As they vanished, he finally realized that there was only one thing left.

It was a short sentence, something akin to regret.

"I'm sorry."

He should have said that to Myuri, even if she ignored or rejected him.

There must have been some air trapped in his heavy clothes, as even though he barely moved his arms and legs, he bobbed up to the surface at every wave like some sort of sick joke.

He only wanted to drown.

A sleepy surrender began to eat away at his body, and he closed his eyes.

He once heard that people dreamed as they died.

It seemed his was just beginning.

"Brother!"

From the stern of the boat that grew distant in his vision, Myuri jumped into the water.

He watched her and vacantly thought, *Your clothes will get wet.*

She hit the water with a splash.

It was only when he saw her head emerge above water and she began swimming desperately toward him that he understood he was seeing reality.

"Brother!"

"...Myu...Wh...why...?"

He could no longer speak. As though his back teeth had melded together, his jaw was stiff. His teeth were clenched together, and he could not move them.

Myuri was swimming in such thin clothes that he almost sighed; perhaps she had removed her bulky outer garments before jumping in.

He wanted to say, *You'll get sick.*

"Brother, Brother!"

Her hands reached his face, and a particularly large wave washed over them.

He only reached the surface because Myuri held him as she swam.

"Wh-why...?"

Why had she jumped in? He questioned her with his eyes, and as though she had jumped into a lake in summer, she shook her head, water spraying from it.

"Didn't I tell you?"

She clung to him, and she was so warm it almost made him sleepy.

"I would absolutely jump in after you if you fell into the cold, dark ocean. I would never leave you alone, and I would be fine at the bottom of the ocean as long as I'm with you."

He looked at her, and her expression was twisted as though she was about to cry in happiness.

He thought absently about how much she loved him. Myuri truly believed in her feelings, and she would give her life for them. Even though he had done something so terrible to her.

He mustered all the strength he could in his stiffened body to return her embrace.

Though he could not murmur words of prayer to God, his mouth breathed his last words.

"Myu...ri..."

"Yeah?"

Her reddish eyes looked at him happily.

"I'm sorry...I was so terrible to you..."

Or perhaps, he dreamed he got the chance to say that.

The world went quiet, and his body no longer bobbed with the waves.

Just as he understood that he was sinking, he thought—

Where was the Black-Mother?

He was not speaking cynically of others' faith but rather wishing for her to see him off.

He could not feel the cold of the sea.

His consciousness, too, quietly sank.

CHAPTER FIVE

After a sudden attack of breathlessness, he coughed.

But what came from his throat was not a cough but water. He heaved violently, and once he was able to breathe again, he bent over, gasping.

"Guh...Geugh...Ack..."

Col kept coughing, as it was painful to breathe in and out. Once his breathing calmed, his throat felt like it was burning.

He did not understand.

Was the afterlife supposed to be this vivid? Was it because he had been unable to enter the kingdom of heaven and had fallen into the underworld?

With this in mind, he looked around. He was in a small and simple stone room that resembled a prison cell with a small fire burning. Apocalyptic winds raged outside, and snow blew in from the windows, open squares cut in the walls. When he took that all in, he shivered.

This was the monastery. Col was in Autumn's monastery.

A sudden chill ran down his spine that was not due to the cold. Had everything that just happened been a dream? Had he simply been sleeping in the monastery? When he jumped onto the dock from the boat, had he slipped and fallen into the sea?

That was the only explanation that made sense. Because he had fallen into the water, and then...

"Myuri!"

He finally understood what he saw before him.

There, Myuri lay on her side. There was no sign of life in her pale face, and her entire body was soaked.

"Myuri! Myuri!"

He screamed her name and shook her, but she did not open her eyes. Rather, when her head limply rolled to the side, water spilled from her lips.

With a nauseous feeling of despair, he pried open her lips with his fingers and turned her over. Water emptied from her mouth, but her breath did not return.

Before calling for God's help, what crossed his mind was the war story he heard from the mercenary company that inherited Myuri's name. Not all those whose hearts stopped were fated to die. If she did not move, then he would move her himself.

He smacked Myuri's back as hard as he could. It was like he was trying to wake her. He hit her back many, many times, and when water finally stopped coming out of her mouth, her body shivered and she began to cough.

"Myuri!"

He called her name, but she did not open her eyes. He lowered his ear to her mouth, and he could hear the faint sound of her breath. But her body was growing cold like ice. He had to warm her.

He stared at the fire as though begging it for help. The faint flame danced upon only a few skinny pieces of driftwood.

"Hmm, you are lucky."

He almost jumped around in shock when he heard the sudden voice.

It was Autumn, looking out from the next room.

"Y-you're…Why…?"

"This is my monastery."

Autumn spoke quietly and tossed him a tattered blanket.

"This is all I have here."

Then he turned his back to Col and withdrew.

The blanket smelled moldy and was wet from the seawater, but it was better than nothing. Myuri had inhaled quite a lot of water; he removed the sash around her waist, wrung the water out of her hair, removed her shirt, and wrapped her in the blanket.

Her lips were beyond blue and were so pale he could not see the difference between that and her skin.

He desperately rubbed her with the blanket she was wrapped in, but there was no visible effect.

"Please hold on," he said to her and stood up.

But as Col rose, violent dizziness immediately assaulted him. He crashed into the wall and threw up on the spot. What came out was salty seawater. As it left his body, he wondered where all this water was being stored inside of him. That was the moment he finally realized that they had indeed fallen from the boat into the water and nearly drowned.

But he had no memory of how they managed to get here, nor could he imagine why such a thing had happened.

When he was finished, not waiting for his breathing to recover, he crawled into the next room, and Autumn was there, fiddling with a figure of the Black-Mother.

"Do you have something—something I can burn?" he pleaded.

With the tip of his chisel, Autumn whittled a design on the figure of the Holy Mother and scrutinized the light burning on the candle.

"This is a house of faith. You may burn your faith."

Col stood, his anger certainly ablaze, when Autumn finally looked at him.

"Everyone dies. Why not celebrate the moments that extend the deadline? Had you not escaped from the treasure repository in the chapel, you may very well have lived out the rest of your life in peace."

His second bout of dizziness came from fury.

But not a single emotion stirred in Autumn's expression.

"When I returned from the banquet, you had washed up on my shore. It must be the Black-Mother's providence."

His quiet eyes only looked as though they were simply relaying the facts.

"What you were trying would have rendered my decision worthless."

It sounded like he was demanding thanks for simply giving them a blanket.

No—Col told himself that was only his own assumption. Because, as he could see for himself, there was nothing here. Autumn himself only wore tattered rags. The only other things present were the Black-Mother figures, raw jet for material to make more, a few candles, and some food sitting exposed on the floor. There was no doubt that even the burning driftwood was the very most he could do for them.

That faint flame was the monastery itself.

"The Holy Mother, the savior of this island, will indiscriminately show miracles to those who interfere with me, the one who protects this island. What is your faith compared to that?"

Col had no argument.

"There is nothing more that can be done to aid your companion. These islands are filled with things that cannot be helped. I can only pray to God and thank the Holy Mother for the luck that I was able to save you."

Everything he said made perfect sense. Col had to acknowledge that.

However, Myuri was dying right by his side, and there was still time to save her.

He wanted to convince Autumn of that with everything he had, but the words did not come out of his mouth because he knew nothing would happen. There was nothing here—only prayer.

Autumn looked away quietly. He may have imagined the uncomfortable look in his eyes.

"Pray. I shall pray for you as well."

Autumn turned his back to Col, gripping the Black-Mother as he spoke.

Reeling once he realized the holy man had rejected his request, Col returned to Myuri's side and crumpled to the ground. The always energetic and mischievous girl looked like a princess who would sleep for a hundred years.

There was nothing left to cry, laugh, or get angry about. Even though he had done something so terrible to her, she still jumped into the sea after him and likely without any hesitation. He clearly remembered her smile and how warm she felt in the water.

At this rate, he was powerless to do anything but watch as her life flickered out.

He had read much of the scripture. He had talked to many who pursued theology. Every morning and every night, he prayed with all his might. And this was what he would end up reaping?

It was painful to acknowledge that all he had done was a mistake.

But it was nothing compared to losing Myuri.

He could voice his complaints to God later. When he thought about burning something, he realized he may be able to burn his clothes. He quickly removed some, wrung out the water, and held them by the fire. In his irritation, he held them as closely to the fire as he could, but it seemed like the flames might go out instead.

Though he knew that he might be able to light his clothes on

251

fire if he dried them, he also could see the driftwood burning up and going out before then. And with it, Myuri's life.

He desperately held back the urge to yell in despair and rubbed her hands and cheeks and any other part of her body as hard as he could.

It all felt in vain, as his hands that were doing the rubbing were also cold, but he had to try.

He wanted her to wake up and look at him. He wanted her to say, *Why are you making that face, Brother?*

It was now, of all times, that he needed God's help. But like Myuri said, he would not suddenly appear from the scripture to help him. The Black-Mother, too—he screamed in his heart, asking why would she do such a cruel thing? They should have just drowned together. An ending like this was no miracle.

The Black-Mother was an ancient, nonhuman spirit, and her figures were nothing but worthless material that was found with peat and coal. They were simply worshipping an imitation.

At that moment, he recalled a certain memory.

"...Worth...less...?"

He rewound the events in his head back to Atiph. He recalled what Hyland had said in the tavern where the fishermen gathered. The Black-Mother was made of jet. It was similar in properties to amber, and by scraping it, one could produce sand and wool, and then? And then what?

"There is a way." he murmured and gulped.

Blood began to rush throughout his body with the loud thumping of his heart, and his head grew hot.

Of course, there were things he could burn here.

He could burn the Black-Mother figures.

Autumn's uncomfortable gaze had likely been because he chose not to mention it. Jet was precious, found in the dwindling coal mines, and it was something the islanders clung to and always kept on their persons.

The fisherman who had let them borrow his boat at the port said they would eventually buy it from other countries, but there was no way the islanders had enough money.

But people's lives should be more precious. Autumn, a monk, should understand.

Col stood and breathed.

This time, he was not dizzy.

"Lord Autumn."

He called out to him, but Autumn did not turn around, nor did his hands stop.

"May I have a figure of the Black-Mother?"

Autumn finally turned around to look at him.

"Will you be praying?"

His question implied that he saw right through him.

"The only thing here to burn is faith."

Autumn's eyes widened slightly, then narrowed. It was the expression of someone who did not want to accept a harsh reality.

"No."

His answer was curt, and Col could see him grip the chisel even tighter in his right hand.

"There are only so many of these figures. I cannot give one to someone it may not help. Give up."

He turned around.

"I have said the same to many."

There was a leaden weight to Autumn's words that over-whelmed him. Col had seen with his own eyes exactly what he carried in those words. That was how this region developed. It was the prayers to the Black-Mother that somehow preserved this precarious balance.

It was a mistake to set fire to this Black-Mother for the sake of one person who might not even be saved. The scale did not balance out. It was the typical question of the devil, often brought forth by priests who preached philanthropy.

To leave one person to die and save a hundred—what would you do?

Autumn did not look away. He was prepared for hatred, but he had no intentions of bending the rules. It was a silent statement of responsibility for everything he had done in his past and that he was here now, after choosing to save a hundred people.

Col's instinct told him there was no chance of convincing him.

He turned around, like he was running away.

They had certainly died once in that moment. And Myuri had jumped into the water, prepared for that. And then, in a miracle, they had washed up at the monastery. There was no deceit in what Autumn had said. Everyone will die, and one should celebrate every moment a life is extended, giving thanks to God.

His logic was unassailable. There was not enough room for even an ant to slip through.

But whether Col could accept that or not was a different story.

He could not leave Myuri to die. He could not. That was the only impossibility.

Since coming to this island, it was experience after experience that could have lost him her trust. He had seen how hollow he was inside. But there was just one thing, one thing he vowed in the past that he would never, ever compromise on.

That was—

"I will not leave Myuri alone."

The one soul who truly believed all the words of this ignorant man, who wished to one day become a holy man in the hopes of saving others, was Myuri.

He did not know if his prayers would reach God, but Myuri's

prayers reached him. Whether they came true or not depended on his actions. He was the object of her faith.

If he could not answer her prayers, then how could he pray in the same fashion to God?

The light from the fire illuminated her profile, as the light of her life dwindled.

Such a straight face did not suit her. She was supposed to be expressive, even in her sleep.

He would not leave her. Even if she had to die in order for a hundred to survive, he would choose to stay by her side.

He had promised that he would always be her friend.

"I, too, do not mind if you hate me."

Col himself was not particularly great-looking, but Autumn was much too thin. He likely was not eating properly and only holed himself up in his monastery to work.

But he gripped a chisel in his hand. A dull, worn-out chisel that only just managed to whittle the jet. It was something that looked like it could break skin if he put all his strength into it.

Col thought about how if it was a sharp sword instead, the fight would be over in an instant.

They both knew this would not end safely for either, that it would become a terrifying thing.

But did he care?

There was never any mercy with God.

"Myuri."

He murmured her name the moment Autumn was about to attack him.

"Humans are all the same," Autumn said.

"They forget their debts and become possessed by self-interest."

The reason he couldn't move his legs was not because the conversation dulled his determination. He froze due to something else entirely.

As Autumn stared at him, his beard and hair that reached his stomach puffed outward, as though he had taken a deep breath. Col thought for a moment it might be an illusion, but it was not. Autumn's body was growing larger.

"It is not enough to demonstrate miracles. Only through punishment do humans recall their faith. The one who saved them, as well as that which must not be forgotten; I will engrave it all into this land."

Though he remained sitting, Col had to look up to see him. Like some sort of joke, Autumn looked down at him in his cramped position.

Autumn was not human.

Col then realized how shallow he had been. Myuri had commented that he did not smell like an animal.

What had been the god of his own hometown?

"Hate me. I will be conscious of sin, just as you think of cows and pigs."

His blackened hand reached out to Col to crush him.

He could not run; even if he did, he would be leaving Myuri behind.

Oh God!

At that moment, something slid by him.

A silver mass flew at Autumn, its tail streaming out behind it.

"A beast?! Why here?!"

Myuri had turned into a wolf and flew at Autumn.

Autumn gave a yell and his posture crumpled, his floating backside falling to the floor. The ceiling cracked, and the figures standing by the wall scattered across the floor.

But as he flailed his arms about, desperately trying to chase Myuri away, it was not long before he noticed.

There was no silver wolf to be seen.

After a moment of uneasy silence, Col felt the blood drain from his face and he turned around.

Myuri lay there quietly.

He thought he saw the slightest smile at the corner of her mouth.

"Myuri! Myuri!"

That may have been her spirit.

He touched her cheek and her neck, but she was still terribly cold. He did not want to believe it, pulling the body so limp it seemed it would fall to pieces into his arms. He drew his ear near her mouth, finding that she was still only barely breathing.

But she did not have long left. He knew that she had squeezed out the last of her strength to create a miracle.

He peeled off the blanket and embraced her. He could only pray that, as he had in the sea, the last thing she would feel was his warmth. He wished he could tell her—*I am here. As you were by my side in my final moments, I, too, will be your friend until the very end.*

He immediately felt a presence behind him, but he did not turn around. There was no time to do even that.

If Autumn were to kill him, he wished he did it quickly. It no longer mattered if he lived or not.

Rather, he wished he could curse his powerless self for still being alive.

"Use it."

With a high-pitched *thunk, clunk*, a mass of black rolled to his side. There were stonelike pieces, unfinished pieces, and spectacular decorative pieces.

He turned around and Autumn, still ballooned up, stared at the girl in his arms.

His expression was pained, as though he had questions to ask.

Perhaps it was something among nonhumans. He did not know what it was, but now was not the time for that.

Col immediately gathered the jet, threw it against the wall, and fed the pieces to the fire.

After a few moments, the fire shrank. It was not something that caught right away.

He wanted to cry in frustration, but a voice hung over him.

"You need to make sure the wood does not collapse."

Without a moment to think, there was the sound of a deep inhale behind him. He immediately reached out, grabbed a part of the driftwood that had not lit yet, then suppressed the embers.

An instant later, a large gust blew through, like the kind he would feel standing on the deck of a ship.

It fanned the fire, and a piece of jet suddenly ignited.

"Here comes the smoke," Autumn said and put his absurdly large hand to the window.

He altered the stone wall like it was clay and widened the window, and all the black smoke rushed out of the opening at once.

He retreated to the other room for a moment and returned shortly. His hand extended over Col's head, and after crushing the jet in his hands over the fire, he sighed again.

The small fire instantly burst into flames. It was so hot it felt like it would burn his skin.

"I..."

He heard Autumn's voice and the soft *thud* as he sat down.

"I did not know what to do."

Col turned around, and though the size of Autumn's body had not changed, he looked withered.

He was hunched over, at a loss, staring at the figures of the Holy Mother scattered on the floor.

"Humans multiply. They proliferate without thinking. They spread, knowing it will ruin them. I never knew why *this* threw away its life for the sake of such humans."

He touched the Black-Mother figure with his fingertip, as though stroking it.

"...You're..."

Col gulped.

"You're not human. Just like the Mother."

Autumn's eyes slowly turned toward him, and they looked somewhat resigned. His oddly blackened eyes were clearly not human, but the way they expressed his wish to tell someone the truth was very human.

"...Long ago, I was worshipped as the dragon of the seas."

He hunched over further, like a fallen king.

"Humans called it a whale."

A giant body big enough to stop the flow of lava, the miracle on the boat that Yosef told them about. The story of a wave putting out the fire on a burning boat. And then, the puzzlingly prosperous fishing harvest.

Everything came together neatly with a single thread.

It was understandable that Myuri could not sniff out his true form. It was her first time at sea after all.

"I can no longer remember if this was a blood relative or a companion. It must have had a name, but I cannot recall. It was so long ago that it left to travel. I did not mind at first, but I suddenly yearned for it and went to search. When I finally found it, it had already become cinders."

The fishing became prosperous after the Mother volunteered her body and saved the town because a whale, who naturally had to eat quite a bit, was suddenly gone. What the fishermen had said was true. A dragon did once live at the bottom of the sea.

"I could not understand. Humans are foolish creatures. Leave them alone and they destroy themselves in an instant. But I knew there must have been a reason why it gave its life to save them."

"So you decided to maintain the islands for that?"

Autumn was about to nod, but he stopped.

"No. Without inhabitants on the islands, people would forget. So I decided to raise the humans here, so that the memory passes down from one to the next. So they do not forget."

Raise humans.

That was a difficult phrase to swallow, but Autumn continued.

"The sea is vast and deep. I could have drifted in the waters for eternity, because I thought *this* was somewhere out there. I thought I would have been able to see it anytime."

Autumn's solitude was here.

"Were I the only one to remember, then one day, I might mistake it for a dream. I could think that I truly had been alone from the beginning. How terrifying the thought is. The oceans are bottomless. It is truly silent."

Col could not say he understood the pain of those who lived for time eternal, but he had watched them as they suffered through it.

"It seems, however, that what I truly wished for was something else. Now I realize that."

Autumn looked at Col's arms.

"Even on the brink of death, that wolf showed herself to save you. Then…Then why, at the time of its death, did this not appear before me?"

The lone monk held the figure of the Black-Mother in his hand, on the brink of tears.

"I knew that, in order to sustain this island, I had to prolong the people's suffering. But it was not so that they would hand down *its* name. Had that been all, there must have been a different way. In the end, I continued to watch the people suffer because…"

Autumn took an extended sigh.

"It was nothing more than a fit of jealousy. I was jealous because I knew that when this died, it had not been thinking about me but the people of the island…"

That was not something Col could laugh about, nor could he blame him for.

Autumn may not have found another companion besides the Black-Mother in the endlessly vast, deep sea. Col could not say he completely understood the extent of his loneliness.

But he did know Myuri, who had stared powerlessly at the world map. He had borne witness to the helplessness of those who knew they had no place in the world, despite how vast it was.

Autumn's wish of praying to his only friend was a rather modest one.

And Col was learning that there were many ways to look at things.

"…Even if it was jealousy, it is fact that you have supported these islands. There are those you have saved, and there are many who thank you."

For the first time, Autumn smiled.

"I was not expecting words of comfort. A true fool."

He seemed astonished.

"But before anything else, I must say this."

Still holding Myuri, Col looked at Autumn.

"Thank you so much for saving us."

It was not a coincidence that they had washed up here. Autumn had saved them. Every time in the past people threw their Black-Mother figures into the sea when they encountered trouble on the waters, he followed the scent and rushed to save them.

Col could not imagine it was all simply out of jealousy, as he claimed.

In his own mind, he thought that Autumn was doing all he could to protect the land his friend once saved.

"It was only a whim." Autumn spoke quietly, a bitter smile on his face as though holding back a cough.

"It may have been a whim, but I am glad I did. I had not realized she was not human. Or perhaps, it was the hand of God."

Autumn spoke words that even the most extraordinary of theological scholars would not know how a person should respond to that.

"I have discovered what I should truly be, thanks to that wolf."

Then he took the figure of the Holy Mother in his hands and fed it to the fire.

It was like a farewell.

"I shall return to the deep oceans and forget everything. The humans, too, shall forget everything. What strange creatures they are. They can swallow pain and sadness much greater than themselves," he said and nodded like a monk.

"Perhaps that is what faith is. We have no such thing."

He lifted himself slowly.

It almost seemed as though he was going for a short walk.

"You may use any of this to keep the fire going. Once the blizzard passes, someone will come. Then have them take you on their boat."

"...Are you leaving?"

"What is left for me to do here? I cannot save this place. I truly could not save the Black-Mother. Had *this* not given its life rather, then the pain here would have ended long ago."

That much was true.

But what was right, and what was wrong?

Everyone had their own reasons and their own judgments.

They were each right in their own way, but for some reason, when brought together, they no longer worked.

Without Autumn, this island would no longer be able to sustain itself, eventually falling into devastation and dying out.

No one would have to endure pain after that. Perhaps that was salvation in itself.

"My negotiations that were inconvenient for you will sustain the islands for a short time. The smarter humans will leave. And that will be all for those who cannot."

Or perhaps, Col thought, that Autumn had finally found a way to get the islanders out of this land by way of the slave deals.

He believed that even if they were in a distant land, separated from their families, it was much better than staying here.

He did not think it was that reckless. He, too, had tried to do much the same with Reicher.

"Without me, they will not be able to settle the negotiations. Then, it will all work in favor for your Winfiel side."

For some reason, he did not seem at all happy.

"If only gold appeared from the island itself…that would solve everything."

He knew that such a convenient miracle would never happen. There was an extent to what sort of miracles even the Black-Mother could bring about. Nonhumans lived much longer lives than humans, and compared to mortals, they almost seemed to possess unrivaled power. But there were only so many things that those powers could prevent.

Myuri's mother, Holo, had also warned her of this—do not rely too much on your fangs and claws; there is only so much she could do with those. Autumn had used his powers in accordance with the ways of the human world, so the region ran smoothly. In that sense, he had supported it well.

And in the end, he saved no one. Not even a glimpse of what had improved remained. What a terrible end.

"Ah, right."

Autumn was about to leave the building, as his head poked out of the sharkskin that hung over the entrance, then he came back.

"I will take one with me. Even if I forget it all, I may recall what was important when I look at this."

He retrieved a figure of the Black-Mother, then tilted his head.

"What a strange story. Here, this is more valuable than gold."

Then the embodiment of the whale left as black smoke billowed from the raging, burning fire. Col's clothes had already dried, and a bit of warmth had returned to Myuri's body.

Autumn's words had been deep.

In this moment, there was no doubt that the jet was much more valuable to Col than gold would have been. It had saved Myuri's life, and he wanted to spread the story around as a miracle of the Black-Mother—*This really happened!* Who cared if it was actually the remains of something the avatar of a whale once burned?. Whether or not a whale that could turn into a human fit into the teachings of the scripture was hardly worth thinking about.

It was essential that people learned and believed that a miracle had truly happened to them. The most important thing was that they had been saved.

"Then?"

He stared at the figure of the Black-Mother in his hand. The wavering light of the fire lit its gentle expression. Illuminated by such a strong light, it glinted, like it truly had turned into gold.

No—wait.

It had actually turned to gold in his hands!

When it occurred to him that there may be a way to save the people of the islands, he lost himself and tried to stand, almost dropping Myuri's head. That made him snap back to reality, and a bitter taste filled his mouth.

He was a shallow human who read some books, obsessed over theology in his little hot spring village of Nyohhira, then assumed he knew everything there was to know when it came to faith. All the actions he had considered so deeply and taken were all nothing but ignorant, fruitless efforts. And when he had guessed wrong and imagined acknowledging the reality, he grew scared and could not move.

This region had somehow managed to develop, thanks to a person like Autumn governing over it. It was rather odd to think now that an outsider's ideas would decide the direction of the land. He wanted to pretend like he had not noticed anything and warm Myuri. Then, when she woke up, he would celebrate her good health as though it had been his own achievement.

"But…," he murmured and looked at Myuri.

At the moment her life was about to be snuffed out, she had shown him a miracle. She was a girl who wanted him to be impressive, he who was a fool that only got older and older.

If he could not be the least bit brave for her now, he would be too ashamed to face her once she woke up. Even if she did not notice, he would not be able to forgive himself.

It would make jumping into the cold, dark sea seem all for naught.

There must have been something even her useless big brother could do. There must have been a way to live where she would not laugh at him.

No matter how foolish it was, he had the obligation to continue believing that the world could be a better place.

He patted her head, brushed his fingers through her hair, then placed her softly on the floor.

"I will be right back."

He stood and went into the next room. He stepped across the figures of the Holy Mother strewn about the floor and pushed aside the sharkskin, wind and snow blowing in from the gaps.

The cold suddenly beat against his face.

He squinted his eyes and undauntedly moved toward the dock.

"Lord Autumn!"

He made his way to the water and called out the name with all his might.

But the wind drowned it all out, and the darkness dominated the seas.

"Is there something you need?"

That was not the darkness.

Col could not tell where the voice was coming from. He looked to the left, to the right, and up into the sky; he could not tell where the beginning or end of the massive body was.

As he stood in shock, the darkness spoke.

"If you do not need anything, then I shall be off."

"P-please wait!" he said and desperately rearranged the thoughts in his head. "Gold will come from the island."

"What?"

"Gold will come from the island. No—"

He raised the figure of the Black-Mother he gripped in his hand and said:

"We will turn this into gold."

Such a thing was possible in the event of a miracle.

Yes.

They just need a miracle to happen.

It was still true, however, that that would not be enough. It was easy to cause things that could only be called miracles by using nonhuman power, but it would be nothing more than a make-shift measure without the proper forethought. The large fangs and claws of nonhumans were, at the end of the day, nothing but powers that existed largely in ancient myth. There was only so much that they could accomplish in this new human world. In order to save an entire land of people, it was necessary to organize a structure that fit into the framework of the human world.

If he had to point out a problem, it was that Autumn's miracle had been used to endure hardship. There was no doubt that it was the best method he came to after thinking about it in his own way. Col also thought that it had actually worked well.

But speaking, from his own faith, Col thought that miracles should be things that always gave others reason to smile, and there should be many more possibilities for them in the work-ings of the human world. He had learned that from his journey with a master merchant and from his conversations with theologians who gathered all sorts of conclusions from the words of the scripture.

He should be able to create a new light by putting everything he had in his hands together.

"With your power, it is possible."

"..."

"We should be able to bring back the smiles of this land by using the power of everyone involved with this island."

Autumn was silent, then spoke slowly.

"*Truly?*"

He had no guarantee it would go well, and what he was trying to do was to fake a miracle and use that to create a permanent system. No matter what excuses he used, it would clash with the actions of a good believer as described in the scripture.

But he had thought about it in that shrine of lava. Faith was not right or wrong. What mattered was whether the outcome was right, and he could say with confidence that to return the people sold into slavery to their families could not possibly be wrong.

And then, even if he became the subject of scorn of all the clergymen in the world, at least Myuri would smile for him.

"Truly."

If it did not go well, he thought about how Autumn might eat him or perhaps drag him into the bottom of the sea. But he had already died once. Col was not afraid.

"Truly."

The moment he repeated himself, there was a spectacularly big wave, and then Autumn was there, standing at the edge of the docks.

He was looking at Col fiercely, emotion laid bare in his eyes.

"I believe you."

They were fitting words for a monk.

EPILOGUE

One reason why the Church became corrupt, drowned in riches, and ended up in its current state, was because faith could be sold at a high price.

People would empty their wallets as a way of thanks in order to earn blessings, protection, and comfort in the big milestones in life—birth, weddings, funerals; protection on a journey; prayers for well-being in sickness; guidance in old age. Many people would give all they could for what they desperately wished for.

Faith was money.

The sky was a clear blue, the blizzard of the past few days now nothing but a dream.

It was a beautiful day, a sign that the end of winter was slowly coming northward, and a new season was on its way.

The waves on the seas, which had been raging just a little while ago, were gentle like a baby's sleeping breath as they caressed the shoreline.

Gliding on the calm waters was a giant ship.

From what he had heard, a hundred people were about to be sold. Officially, they would have been volunteering their labor for the holy Church. Only God knew if that was true or not.

Though no one in the port of Caeson raised their voices, the whole town was wrapped in sadness. The only ones smiling were the archbishop and the wealthy merchant. Reicher and the others simply drank themselves to sleep. The islanders took the gold and were made to promise they would side with the Church in the coming war. But it was not what they wished for. Whenever the giant ship crossed the islands here and there, the families who had sent one of their own watched them go.

Autumn, who had come from the waters, told Col all this. They confirmed their plan and preparations once more. It was not that complicated, so it ended quickly.

Ever since that night, Autumn, who had been quite business-like, would glance at him before returning to the water.

"You have not said anything about compensation."

Col had come on behalf of the Kingdom of Winfiel to see if the people of this land would be suitable allies in war. Autumn, who had collected the veneration of all the islanders onto himself, would be able to have a notable influence on them.

"Have you forgotten? You saved our lives. What else would we ask you give us?"

Autumn did not smile.

"These proud sailors will not side with those who buy islanders for gold to take them hostage."

"But my plan is to sell faith for gold."

Autumn peered at him with quiet eyes between his hair and beard.

"People place different value on things, even if it is the same fish. I suppose that is what the fishermen sigh over."

Though Autumn had said his human identity was temporary, answers like this made it seem more and more like he truly was a monk.

"At the very least, I will appear to you wherever you are in the sea when I hear your voice. Whether the people of this land will follow me, well…Only God knows."

Just as Col thought he saw a grin on Autumn's face, the avatar of the whale had already returned to the sea. The hole in one of the rooms in the monastery that led to the water had been for him to come and go when it was clear outside. As he watched Autumn disappear into the shining, green-lit waters, what he felt was not the satisfaction of successfully carrying out Hyland's mission.

It was happiness, knowing that he had perhaps been able to aid Autumn, who had supported this land all by himself.

All that was left was to fulfill the job he had been given.

He left the monastery and headed to the dock.

Several small boats were tied there, and each had one person inside. Among them was Yosef, but the majority were pirates.

"Lord Autumn has spoken. The Black-Mother is angry."

"Oohh…"

The anxiety spread. The pirates especially grew pale. That was because what they had done to Col had played a rather big part in that.

On the night of the blizzard, the pirates all had been told to capture any suspicious-looking ships on the water. And while it had gone well until they tackled Yosef's boat, a fool had fallen into the sea, and yet another jumped in after. And the one who had fallen in was, of all things, dressed like a priest.

The expressions on the pirates' faces when they saw he had lived would stick in his memory for quite a while.

There were those left speechless, who doubted themselves, who fell to their knees before Col, and even those who burst into tears. Their reactions had become even more intense ever since Autumn declared him a soul who had received all of the Holy Mother's protection.

As though listening for their judgment in hell, those pirates carefully heeded every word he said.

273

The Black-Mother was angry. There was someone trying to harm the islands.

"You must know that the Black-Mother does not only offer salvation."

Those who discerned the deeper meaning behind those words were the only ones who knew the Black-Mother's true identity.

That being said, the expressions of those who submitted themselves to faith stiffened.

"However, as long as we are good followers, she may be benevolent with our sins."

It also meant that she would forgive them for what they did to him. The pirates seemed slightly relieved.

"The Black-Mother has announced the coming of a miracle, and punishment will come before long. We must show those people mercy and receive her true teachings."

Those sitting in the small boats all nodded. Each of them either gripped their figures of the Black-Mother or patted their chests where they kept them.

"We must have them understand that the Black-Mother will show us a true miracle."

Though he had not raised a battle cry, everyone quietly understood what they had to do. Once he said, "That is all," the pirates paddled their boats back to the galley anchored off shore.

Yosef's ship stood beside it. The left side, which had been hollowed out in the pirate attack, seemed unhindered in sailing thanks to emergency measures.

"Master Col."

As the pirates headed toward the ship, Yosef stepped onto the dock.

"Will salvation really come to this land?"

Col took a deep breath when he heard his serious question.

"We can do nothing but continue to believe in true salvation. However, I can only promise that great salvation will come."

He had not lied. It was not as though they would come across fortune in their sleep.

The miracles of nonhumans were nothing but a beginning.

In the end, for humans to live on, they themselves needed to act.

"I would not mind that. It would be better than what we have now," Yosef said and returned to his ship.

He watched them off from the dock, and once it fell silent again, he headed the opposite way of the monastery shore.

The sun was bright, the wind calm, and the water was so clear he could see all the way to the bottom.

One step and another—he made his way forward as his feet caught in the small pools and rough rocks and soon made it to the water.

Squinting, he could clearly see the gallant figure of a giant ship making its way calmly and confidently over the water.

A bolt from the blue, as it was often called.

For a moment, the ship soared in the air.

Though he knew what was happening, he was still surprised to see it, and it could not compare to what the people on board must have been feeling. It looked like the ship had risen into the air before it sank back into the water with a magnificent spray of water, making it seem like time had slowed down. The moment he thought he could see a distant rainbow, he heard a loud *boom* like a drum.

The giant ship had, of course, not escaped unscathed. It leaned far to the right and looked as though it would capsize at any moment.

The pirates may have seen it, too, if they looked carefully—the ship, full of islanders, appeared to be astride the back of the Black-Mother, and was about to be flipped over.

"Lord Autumn...That's too much..."

When Col unwittingly murmured that out loud, Autumn's back sunk into the water again and the ship was back to normal.

The oars extending from the ship made it look like a comb that was missing teeth, but they began to paddle at the water in a hurry.

Then Autumn must have attacked once more with his giant tail fin, for this time, the ship's stern rose into the air, pitching forward. Once the ship returned to the water, the stern looked as though it was sinking. Perhaps a hole had opened and it was capsizing.

Everyone on board must have been in pandemonium.

Col was thrilled, especially since he knew what was going on behind the scenes, but then the shaking of the boat suddenly stopped, and it began to move even though the oars were not. The sinking stopped as well.

Someone must have thrown a figure of the Black-Mother into the water.

Anyone would feel the need to pray if that happened to them. There was nothing else they could do after all.

Then, led by a mysterious force, they would be cast ashore on a nearby island. While they were at a loss, the people of the island would at the same time be led by the Holy Mother and come help them. They would ask, *Brothers, are you all right?*

The archbishop would immediately understand why this happened to them. That was because the ship was full of people sobbing in despair, and what they threw into the sea were figures of the Black-Mother.

Then he would without a doubt understand who caused this miracle, even if he did not want to admit it. There was no doubt he would understand what they had all thrown into the sea.

Even merchants knew of these kinds of stories, and clergymen were even more familiar with them.

Relics.

"Ooh, we're doing something bad."

Col turned around when he heard the voice.

"Are you okay to be up and about?"

Blanket wrapped around herself, Myuri's complexion was still pale. But a bit of color had returned to her cheeks as they were lit by the sun.

"I'll only be punished if I sleep through such a nice day like this."

"Why are you always…?"

What worried him was that though her life had been saved by burning the Black-Mother, she then grew feverish and had nightmares in the days that followed. Though her fever had finally broken, it would be a while yet before she was fully recovered.

"And I still have work to do, don't I? I can't let myself get rusty."

Myuri spoke as she gazed far out across the water.

Myuri's power was necessary in order to complete the plan Col had thought up.

He was just a powerless young man after all.

"Like how Mother dug up water for Father, I'll be digging up rocks for Brother."

A wolf's nose and claws. With those together, she may be able to find new mineral veins on an island that everyone assumed was barren. Jet may appear here once more. And then they would offer a proposal to the archbishop.

These Holy Mother figures were fragments of the Holy Mother's body, who descended to earth so she could save this island. By keeping a figure close at all times, the faithful could bring blessings and open up possibilities in the future. What's more, the world was currently wavering in regards to what was righteous faith and what was not. Who would not want to be on the side of righteous faith? Were there not a great many who wished to be in the favor of righteous faith as well? Would not a relic of a true miracle be worth much more than any mountain of gold?

Members of the Ruvik Alliance came and went through the Caeson port daily. Autumn would create figures of the Holy Mother from the mined jet, which would then be sold for a high price as a relic. Reicher could take care of selling negotiations. There were legends of alchemists who could turn lead into gold, but faith could turn coal into gold. Col had strung together such a plan and told Autumn that one blizzard night that it may keep the island going for a little while longer.

Col was much too meager to stand with his faith, and even if he did sacrifice himself, he would not even know where or how to push forward.

But as long as the road he had lived so far still continued into the future, then this could be a place where he could compromise when it came to his place in the world.

It was none other than Autumn who had shown him that by praying earnestly, God would forgive any sins he committed.

He had no choice but to pray more than he ever had before.

Should prayer be able to bring someone salvation, then faith was not something to toss away.

"A whale as big as a mountain…Whatever exaggerated stories I heard in Nyohhira are nothing compared to this."

Myuri chuckled.

At the end of the day, stories were things that humans came up with, and if God had truly created this world, then it was logical to be more impressed by reality.

"Come now, you should return to the fire soon."

Though the weather was nice, the air was still cold. Col placed his hand on her shoulder to guide her, and after a moment, Myuri spoke.

"The story about the whale also sounds fake, but I still can't believe you finally made up your mind, Brother."

Myuri grinned and slid up beside him.

Col unconsciously pulled back, as though trying to escape, but a towering rock face immediately blocked him off.

"...How many times do I have to tell you? You misunderstand."

And then, after he spoke, Myuri drew even closer.

"Misunderstand? What do you mean, misunderstand? Even though you were so terrible to me, I didn't hesitate one bit to jump into the sea after you, turning into a spirit to rush to your side. So tell me, what kind of misunderstanding am I making?"

Every single thing she mentioned was either a debt of gratitude he could never repay or a blunder he could never make up for.

But he had no choice to keep telling her that what she was talking about was, without a doubt, a misunderstanding.

"That's...That was because I knew that there was no fuel left to keep you warm until the blizzard passed. Were you not taught this in Nyohhira? It is what you are supposed to do when someone has fallen into the river in the winter and there is nothing to use. You could also say that is the wisdom of those who often travel in cold regions. It is normal."

He persisted in his logic that the problem lay with the methodology. To show that he was not deceiving her at all, he puffed out his chest and stood up straight.

Myuri watched him and tilted her head, staring at him with a suspicious expression.

She would quip at him any moment now.

As he braced himself, her wolf ears and tail suddenly appeared.

"Maybe we should ask other people if they think it's a misunderstanding?"

She was smiling calmly, as though there was nothing for him to be angry about.

But he had acted with a selfless heart. It had been nothing but goodwill. He was confident about that. Myuri knew that. She knew but disregarded it.

"I remember it *reeeaaally* well."

This girl, who was of age, shrugged and placed both hands on her cheeks, embarrassed.

That night, Col had removed his clothes to warm Myuri with his body heat. It was true that even travelers knew that it was the best way to warm up, and there should have been nothing to be ashamed of.

However, Myuri regained consciousness unexpectedly, and when she immediately realized what situation she was in, she said—

"Am I your wife now, Brother?"

There were many reasons why he could not look directly into her sparkling eyes.

"When you write a letter to Father next, be sure to include that, okay? Brother and I were naked under the same bla— *Owwwwwww...!*"

She rubbed her head but was still smiling.

"But it's true that you've improved so much that I'd be happy to become your bride."

The foul look in his eyes he showed Myuri was no act.

"I could not do anything. I have been powerless ever since we came to this land."

"Really?"

"Yes. I could not protect you, and what I proposed to Autumn was nothing more than child's play. It is quite possible that it may only work temporarily."

But Myuri continued to smile.

"That's true, but at least from what I heard, I think this place might become a little happier. It might not be enough for you, but hmm, how should I say it?"

She closed her eyes, like she was listening to the voice of the wind.

"It's totally different from what that old beardy guy was doing. You know, it smells a lot like you."

"…Smells like me?"

"Yeah. It smells like a sheep, one that only sees half of half of the world."

He thought for a moment she was making fun of him, but when Myuri opened her eyes, she was staring directly at him.

"You weren't looking for a way to endure hardship but a road that leads people to more happiness. Even if something really small, even if everyone thinks you can't do it, you still believe in the warm sun and just go for it. There's like a brightness to that. You have such a stubborn mind-set that trusts the world isn't some huge barren wasteland, and things will get better if everyone works together. That's what it smells like."

She stared at him in fascination with her clear, unclouded eyes. What she had pointed out was the good side of only seeing half of half of the world.

"You actually did fail several times, but you thought of another way in the end, didn't you? Even I would learn the hard way and run with my tail between my legs if I got all beat up like that. But you even thought of getting the help of lots of other people, not just me."

Col had truly been on the verge of giving up. He had the choice of swallowing what he had thought of and waiting for Myuri to wake up. But he did not do that. He could not. That could be called faith, but it could also be called clumsiness. He even thought it was a bit stupid.

His voice caught in his throat, but it was not because he could not think of what to say in protest.

Still gazing up at him, Myuri giggled and grasped his hand.

"Brother?"

He did not think she was going to tease him. She spoke softly, and though there was a teasing expression on her face, he could tell she was about to say something important.

Far away, the broken boat was being carried to a nearby island.

Col watched that for a while before surrendering and turning to face Myuri.

"What is it?"

As her wolf ears and tail swayed in the gentle breeze, the same strange mix of ash and flecks of silver as her hair, she spoke.

"Can you take me along on your next journey, too?"

He would never find such a phrase containing as many different interpretations in the scripture.

This was what happened when so many conflicting feelings inside Myuri bubbled up around one another and coursed into her hand as it squeezed his.

There was no method on this earth that could cleanly divide them all.

But to know which piece of bread he had that would make her happy, he only needed to look at his hands.

"As long as you are a good girl."

Myuri shrugged and narrowed her eyes.

"Fine."

He caught a glimpse of her pointed canines when she smiled.

She stood close to him, and Col put his arm around her shoulders, then returned to the fire inside the building.

Myuri's fluffy tail playfully bumped up against his leg.

The sky was blue, and the sea was calm.

While he still did not know if God existed, he knew that the truth was here.

AFTERWORD

Hello again, everyone. This is Isuna Hasekura. This is the second book. Six months have somehow passed. I'm sorry. I think I managed to release a book once every four months right after my debut, but I no longer remember how I managed to do that... which is pretty discouraging, but then I remembered I was also writing a short story collection for *Spice and Wolf*. Thank you for those who are reading that as well as *Wolf and Parchment*.

This time, I also aimed to write a book where you can open to any page before you fall asleep to find cute, fuzzy things jumping out at you, but I think the latter half got very serious. It got quite off track from the plot, and since I always feel my way through when I write my novels, I can't predict it too well. But since the road was quite serious, I rather like the last scene. I would be quite happy if you enjoyed it as well.

I thought I had written enough for the afterword, but I've only filled about a third of the space...It's taken me about an hour to write this far.

I was wondering what I should write about...but now I

remember I have had my face stuck in the world of VR for the past year, so I will talk about that. You know VR. It's that familiar thing with the Sword and the Art from *Dengeki Bunko*. It's only our sight that can enter the 2-D world at the moment, but it feels incredibly immersive. So much so that things like horror are much too frightening, and I think some kind of accident (like a heart attack) will bring about regulations before long. You can really appreciate its power when a girl character is right in front of you. You may think I'm lying, but when a character reaches out to touch you on the cheek, it feels warm. I was so deeply moved at first, thinking my delusions had finally reached a new point…but it turns out those sensory illusions have been confirmed academically. I'm a bit disappointed but also relieved.

But it's still in its infancy, and there is not a lot of content. I was very upset to see there was a special lack of moe, so I planned it myself and made something with the help of many people. I can remember it now, being so busy from summer to winter last year…I think it may be how old I'm getting that I now forget everything when I have a chance to rest. For those interested, please search for *Project LUX*. We are making a long anime series with VR with the zeal of someone who is very excited to go to the 2-D world. There was much to learn working in unknown territory, so there was also a great sense of adventure in the development itself. I almost want to write a novel about it next time.

The page filled up as I was rambling about all that.

I appreciate all your continued support. Thank you.

Isuna Hasekura